W9-BSL-657

THE HOCUS GIRL

THE HOCUS GIRL

A Simon Westow mystery

Chris Nickson

This first world edition published 2019
in Great Britain and 2020 in the USA by
SEVERN HOUSE PUBLISHERS LTD of
Eardley House, 4 Uxbridge Street, London W8 7SY.
Trade paperback edition first published
in Great Britain and the USA 2020 by
SEVERN HOUSE PUBLISHERS LTD.

British Library Cataloguing in Publication Data
A CIP catalogue record for this title is available from the British Library.

ISBN-13: 978-0-7278-8935-5 (cased)
ISBN-13: 978-1-78029-649-4 (trade paper)
ISBN-13: 978-1-4483-0348-9 (e-book)

All Severn House titles are printed on acid-free paper.

Severn House Publishers support the Forest Stewardship Council™ [FSC™],
the leading international forest certification organisation. All our titles that
are printed on FSC certified paper carry the FSC logo.

Typeset by Palimpsest Book Production Ltd.,
Falkirk, Stirlingshire, Scotland.
Printed and bound in Great Britain by
TJ International, Padstow, Cornwall.

ONE

Leeds, May 1822

The man uncurled his fist to show the pocket watch. Candlelight reflected and shimmered on the gold.

'Open it up,' Simon Westow said.

Inside the cover, an inscription: *From Martha to Walter, my loving husband.*

'See?' the man said. 'The real thing, that is. Proper gold. Keeps good time and—'

The knife at his throat silenced him.

'And it was stolen three days ago,' Simon said. He held the blade steady, stretching the man's skin without breaking it. 'Where's the rest?' With a gentle touch, he lifted the watch out of the man's palm and slipped it into his pocket. 'Well?'

'Don't know.' The man gasped the words. His head was pushed back against the wall, neck exposed. 'I bought this from Robby Barstow.'

'When?' A little more pressure, enough to bring a single drop of warm blood.

'Last night.'

The man's eyes were wide, pleading, the whites showing. It was the truth. He was too terrified to lie.

'Then you'd best tell Robby I'm coming for him.'

'What—'

'About the watch?'

'Yes.' He breathed out the word, trying not to move at all.

'Consider it a bad investment.'

Outside, he blinked in the light. A coach rumbled past on the Head Row, the driver trying to make good time on his way to Skipton.

Simon would hunt for Barstow later. The watch was the important item; Walter Haigh was desperate to have it returned, a gift from his late wife. He'd promised a fine reward.

That was what a thief-taker did. Find what had been stolen and return it for a fee.

Market day. Briggate was packed, trestles set up on either side of the street. People forced their way through the crowds. Carts were at a standstill below the Moot Hall, horses waiting patiently in their traces.

'No taxes, no charge for the post, porter a ha'penny a gallon. That's what we need.' The voice rang out sharp and clear, keening high above the hubbub to make people stop and stare. 'The kingdom of Shiloh is coming, and after it the Angel of the Lord will bring an earthquake to sink the world.'

Simon paused, amused. The country was full of fools with visions. This one was an old man in dusty, tattered clothes, with a white prophet's beard hanging down to his chest. He drew in a breath, ready to bellow more. But before he could continue, two members of the watch pinned him by the arms and dragged him roughly away, kicking over the small pile of tracts by his feet. Simon picked one up, glanced at it briefly, then tossed it back with the others.

He spotted Rosie. The bright blue plume of her hat rose tall over all the heads around her. Reaching her took longer, squeezing and pushing, easing between the press of bodies. He saw a young girl deftly stealing two apples while the stall holder's head was turned. A man cut a woman's purse strings, sliding away before she could notice.

Leeds, Simon thought. Its greedy heart never changed.

'All done?' she said. She hadn't turned her head; she simply seemed to know he was there. She wore a gown that reached to her ankles, a deep shade of indigo with a patterned bodice and puffed oversleeves. Dressed up in her finery, just like him in his black frock coat, close-fitting trousers and neatly striped waistcoat. And armed, always; Rosie carried a knife, hidden away in the pocket of her dress. Simon had three; one on his belt, another in his boot, the third in a sheath up his sleeve. He'd taught himself to use them well; the job was dangerous.

'Yes. Simple enough.'

'Take a look at this.' Rosie's fingers rubbed the worn velvet of a dress, russet and gold.

'What about it?'

'It used to belong to Katherine Wainwright. I remember her wearing it.'

She'd been Rosie's closest friend, older, softer, then gone, dead for five years now. A sickness that arrived in the night, robbing her of breath and filling her lungs with liquid.

'You can't bring her back,' Simon said gently.

'I know.' She laid it on the trestle and stroked the fabric once more. 'I just wondered how many others have worn it since.'

She put her arm through his and they began to move. Past farmers selling butter and cheeses brought from the country. Last autumn's fruit. Sacks bulging with onions and potatoes. A tinker offering mended pans. And everywhere, talk and more talk. A constant, roaring ocean of sound to fill the town.

Simon watched, noticing every face as his wife chattered. People, information; they were his stock in trade. Down near the Old King's Arms, she nudged him.

'Isn't that George Ericsson?'

The man strode up the other side of Briggate, eyes fixed straight ahead. Tall, with wide shoulders and a grave, solemn face.

'It is. I'd heard he was back,' Simon said.

Ericsson was a timber merchant, a Swede, with a warehouse down on the river. For the last five years he'd been in Stockholm, leaving his oldest son Jonas to handle business here. The lad had done well; with so many factories and houses rising these days, the demand for wood was high.

'He looks a lot older,' Rosie said, staring.

True enough, Simon thought. Time hadn't been kind to the man. It had worn down the planes of his face and turned the pale blond hair a sharp, brilliant white.

'His wife's returned with him, too,' he said. 'Rounder than ever, someone told me.'

'Hardly surprising. She used to eat everything in sight.'

'I didn't think you knew her.'

Rosie shook her head, hair rippling under the broad hat. 'I used to see her in the shops. She always expected a special price, as if she was doing them a favour by gracing them with her custom.'

'Did they give it to her?'

Rosie gave him a withering look. 'Don't you know better than that, Simon? They'd quote something higher, then make a show of taking that off.'

He laughed.

It was rare for them to have time together, the two of them alone, a luxury worth more than money. Just the chance to stroll, to observe, and to enjoy the May sunshine. Their boys, Richard and Amos, were in Kirkstall for a few days, staying with Mrs Burton and her husband to enjoy the early days of good weather.

Jane, the girl who worked with him, was off somewhere. He'd heard her leave the house first thing that morning, sliding away into the dawn.

They turned the corner on to Swinegate as Rosie talked. She had a sharp eye and a wicked tongue, and she relished taking aim at the great and good ladies of the town. Simon let the words flow over him. Then she halted in mid-sentence, standing still on the pavement.

'That's Emily Ashton at our door.'

He narrowed his eyes, trying to make out the figure by the step. In her early forties, wearing an old calico dress, a shawl across her shoulders, turned away from them. Only the dark red hair gave her away, coiled up on her head.

'You're right.'

TWO

The Ashtons had looked after him. He'd walked away from the workhouse, aged thirteen, a boy filled with anger, trying to pull together a life he could call his own. Too often he'd gone hungry or slept out in the bitter cold. But when Simon could take no more, desperate for warmth or a meal in his belly, he could go to see Emily Ashton and her brother Davey at their house on Mabgate. They gave him sanctuary.

Emily would feed him and put down a blanket by the hearth.

Her brother would fill his head with words. Ideas. Equality, brotherhood, dignity, hope.

They saved him. They shaped him.

'Emily,' he called.

She turned and began to run towards them, the panic plain on her face. Simon wrapped his arms around her. Emily shook, tears running down her cheeks.

'What is it?'

'It's Davey.' The words were a helpless sob, choking in her mouth. For a moment he thought the man was dead. 'They've taken him.'

'Taken him?' He didn't understand. 'Who?'

'The government.' Her hands gripped him tight, holding on to him like an anchor. 'They said they're going to charge him with sedition.'

Jane stood in the shadow of a building on Vicar Lane, watching the people pass. Back in the gloom, the shawl pulled over her hair, she knew she was invisible. The night before, she'd heard a rumour that Stephen Bullock was back in Leeds and staying with Isaac Palmer.

Bullock was a servant who'd thieved from his employer, vanishing three months before with five pounds in coins and two pieces of silver plate. All the money would be long spent by now, but his master hadn't forgotten. He wanted to prosecute. Catch him, and she and Simon would receive their fee.

She tensed as the door opened. But it was only Palmer, looking as if he didn't have a care in the world. No matter. She had plenty of patience.

'Let's go inside,' Rosie said quietly. She put an arm around Emily, guiding her down the hall and into the kitchen, sitting her on one of the chairs then pouring a glass of French brandy. 'Drink that.'

She swallowed, coughed. But a little colour came back to her face and the wildness began to fade from her eyes.

'What's he supposed to have done?' Simon asked. It was strange; people should have been talking about it at the market, the gossip moving from mouth to mouth. But he'd heard nothing.

'They wouldn't tell me.' She began to cry again. 'Just pushed me out of the way and marched him off. A magistrate and soldiers with bayonets.'

Davey Ashton read books. He went to meetings and talked into the night with other men about a better world. About reform. Words and hope.

Sedition . . .

The government had passed their Six Acts just two years before, after the Peterloo massacre in Manchester, a way to muffle all criticism and rebellion. But it hadn't worked. Fury still simmered constantly, boiling over as demonstrations flared and faded across the North.

Sedition.

Guilty, and Davey could be sentenced to spend the rest of his life as a convict in Australia.

'They went through the house,' Emily continued. 'Took some of his papers and his books.' She started to rise, eyes wide with panic. 'I need to go home and clean it all up. You know how he likes everything in order.'

Rosie put her arms around Emily's shoulders and eased her back down.

'Stay here tonight. You'll be safe with us. Tomorrow,' her voice was soothing, 'we'll go over there in the morning. Together.'

He watched them, but this was a place where he wasn't needed. His wife would look after Emily. Quietly, Simon left, back into the street with its noise and stink.

Why in God's name would they arrest Davey? He wrote, he spoke, but only words and thoughts were his world. He was harmless, a gentle soul who believed in justice. Nothing more. Or perhaps that was enough these days, with a government so scared of its own people.

Someone would have seen, must have heard. Were they all so terrified that they were keeping silent? What had happened to this town?

The market had ended, but Briggate was still bustling. The crack of a whip as a coach turned out of the Rose and Crown and headed up the street, forcing people aside. A woman tried to sell old bunches of heather from a tray, crying out, 'Luck!

Good lucky heather! Be sweet for the day, be sweet for your love!'

A haze lay over Leeds, thin smoke from the factory chimneys, growing thicker and thicker year on year. Simon looked up at the sky as he walked. A few still hoped for clean air, but money would always win out. Profit and business paid the piper. They called the tune.

Near the top of Kirkgate, Simon pushed open the heavy door of the gaol. The place was old now, mortar crumbling between the stones, cold even in the spring sun. The clerk at the desk raised his head.

'Mr Westow,' he said in surprise. 'Have you brought someone for us?'

'Davey Ashton. Do you have him in the cells?'

'No, sir.' The man frowned and pushed the spectacles up his nose. He put down his pen and rubbed the fingers of his right hand. 'There's no one by that name. When was he arrested?'

'This morning.'

The clerk's expression cleared and his mouth turned down. 'Is this the sedition case?'

'Yes.'

'They're questioning him at the Moot Hall. I'll warn you now, though, they won't let you in. It's supposed to be secret, but I've heard there have been arrests all over the West Riding. Breaking up a rebellion, that's what they're saying.'

Simon felt a chill rise through his body. Rebellion was a capital crime. The death penalty. Hanging. In God's name, what was going on?

'Who's the magistrate?'

'Mr Curzon.'

He knew all about Curzon. A mill owner, a rich man who paid his workers as little as he dared and worked them as hard as he could. A man who'd honed away his compassion and conscience and replaced them with gold.

He'd be putting his questions, damning Davey to hell and threatening him with transportation for life or the noose. Simon felt the desperation clawing in his belly. He had to do something. But he wouldn't even be able to see Davey until Curzon was done. And he didn't know how he could save his friend.

'I see. Thank you.' A nod and he left. At least he knew his enemy now.

He could have found his way out here without looking. Across Sheepscar Beck at Lady Lodge, then follow the road past Quarry Hill and Mabgate.

The house had belonged to Davey and Emily's parents. Along with a small annuity that barely saw them through each year, it had been all their father had to leave. A cottage with a plot of land, every room crammed with pamphlets and books and an air that smelled of freedom. It stood alone, silent in its garden, close to where the old dyeworks had once been.

The key was still tucked away under a stone by the gate. He'd used it often enough when he was young. Sometimes he'd arrive after dark, long after the lamps had all been doused behind the windows, let himself in and curl up on the rug, warm and safe for another night. In the morning, Emily would feed him thick, sweetened porridge and bread smeared with butter. Davey would talk, educate him. Simon had taught himself to read. He'd thought that was enough. But Davey showed him that it was just the beginning. He fed Simon ideas, showed him how to think, to weigh arguments, to understand.

All history now. From a time before he became a thief-taker, before he ever met Rosie. When lasting one more day was as far ahead as he could imagine.

He turned the key in the lock and pushed the door open. Inside was chaos. Papers were strewn across the floor, books tumbled off the shelves and scattered. Simon walked around carefully, bending to gather things. Thomas Paine's *Rights of Man*, its spine broken and pages loose from years of reading. Wordsworth's poems. Mary Wollstonecraft's *A Vindication of the Rights of Women*, pages trampled into the floorboards. Copies of *The Black Dwarf*, the *Weekly Political Register* and *Republican*. More, so much more.

Davey Ashton owned the first library Simon had ever seen. He'd never even heard the word before he came here. It had opened a new world, bigger than he'd ever imagined. One that welcomed him with its knowledge.

Now he worked, collecting everything and trying to fit it back on the wooden shelves Davey had built all around the parlour and in his bedroom.

An hour and things looked better; at least the floor was clear. Simon took a broom and swept the boards, pushing the dust and dirt into the garden. When Emily came home in the morning she'd find something approaching order in the house. It might make things a little easier for her. He stood and looked around. The room was hushed. Worn, weary, but calm again with the familiar, comforting smell that carried him back through the years.

He had to help Davey. But what could he do against the government? Rebellion? Davey Ashton was a man of ideas. He wouldn't know how to lift a hand in violence. It simply wasn't in him. But these days the smallest thing could be treachery.

Jane stood close to Lady Bridge, hidden away among the trees. Without thinking, she kept turning the gold ring on her finger, the only thing of value she owned. She kept her eyes fixed on the path, waiting until Simon came out of the house, watching him stand with his fingers tight on the door handle, frowning in concentration for a moment, then striding hurriedly towards her.

His head turned as she appeared at his side, matching him stride for stride over the bridge and back towards town.

'I saw you on Vicar Lane and followed you out here,' she said. 'Is something wrong?'

'Yes,' he answered. He didn't explain. 'I want you to wait by the Moot Hall. Listen for anyone talking about a man called Davey Ashton.'

'Why?' Jane asked, but he ignored her question.

'If he comes out, I want to know.'

'What does he look like?'

'Davey's tall, he's got stooped shoulders. His hair is going grey. Thin. There's a scar across the back of his left hand. He'll be dressed in old clothes.'

'What's he done?'

Simon's face was hard. She could feel the anger flaring inside him. 'I don't know. Probably nothing. But Curzon arrested him. You know what he's like. He'll do anything to convict.'

* * *

Simon needed information. More than the fragments he had if he was going to make Davey a free man again. Governments and mentions of sedition scared people into silence. They might be next. Keep them quiet, keep them down.

He needed someone who had friends at the Moot Hall, someone with a keen ear for the truth and a mouth that could be loosened with a little money.

Bradley's beershop. It was the parlour of a small old house on High Court. Bare and basic, a few benches and tables and a barrel with a tap sitting on its cradle. The place was almost empty, two old drinkers in the corner and the landlord paring his nails with a knife. No sign of the man he needed.

'Joshua Miller,' Simon said.

Bradley shook his head. 'Not been in today.'

The same reply in three other places up and down Kirkgate. Then, in the Yorkshire Grey, he spotted the man, hunched over a mug as he read the *Intelligencer*.

'You're a hard one to find.' Simon slid three pennies across the table and watched them disappear into Miller's bony hand.

'No, I'm not.' He looked up with a sly smile. 'I always know where I am.'

'Curzon,' Simon said, and the other man nodded. 'What's he up to?'

'Him?' Miller sneered. 'I thought you were cleverer than that, Simon. Are you going soft? The only aim in Thomas Curzon's life is to glorify the great and wondrous name of Thomas Curzon. He wants to end up a sir or a lord.' Miller drained the beer. Simon signalled for another. 'Have you heard he's even got himself a bodyguard now?'

'Why would he do that?'

The man shrugged. 'Makes him look powerful, I suppose. He wants people to think that his job is full of danger. About the only thing that's for certain is we'll be the ones paying for it.'

Miller had been an important man once. A position as the town's head legal clerk, with his own office in the Moot Hall, and a staff working under him. It lasted until the day a mail coach overturned on Briggate. Miller's arm had been trapped between the iron rim of the wheel and a wall. By the time he'd been freed, his right hand was crushed. Only the stubs of the first three fingers remained, and the other two were twisted. A clerk who could no longer write was useless to the council, and suddenly Joshua Miller was out of a job. No pension, no status, nothing at all. A very swift tumble, down and down, all the way to the bottom of society. These days he pecked by on charity, nursing his bitterness while his wife took in washing. He spent too much of his time sipping at poor ale and exchanging information for whatever anyone would pay. Very little, it seemed; his dowdy old coat was patched at the elbows and collar, the leather of his shoes peeling away from the soles. His skin had a grey, sad pallor.

'There's something going on across the West Riding,' Simon said.

'So I've heard. The government's cracking down again. Sedition.' He took a sip of the fresh drink and smiled. 'Mother's milk, that is.' He looked around, making sure no one was paying attention, then leaned forward and lowered his voice to a whisper. 'Someone told me they sent a man up here.'

'What? An investigator?' Simon asked, but Miller was shaking his head.

'A spy.'

Jane found a place to watch the entrance of the Moot Hall. Set back from the street, in the shade that fell across the entrance to a yard. Close enough to reach out and touch the people as they passed on Briggate. But not a single one of them realized she was there. And they never would. The invisible girl.

She'd been eight when her mother threw her from her house. Another child of the streets, one of hundreds. But where so many had died, she'd lived. She'd learned when to share and when to be ruthless. How to steal, to kill when she had to. To make sure she survived. And she'd discovered she could follow people without being seen. To become unnoticed, not there at all.

Maybe it was a gift, a skill; or it was simply her nature. A few times it had saved her life; now it made her money, more than she could ever have dreamed. Jane had over three hundred and fifty pounds wrapped in oilcloth and buried in the woods beyond Drony Laith. That was her freedom. Enough to live like a lady for the rest of her days if she ever wanted.

But she didn't have the desire. Possessing the money was enough. She worked with Simon, sharing the fees when they recovered the things that had been stolen. What little she owned, she carried in the pocket of her dress. She had the bare attic room in Simon and Rosie's house, but it was nothing more than a place to sleep. If the moment came, she could walk away without a trace and become a new person in another town.

Pain had been a good teacher. Jane built a wall to keep the world at a distance. It was safer to never let anyone too close. In the end, she could only rely on herself. Somehow, in some way, everyone else failed. There were two people she trusted. But not Simon, not Rosie; not completely. They were just there.

She stood still, listening to the prattle of housewives and servants as they hurried by. After half an hour, the door of the Moot Hall opened and a figure came into the daylight. Not the man Simon had described. Jane knew this one – Curzon the magistrate, with his beak nose and sleek, shining dark hair. Another man appeared behind him and they ambled away, heads together as they spoke rapidly.

As they passed, Jane caught a single word, a name. Ashton. She clutched the shawl under her chin and ducked her head, about to follow and listen. Then, from the corner of her eye, she caught a movement, a man easing from a doorway on the other side of the street, following Curzon and glancing around, eyes narrowed as he assessed everyone he saw. Broad, muscled, with a face full of violence.

She slipped back into the shadows, reached into her pocket and wrapped her fingers round the knife hilt, listening as her heart beat twenty times before she emerged. The men were easy to spot, easier still to follow in the crowd on Briggate.

THREE

'The government's spying on Englishmen?' For a moment, Simon wasn't sure he'd heard properly.

'You make it sound as if that's something shocking,' Miller snorted. 'They've been doing it for centuries. They're petrified, Simon. Terrified. With the price of food so high and wages low, they're afraid we're going to rebel like the French did thirty years ago and send them all to the guillotine.'

'More Peterloos.'

No one would ever forget the day when a Manchester magistrate sent the cavalry to break up a political meeting. Fifteen had died, hundreds were wounded.

'Or worse,' Miller continued. 'They're taking no chances. So they're sending agents to spy on people.' He shrugged and drank again.

A spy. Simon considered the idea.

'What else do you know?'

The man shook his head as an answer. 'That's it, Simon. Little things I've heard and put together. It *might* not be true. But I'll wager good money it is.'

It was. He could feel it in his bones. He took out another coin and slid it across the table.

'I'd like to know more about this spy. If you can find anything. Anything at all . . .'

Miller rubbed the thumb and the stubs of two fingers together. Money. 'I'll let you know.'

Curzon didn't go far, no more than a hundred yards. Outside the Bull and Mouth he shook his companion's hand, then strode through the door. Jane let herself be pulled along, lost in the crowd, seeing the big man hesitate a second before disappearing under the arch and into the yard of the inn.

She waited. Just five minutes later a carriage sped out, its bodywork a brilliant, dazzling black. Curzon sat inside, absorbed in a newspaper, oblivious to everything around him. A few moments after, she heard the sharp clatter of hooves on the cobbles and the big man was there again, seated high on a horse. He examined every face he saw as he patiently guided the animal up Briggate, as if he was committing them all to memory. But he never saw her; Jane made certain of that.

Go back to the Moot Hall? No, she decided. By now she might have missed the man Simon wanted. Instead, Jane walked and listened.

*   *   *

Simon hurried back through town. All the debris of the market, cabbage leaves and rotten fruit, scraps and rubbish, had been scavenged. Too many were hungry these days for the smallest thing to be wasted. He crossed the Head Row and pushed open a door.

For a moment, the smell of ink overwhelmed him; he had to stop and catch his breath. George Mudie stood by his printing press, turning the handle and inspecting each sheet as it emerged.

Finally he was satisfied, pulled a rag from his leather apron and wiped his hands.

'Eager for the latest ballad, Simon?' He peered at the paper, grimaced and shrugged. 'About some hanging in London. That should sell a few copies.'

A few years before, Mudie had been the editor of the *Leeds Intelligencer*. A new owner had disapproved of his ideas. After that, he tried running his own newspaper until it failed. These days he scraped a living from his printing press. Pamphlets, notices, whatever paid; a new broadside always turned a profit. But news about Leeds still ran through his blood.

'They arrested Davey Ashton this morning. Sedition.'

'They?' Mudie wiped his hands again. It was a hopeless task; after all these years, the ink was ingrained in his skin. 'Who?'

'Curzon was in charge, but he had soldiers with him. Someone told me there's a spy up here.'

Mudie raised his eyebrows but said nothing. He took a bottle of brandy from the shelf and poured himself a glass.

'Dangerous times,' he said. 'Are they going to charge Mr Ashton?'

'They've taken him to the Moot Hall for questioning. It looks as if they'll bring him to court under the Six Acts.'

'You know what that means,' Mudie said.

'Of course I do. I need to find out what's happened, who's involved.'

'I can ask, if you like.' He knew people who might have some answers.

'As soon as you can. His sister's falling apart. She's at our house.'

Mudie cocked his head. 'You and Ashton are good friends, aren't you?'

'He did a lot for me when I was young. I want to save him.'

Mudie snorted. 'That's not like you, Simon. Not a penny in it? And how are you going to rescue him from the government? I wish you luck. Still, I'll let you know if I come across anything useful. Spies.' He stared into his empty glass. 'Our masters are feart.'

There were still too many things he didn't understand. Why Davey? What had he been doing? He needed to talk to Emily again, to try and make sense of it all.

But he found only Rosie in the kitchen, cooking and tasting from a spoon.

'I gave her another glass of brandy after you left,' she said. 'She was still frantic. It calmed her enough to rest. She's up in the boys' room. I looked in on her a few minutes ago. She's asleep.'

He told her what he'd discovered, watching her expression darken.

'Is it true, do you think? About the spy?'

'I believe it,' he said. 'I'm going to find out.'

She placed her hand on his and stroked it gently. 'Be careful, Simon. This isn't some thief. It's the government.'

'They're going after Davey. That makes it my battle. Has Jane come back yet?'

Before she could answer, they heard the quiet click of the latch and she was there. Grown from a child who'd been thin as wire into a young woman. But still the same dark, distrustful eyes that saw everything and found it all wanting.

'Have they released him?' Simon asked hopefully.

Jane shook her head. 'That magistrate came out, so I followed him.' She paused. 'There was someone else with him, too. Trailing behind. A vicious-looking man.'

'He has a bodyguard,' Simon told her. 'Where did they go?'

'Left in his carriage from the Bull and Mouth. The other man one came out later on a horse. After that I walked around and listened to the gossip.'

'What did you hear?'

'Just the usual things: people complaining about the price of everything. Nobody was mentioning the name Ashton. Who is he?'

He explained, a few words. It was enough.

'What do you want me to do now?' Jane asked.

'I don't know yet,' Simon admitted. There was so much, everything urgent. Talk to Emily. See Davey. Track down this spy. Put all the pieces together. 'Oh,' he added. 'I found Haigh's watch. Robby Barstow has the rest.'

Jane nodded. 'I'll track him down tonight.'

That was enough. He knew she'd take care of it.

They'd eaten by the time Emily appeared. Her face was pale, still puffy from sleep, dark circles under a pair of lost eyes. The red hair was unpinned and trailing over her shoulders.

'Come on,' Rosie said, 'Sit down. I've made some food.' She obeyed like a child.

'I'm sorry.' She looked at them. 'The brandy . . . I . . .'

'You needed to rest,' Rosie told her.

'But Davey's in gaol.' Panic brimmed in her voice. 'I should—'

She could only think in shards, he realized. Tiny pieces bobbing in her mind.

'I'm doing everything I can,' Simon said. He reached across the table and took her hands as he glanced at his wife. 'I have to ask you a few things.'

Emily took a deep breath and gave a small, tentative nod.

'Has Davey met anyone lately? Any strangers around?'

'No. No one at all.' She raised her head in surprise. 'He's been poorly for the last month with his chest. He was just starting to feel well again. He hasn't even written a letter for weeks.'

'Were there any visitors that you don't know?'

Emily frowned. 'A few friends, that's all.'

Simon felt guilty. He'd been out of touch with them; he hadn't even known Davey was ill.

'Have you heard of anyone asking questions about him? Or about anyone else?'

'Nothing.' Her eyes flickered with fear. 'Why? What's going on, Simon? Tell me.'

'It seems there were quite a few arrests all over the West Riding. Davey was just one of them. Someone told me the government has a spy up here.'

'But—' she began. 'Why?' Simon watched her carefully. She

didn't have the words, just a helpless shake of her head. 'What's going to happen?' she asked finally.

'I wish I knew,' he replied. 'I'm going to do everything I can.' He wasn't about to promise her anything he couldn't deliver. 'I went to your house and tidied it a little.'

'Thank you. I—'

'You're staying here tonight,' Rosie said gently. 'No arguments. We'll look after you.'

'Yes,' Simon agreed as he saw her hesitation. 'Just tonight.'

'I'll go back with you in the morning,' Rosie said.

Up in the attic room, Jane stood by the window, staring down at the street. People passed, but none of them glanced up. They never did; they missed so much, only seeing what lay right in front of them. Danger could be waiting anywhere. Live with it long enough and you knew. You were ready. She reached out and ran her fingertips over the sill, feeling the smooth grain of the wood.

The sky was darkening. Almost evening. A little while longer and she'd go out. She trusted the night. It hid her, and brought a curious comfort. Out there she could be anyone. Sometimes she'd simply wander, easing herself into the places where the homeless gathered. Around them she was silent, just another shape in the gloom. Someone and no one at all. She'd sit away from the small fires they built and listen as they talked, then glide quietly away without them realizing she'd ever been there.

The men who prowled in the darkness didn't scare her. They were searching for victims. Jane wasn't one. She was always prepared, one hand over her knife, ready to use it. She'd killed before, with no remorse or regret. She'd do it again. The world was better without men like that.

Jane took out the blade and began to hone it on her whetstone. The knife was still new, perfectly weighted, its edge already sharper than any razor. But this was her ritual, letting her mind roam as her fingers moved, a soft rhythm for her thoughts.

She finished and slid it back into the sheath. Time to leave. Time to find Robby Barstow.

*   *   *

He saw all the chimneys pushing at the sky. Dozens of them, spewing out smoke day and night and making money for their owners. More of them every year.

Simon could remember when the idea of a manufactory was still new, when each of the tall chimneys was enough of a novelty to make everyone gawk and point in wonder. None of them imagined what Leeds would become. The soot that floated in the air, caught in the throat and stained the washing as it hung to dry, the haze that covered the town.

The factories and machines had drawn people from the country-side, filled with the promise of a fair future. They learned the truth quickly enough.

But the factories kept rising and the families kept arriving. Every year, every week, dreams of fortune that quickly dwindled to regret. As Simon crossed the bridge over the Aire, he saw two forlorn families staring down at the water.

He walked past them, beyond the solid brick of Salem Chapel and Sykes's Brewery before cutting across the open ground to Hunslet Lane. Gas lamps twinkled along the road, each one illuminating a few feet of pavement. A new idea from the council, and barely worth the money they'd spent. He stopped at a plain house, one in a row of others all exactly the same. A knock on the door, then a wait before a man answered.

'Tell him it's Simon Westow.'

The click of a lock as the door closed again. Off in the distance he could hear a woman screaming at a child. Half a minute later he was led in, through to the scullery. One man sat at the table, three more standing behind with their arms folded, staring at him with stern, forbidding faces.

'What do you want, Westow?'

His large hands were bunched into fists, eyes narrowed under heavy black brows. He was stark, rough edges and angles, a thug who relished a fight. But his appearance masked a sharp mind. Robert Allston ran a business, hiring his men out as guards. He'd started out keeping factories safe when the Luddites tried to destroy the machines that were killing their livelihoods. That threat faded, but Allston had been intelligent enough to change with the times. These days his men guarded the wealthy and the titled in the area. A thriving enterprise in uncertain days.

'I hear Magistrate Curzon has a bodyguard.'

'What about it?' He took a clay pipe from his jacket, lit a spill from a candle and began to smoke.

'Is he one of yours?'

He shook his head. 'His name's John Whittaker. Used to do some work for the government, the way I heard things.'

'What sort of work?'

Allston gave an eloquent shrug. 'Never asked. Don't matter to me.'

'You heard they arrested Davey Ashton?'

'So? Why are you asking?' He leaned back in his chair. 'Him and a dozen others from around the area, that's what they're saying. Friend of yours, is he?'

'That's right.' Simon glanced round the faces that stared back at him. 'Someone told me there's a government spy behind it all.'

'What about it?' Allston asked. 'It doesn't affect me.'

'I'll pay good money for information.'

'Then you'd better ask someone who's selling.' He turned his head and glanced over his shoulder. 'Right, lads?'

The men murmured their assent.

'I'll wish you a good evening, then,' Simon said.

Allston spoke before he reached the door.

'And I'll give you a word of advice, Westow. Don't bother coming back unless you're buying what we sell.'

At least he knew a little about Curzon's bodyguard now. A name, a hint of background; he'd thought Allston might know. Someone who'd worked for the government. That was interesting, it made the visit worthwhile. Everything else had been hot air and bluster.

Jane passed a new building by the river, a warehouse that towered up three storeys high, pulleys and wide doors facing on to the water. No lights burned behind the tall windows. Last year this had been the ruin of a blacking factory, crumbling walls and charred timbers. Now that had faded into memory. Time raced on, and the past was a country best forgotten.

The world seemed smaller after night fell, as if the darkness pushed everything closer together. She moved along the street down from the old Cloth Hall and the Assembly Rooms, turned a door handle and entered the beershop.

Lamps burned bright inside, casting deep shadows into the corners. Mary Rigton sat on her stool, selling the drink and keeping a close eye on her customers. Men huddled around the benches, the low hum of their voices filling the air. For one bitter winter, this place had been Jane's home every night. Mrs Rigton had let her sleep on the floor, close to the embers of the fire. The shelter and warmth had kept her alive. Jane could still picture herself curled up on the flagstones, letting the heat soak into her body.

'You're got your hunter's face on, girl,' the woman said.

'Robby Barstow.'

Mrs Rigton pursed her lips. 'He hasn't shown his face in here for a while.'

A man squeezed by, placing his tankard on the plank used as a counter. The woman filled it from the barrel and took his coins, pushing them down into the old leather purse that hung from her dress.

'Do you know where I can find him?'

'Jimmy,' the woman called out and a man on the bench turned his head. His skin was dirty, face overgrown with a heavy beard, jacket smeared with filth.

'What?' There was an edge of temper in his voice.

'Robby Barstow.'

'What about him?'

'Where is he?'

'Rose and Crown, probably. Why?'

'This lass is looking for him.'

Jane saw the man stare at her, his lips curling into a sneer.

'If you're in the family way, he'll not marry you, luv. He's already wed.' His laugh turned to a wheezing crackle.

'That's enough,' Mrs Rigton said. No need to raise her voice. She turned to Jane. 'Come back when you have time to talk.'

'I will,' she promised.

After the sun set, the streets belonged to the whores and the thieves. Occasionally the night watch would pass by on their rounds, old men, too fearful and slow to catch a mouse. The lawful stayed behind their shutters or travelled from door to door in the safety of a coach.

The night had its own sounds, its own breath. Jane let it envelop her as she walked. She edged through the door of the Rose and Crown. Barstow was there, lost in conversation with three other men. He was wearing a good suit with a checked weave, legs extended in front of him, the light catching the shine on his boots. No mistaking him, not with that small wart by the side of his mouth. Ugly as the devil and twice as devious.

Jane slipped out again, finding a space in the passage that led through to the stables. She could see everyone who left. Time to wait. All the time in the world.

The clock in the parish church struck eleven as Simon strode up Kirkgate. Leeds was quiet, graceless and black as a grave. He'd gone round the inns and the beershops, listening, asking questions, buying drinks. A few men had heard about Davey. One group even claimed they'd seen him being led through town. But no mention of any government spy. He remained faceless, drifting like fog above it all. Simon made his plans for the morning. See Davey and try to learn more about those arrests across the West Riding. As he crossed Briggate, he glanced up the dark street towards the Moot Hall. His friend was still there, still a prisoner. Helpless, he felt the minutes ticking away.

Men came, men went. Jane stood, watching the door of the Rose and Crown. She heard the bell at St John's ring eleven and grasped the handle of her knife as the door opened.

A creak of hinges and a glow of light from inside, then darkness again as Barstow emerged. She could pick out his figure, dark and solid against the deep blue of night. He stretched slowly, then started to stroll away.

She followed, every step silent and measured, alert for any threat. But Barstow never even looked around, ambling down the Head Row with his hands thrust in his trouser pockets, kicking at loose stones on the pavement.

By the entrance to Rockley Court she crept up behind him and pushed the point of her knife against the nape of his neck. Not a soul around, the only sounds far off and muffled.

Barstow stopped, his body tense, hardly daring to breathe.

'In there,' she hissed. 'Don't turn around.'

Just enough pressure from the blade to prick his skin but
not break it. To keep him in line. Barstow moved stiffly, easing
his hands free.

'Don't,' Jane warned. 'You'll be dead first.'

He was facing away from her, pushed against the cold bricks
of the wall, arms hanging by his sides.

'You sold a watch,' Jane said. Barstow started to move his
head. She pressed the tip a little harder against his flesh and he
halted. 'No need to speak. Nod if you know what I mean.'

A short, tentative dip of his head.

'There was more, wasn't there?'

Another quick movement. Agreement.

'The man who owns them wants them back.'

'But—'

Jane edged the knife deeper, just enough to cause a drop of
blood that slowly trickled down inside his collar. She could smell
his fear over the stink of piss and vomit on the cobbles.

'No.' Her voice was quiet, hard as iron. 'No buts. You know
Mrs Rigton's beershop?'

'Yes.' His voice was a croak.

'Tomorrow morning you'll take it all there and leave it with
her.'

'I—' he began, then took a breath and swallowed. 'I've sold
a few things.'

'Bring the rest. Everything. If you try to cheat me . . .' She
worked the knife a little deeper into his neck. 'You
understand?'

'Yes,' he agreed quickly.

She was gone, off into the night before he could turn. From
a distance she watched as he emerged, following as he made his
way home with a shaky, worried walk.

Jane stopped at the corner of Vicar Lane, standing out of sight
until he took out his keys, looking all around.

Somewhere behind her, a coach rumbled along the road.

FOUR

A dull day. The clouds hung low and a thin wind blew out of the west, as if yesterday's promise of spring had been a tease. Simon dashed up Briggate, dodging between the carts moving on the street and through the heavy wooden doors of the Moot Hall. It had been a grand building, built of dressed stone, with dark wood wainscoting and portraits of the mayors decorating the hallway. Fine inside and out. But its hey days had passed generations ago. Now it was dowdy, worn and scarred and limping to the end of its life.

The office he wanted was up the stairs, tucked away near the end of the corridor. He didn't pause or knock on the door, simply walked in, letting the latch click behind him as the clerk jerked his head up in surprise, then smiled. Simon had dealt with him before, a fellow who'd gladly exchange favours for silver.

A pair of coins landed on the man's desk.

'Is David Ashton still down in the cells?'

There was a small pause before he answered, long enough for greed to swell across his face as he judged whether it was safe to talk.

'He is.' The money vanished into his pocket. 'They'll be taking him to York as soon as they're ready.'

Simon raised an eyebrow in an unspoken question.

'Nobody's told me a day yet,' the man continued.

'What are the charges?'

The man searched through a small pile of papers on his desk and plucked one out.

'Sedition,' he recited. 'Intent to incite against the government and subvert through speech and writings.'

'Does it say when this is supposed to have happened?'

'Seven times in the last two years. The most recent was a week ago. It says there's testimony from someone who heard him.'

A week ago? Impossible. According to Emily, Davey was still

ill then. He'd seen no one, she said, and Simon believed her. He could use that lie.

'Whose testimony?' Simon asked.

The clerk shook his head. 'That's for the trial.'

'Has Curzon finished his questioning?'

A long pause before another coin spun on the wood.

'Yes.'

'I need a pass to go down to the gaol.' Three more silver coins saw the clerk hurriedly scribbling a note.

The cells lay in the cellar, musty and damp. The chill never left the air here, working its way into bone and lungs. The only light came from barred windows set high in the wall. A single desk and chair stood at the bottom of the steps. The heavy man sitting there eyed Simon suspiciously.

A glance at the paper, then he shuffled along the row to a small cell. The key turned easily and silently and the door swung back. Davey lay on the bench. A coin passed from Simon's fingers to the gaoler's palm.

'No need to lock it. He won't try to escape.'

A nod, then they were alone.

'Emily went to you, did she?' Davey sat up slowly. No bruises on his face, and he seemed to move easily enough. At least he hadn't been beaten, Simon thought. But after just a day in here he already seemed older, haunted, with large, dark circles under his eyes.

'Where else would she go?' He stood, arms folded. A thin trickle of water ran down the wall and pooled on the flagstones. Names, dates, numbers had been carved into the stones. The cell stank. 'How do you feel?'

Davey looked at him. 'How do you think? They said they're going to charge me under the Six Acts.' He started to cough, a wet, wracking sound.

'They're claiming the last time was a week ago.'

Ashton shook his head. 'That's not true. I was poorly.' He gazed around. 'I'm not likely to get any better down here, either.'

'You'll be going to York to stand trial.'

'That's what Curzon told me.' Ashton coughed again, fumbled in the pocket of his trousers for a rag and spat into it.

'I've heard talk of a government spy.'

'I don't know. I wouldn't put it past them.'

'I need to find him.'

Davey stared at the floor, painting the picture in his mind, then raised his head.

'The only thing I can tell you is that the magistrate had someone with him when he came to the house. A young man, dark hair, well-dressed, a face like a rat, sharp nose and teeth. He stood there, pointed at me and said, "That's him." Then the soldiers pulled me away while Curzon began searching.'

'Did you know him at all?'

Davey shook his head. 'I've never seen him before.'

'What about a name?'

'I didn't hear one. It happened so quickly. The whole thing sounded . . .' He searched for the word. 'Rehearsed. It had to be.'

'This man, was he local?'

'Simon, I don't know. I only heard him speak two words, not enough to tell. There are thousands of people in Leeds these days. I probably haven't seen half of them in my life.'

Westow sighed. 'They've arrested twelve across the West Riding, too.'

Davey's voice was dull and resigned. 'I'm not surprised. Rumours have been going round for a while that there'd be a crack-down.'

'I'm going to get you out of here.'

'How?' He looked around the cell. 'How are you going to manage that?'

'I don't know yet.' Davey would see through any lie in a second. But he needed to try and give him some hope. 'There has to be a way.'

Ashton shook his head. 'You won't succeed. They're the government, Simon. They own the judges, they own the juries. They can say whatever they want. How am I going to disprove it? You know as well as I do that I've come out with some things over the years.'

And they'd twist every word of it, colour each strand of evidence until they painted Davey's heart pure black and full of hatred for this country.

'I'm not going to give up.'

How could he, after all the Ashtons had done for him when he was young? Some debts could never be paid in full.

'Don't think I'm not grateful. But—'

'The first thing is to find this spy.'

'And what will you do with him after that?' Davey asked. 'Make him recant his statement? It won't help. Who would you fear more if you were him – a thief-taker or the government?'

'I'll make certain he's terrified of the thief-taker.'

Davey gave a small, sorrowful smile. 'For all the good that will do.'

'We'll beat this, Davey.' He reached out and clasped the man's hand.

The gaoler was still at his desk. Simon placed a small pile of coins in front of him.

'As long as Davey Ashton's in here, I want his meals to come from the Rose and Crown. Understood?'

No words, just a nod.

'And he's to have a good blanket, paper, pen and ink. Messages sent and delivered.'

'But the magistrate said—'

'I don't care what the magistrate told you.' He opened his hand to show more coins. 'Here's money that says different.'

'I'll take care of it.'

After the cells, all the factory soot and stench in the air smelled like summer sweetness. Simon stood on Briggate and breathed deep. Davey sounded like a man who'd given up on his own life. In his mind he was already on that ship crossing the ocean.

Simon was going to have to do this on his own.

Jane walked out beyond Drony Laith, where a new building kept rising taller and taller each day. Men shouted and laughed and swore as they worked, laying courses of bricks and hammering timbers. She passed unnoticed, off into the woods beyond.

No one had followed her. She knew that in her blood, but still she was careful, taking a looping route and turning back on herself three times to be sure. A final glance over her shoulder and she vanished between the trees. It was cooler here; the dim air cupped a chill, the shadows deepened as the young leaves seemed to drink all the light.

Her money was buried by the roots of an old oak, tightly wrapped in a tin covered with oilcloth. She dug it up with her knife and pried open the lid. Everything was still there. This place had served her well. Hidden, free, somewhere beyond suspicion. But as Leeds crept closer and closer, it was time to move her savings. Soon all this would be gone, the trees cut down, the ground made over into stone and noise. Nothing was safe here any more.

She knew Simon kept his money in the bank. But he was a man. They'd never allow a girl like her through the door.

Still, there was one good spot in the town, one person she trusted to look after this. She tucked the money into the pocket of her dress, clamped her hand over it, and buried the tin again before she moved back towards the town.

Off the Head Row, Jane cut through Green Dragon Yard. The sound of the road softened. As she slid through a thin opening in the wall to the small court beyond, the noise seemed to vanish altogether, as if she'd managed to step through to a different world. A tiny house stood alone, looking like it had been here forever, forgotten as the rest of Leeds grew around it.

Vines grew in old barrels, climbing in a bright tangle up the stone walls and almost hiding the green door. She tapped on the wood. A few seconds later a small woman was standing there. White hair covered with a cap, her clothes long out of date but clean and crisp, a calm, welcoming smile on her lips and in her eyes.

'Hello, child, I wondered if it might be you.' She stood aside. 'Come in, come in.'

Catherine Shields had lived in the house for years, first as a wife, then as a widow. It was the only place Jane had been where she felt completely safe, utterly free. She always found peace here.

The woman poured two mugs of cordial and settled into her hardback chair.

'You still have the ring.'

Jane glanced at the gold on her finger and looked up in surprise. 'Of course I do.'

Catherine had given it to her, taken it from a box and pressed it in her hand. It had been a keepsake for the woman from her late husband, a token to keep her safe. Jane treasured it, the first gift she'd ever received.

'I told you I'd always wear it.'

'Always is a long time,' Catherine Shields said with a soft smile. 'Especially when you're young. You look like you need something.'

'I do.' Jane took out the packet and opened it to show the money. 'I'd like you to keep this for me.'

Mrs Shields put a hand over her mouth and gasped. 'Oh my,' she said as she stared at Jane. 'Oh *my*. What did you do for it? Nothing bad, I hope.'

'It's mine. I earned it all.'

Catherine raised an eyebrow. 'Then you're a very rich young woman.'

Jane shrugged. She knew it was a fortune, but it was only words and numbers on pieces of paper. Important, she understood that, yet it had little real value to her. It wasn't gold, it wasn't silver. She'd earned this much; she could always make more.

'I'll take care of it, if that's what you really want,' Mrs Shields offered after a moment.

'I do.'

'Then I'll show you where I put it, in case you ever need it.'

She rose from the chair and took the money into the other room. Jane followed, watching as the old woman bent easily, worked a stone from the wall with her fingertips and tucked the packet into the gap behind. A perfect hiding place. If any thief came, he'd never find that.

'Thank you,' Jane said.

'It was worth it to see you smile.' Catherine reached out and stroked her cheek. No one else had ever touched her with fondness and care. Not since she was a child and her world had been a different place. 'You need some joy in your life, child.'

'I'm sorry,' Jane said quickly. 'I have to go. I'll come and visit soon, I promise.'

'You're always welcome here, you know that.'

She left, hurrying away because she didn't want to leave.

'Have you managed to learn anything yet, George?' The print shop was filled with the rich smell of ink. Simon paced up and down the room, racking his brain for anything that might help Davey Ashton. 'For the love of God, there has to be *something*.'

Mudie wiped his hands on his apron. 'Nothing more than dribs and drabs. They've taken a dozen men. Four from Batley, two from Halifax, and six from Dewsbury.'

'Do you have their names?' Simon asked.

Mudie shook his head. 'Haven't heard. If they're not from Leeds, it wouldn't mean much to me, anyway.'

'Why Davey? Why now?'

'Stand back and think about it for a moment. Curzon learns what's going to be happening in the West Riding and thinks he'll have his little slice of glory. And Davey Ashton is an easy target. People know his views. He's never hidden them, you have to admit that. Arrest him and it gilds the Curzon name a little.'

'Then why isn't everyone talking about it? Have you heard people gossiping?'

Mudie pursed his mouth. 'Maybe our friend the magistrate isn't as certain of success as he hopes. Better to keep things quiet.' He shrugged. 'I don't know. That's a guess.'

'Tell me, have you come across any rumours of a spy working around the county?'

'I have,' he replied and paused. 'Look, it doesn't mean much, Simon. You know how things are; there's always talk of government agents in cases like this. Most of the time it's wishful thinking. Usually someone in the group betrays them or they've been stupid.'

'With Davey, though . . .' Simon said.

Mudie shrugged. 'So far it's just words, isn't it? Nobody's seen this man. You don't have a name for him.'

'Davey saw him. A young man with a face like a rat, he said.'

'You're a thief-taker. You should be able to find someone like that.'

'Don't you worry. I will.'

Rosie walked with Emily Ashton. They didn't say much, no more than occasional sentences. Jane followed twenty yards behind, watching with one hand on her knife, eyes alert for anyone who might be a danger. No one at all. They were just three women trudging through Leeds.

On Mabgate she darted ahead, her gaze gliding over the empty spaces and the undergrowth. Everything was clear, open. She found a space in the copse that had grown up around the ruins of the dyeworks. A clear view of the road and the house. Jane sat, pulling the shawl over her hair, and settled down to wait.

Simon sat alone and silent among the talk that filled the coffee house. In his mind he ranged through names and faces. Who'd be able to tell him about a spy?

A small, polite cough disturbed his thoughts. Simon turned quickly to see a cramped man in a low-brimmed hat standing beside him. He had ink stains on his hands and his pale eyes blinked quickly through thick spectacles. But his suit was cut from the best worsted and carefully tailored to hide the growing belly. A clerk, Simon decided, but a very well-paid one. Someone trusted, with responsibilities and some status.

'Forgive me disturbing you, sir.' He had a soft voice, curiously musical and pleasing. 'I've been looking for you. I was told you might be around here.'

'And you found me, Mr . . .?'

'Campion, sir.' He looked flustered. 'It's not for myself. It's for my employer.'

'Go on,' Simon told him.

'Mr Ericsson, sir. The timber merchant.' The smallest of hesitations, then he whispered, 'It's a delicate matter.'

Of course, Simon smiled to himself. Every matter that needed a thief-taker was delicate. For a small moment, he was tempted to say he had no time. Then he glanced at Campion again and saw the pleading in the man's eyes. There was something curious here.

'What's happened?'

The man lowered his gaze again. 'That's for him to say, sir.'

Simon needed to begin the search for this spy; they might move Davey to York at any time. But Ericsson . . . he had money. Whatever he needed, he'd pay. He had powerful friends in this town, too, and that might prove useful. It probably wouldn't even take long. And he had Jane to help.

A nod. 'I'll meet him in an hour. Where?'

'On the bridge, sir.'

'Tell him I'll be there.'

As Campion left, Simon took out his pocket watch. Not long, but he could make a start.

Jane waited. Shadows flitted and shifted. In the distance she could hear the lulling undertone of Sheepscar Beck. Closer, the rhythmic clack of a loom from a house along the road. Not a soul had passed. Rosie was still inside the house with Emily Ashton; she could see their figures moving behind the window glass.

Two hours and nothing stirred. Still she stayed, unmoving, out of sight, with her hand hovering close to her knife.

The door opened. She saw the women hug quickly, then Rosie was on her way back to town, never looking around, giving nothing away.

Jane remained for another hour, then stood, brushed off her dress and moved silently away. In Leeds, she passed unnoticed along the crowded streets. As she approached Mary Rigton's alehouse, she suddenly grew wary, glancing at all faces she saw. There was someone. She could feel it. The tingle, the sense of eyes on her.

Rumour and fact.

Talk swirled and shifted, never quite taking shape. Some had heard of a spy, but none had seen him. No one had met him. He was still a ghost.

But someone had to know. Someone had answers. Simon passed the word, the offer of a reward. Now he had to trust to luck and greed. A glance at the clock on the parish church. Five minutes until the hour was up. Simon strode quickly along Kirkgate, dusting the smuts of soot from his jacket as he squeezed through the press of people and the noise of the town.

Ericsson was waiting, standing on the parapet and gazing down at the flow of the river. Barges were tied two and three deep by the warehouses as men unloaded their cargoes. The bloated body of a dog floated downstream. Thick tendrils of colour moved sluggishly in the water, reds and ochres and blacks from the dyeworks.

Simon settled beside him, elbows resting on the stone parapet.

'You wanted to see me.'

*　　*　　*

She didn't pause, no sign of hesitation to give anything away. Jane pushed open the door and walked into the comforting fug of tobacco and old beer. Five men were sitting, drinking, all of them far from the world. Jane leaned close to Mrs Rigton.

'Did Barstow leave something for me?'

The woman tilted her head. A plain hessian sack lay in the corner. 'Came in just after I opened.'

'I need to leave something upstairs,' Jane told her.

For a moment the woman said nothing. Then: 'Go on.'

There was hardly any furniture in the room. A bed, a table, a chair; Mrs Rigton lived most of her life down in the bar. She only came up here to sleep. After all these years she might have been a wealthy woman, but there was nothing to indicate it in this place.

With great care, Jane emptied the sack. Five pieces made from silver. Barstow had stolen eight. Simon had recovered the watch; two still missing, exactly as the man had said. She stacked everything in the corner, tucked out of sight behind the chair, wadded her shawl and pushed it deep into the sack. A moment later she emerged into the daylight, the fingers of her right hand curled tight around the knife.

Someone was behind her. She could hear him, the way the rhythm of footsteps matched her own. It wouldn't be Barstow; he didn't have the skill or the courage. Not that it mattered. Jane was going to lead him through the courts and yards and finish up behind him. Then she'd make him regret this.

She didn't even need to think where she was going. Leeds was imprinted in her mind, in her feet. She'd walked every inch of the town time and again, she'd lived on its streets when she was a child. Sometimes knowing where to turn and how to hide could be the difference between staying alive and dying.

Ericsson kept his palms flat on the stone surface of the bridge. His eyes looked off into the distance as he spoke.

'In Sweden it's still cold, you know. But summer will arrive soon and there will be hardly any darkness for a few months.' His accent made the words rise at the end of each sentence. 'My wife decided it was time we came back here. Our son has gone to Stockholm to look after the business there.'

'It's been five years. Leeds has changed a great deal since you left,' Simon said. He wanted the man to push to the meat of the matter. This might be business, lucrative business, but it was stealing time from Davey Ashton.

'I can see that.' Ericsson nodded. 'It's uglier now. Dirtier.' He exhaled. 'On Friday, my wife went to visit friends. They have a house near Wetherby. So I decided to go out that night with some of the men I knew when I lived here before. Businessmen,' he added.

Now they were coming to it. 'What happened?'

'One by one, they left. Home to their wives and children. We're not as young as we used to be.' He gave a small shrug, shoulders barely moving in his jacket. 'I stayed. I didn't feel ready to go back to an empty house.'

Of course not. He was a bachelor for a few days, a free man looking for some fun. Simon glanced at him. Ericsson's face was stern, forbidding, his blue eyes cold.

'You met a girl.'

'She met me,' Ericsson corrected him. Naturally. It was always that way. The old, old story.

'Where was this?'

'I don't remember. One place or another. After a while they all began to look alike.' A half-smile of regret. 'I was sitting on my own. She came over to me.'

'And you bought her a drink or two.'

Ericsson nodded. 'The next thing I knew, I woke up by a dungheap in one of the courts. It was still dark.' He reddened at the thought, embarrassed at his own gullibility.

'What did she take?'

'My money, my watch, my suit, my shoes.' He paused for a long time. 'I don't mind those. I deserve it for my own stupidity. But she took my ring.' He held up his right hand, showing a slim band of pale flesh on the third finger. 'My father left it to me. I want it back, Mr Westow.'

'You were hocussed,' Simon told him.

'Hocussed?' He frowned as he ran the word round his mouth. 'I don't know that word. What does it mean, hocussed?'

'She put something in your drink to make you pass out so she could rob you.'

'I have never heard of it. I don't think it happens in Sweden.'

It probably did, Simon thought, and every day of the week. Ericsson had never come across it before, that was all. Rich men, poor men, it didn't matter who they were. If there was anything to take and sell, it vanished, along with the woman.

'What name did she give you?'

'Charlotte Winter. She looked to be about twenty.' Ericsson blushed again. 'Dark hair, plump. She had a sweet smile.'

'Tell me about the ring.'

'It's gold. The stone is amber. There are words in Swedish carved inside the band. A . . .' He searched for the term.

'An inscription. That should be easy to find,' Simon said. Amber was unusual; people would remember it. 'You honestly don't recall where this happened?'

The man shook his head. 'No.' He waved towards the town. 'I tried to find the place again, but . . . no.'

'Was this woman on her own, or did you see a man?'

'I didn't see anyone else. But I was only looking at her.'

It didn't help. There was no trail he could follow.

'Do you know how I work?'

'I do,' Ericsson replied. 'Bring back my ring and I'll pay you well.'

'No promises.' It was something he told all his clients. No thief-taker succeeded every time.

Ericsson nodded. 'I understand. If you find it, come and see Mr Campion. He'll make certain I receive the message.'

'What about the woman? Do you want to prosecute her?' Simon could guess the answer, but he needed to ask.

'No.' A curt reply. Of course not. A court case meant everyone would know, his humiliation on display to the world. 'I want my ring back, that is all.'

'I should tell you, this woman might have already moved on from Leeds. They rarely stay long in one place, it's too dangerous.'

'But she'd have sold what she stole first.'

'Very likely.'

'This is your business, Mr Westow. I'm told you do it well. I hope that's true.'

They shook hands and he watched Ericsson walk away. Firm,

even strides, going south of the river, back to his timber yard by
the water.

It only took five minutes before she came out of a tiny ginnel
to see the figure ahead of her, gazing around, unsure which way
to turn. Jane stopped, staring in disbelief. Not a man at all. A
woman. Taller and heavier than her, several years older, with a
tumble of thick dark hair that hung like a rat's nest over her
shoulders. She wore an old, patched cotton dress too short to
reach her clogs, a threadbare shawl gathered on her shoulders.

For a second, Jane was too stunned to move. Then she breathed
slowly. Man or woman, it didn't matter. This was a threat.

The woman tensed as Jane pricked her back with the tip of
her knife and whispered, 'Why are you looking for me?'

'He paid me. Two pennies.' She opened her fist to show a pair
of coins.

'Who?' Jane wanted to hear the name.

'Him.' That was her only response.

'Why? What does he want?'

'He said I had to see where you went then go back and tell
him.' Her voice shook. 'Please . . . don't hurt me.'

Jane took two steps back. Something was wrong. As soon as
he heard her voice, Barstow would have known exactly who she
was. Every crook in Leeds knew she worked with Simon, and
the thief-taker didn't hide his address. This woman came from
someone else. Who?

'Then you'd better tell him I managed to lose you.'

'I can't.'

Silently, Jane took another pace away from the woman, eyes
fixed, knife ready for any movement.

The woman turned, lunging. Light glinted on the blade of a
long dagger. But all she caught was air. Before she could recover,
Jane was on her. A slash opened the girl's arm and her knife
clattered to the ground. Jane kicked it away.

'Do you really want me to kill you?'

A shake of the head. The girl pressed the edge of her shawl
down on the wound, trying to staunch the blood. Her face had
turned pale.

'Then don't come after me again,' Jane warned. 'Ever.'

For a moment she stared, then turned and walked away. Even as she did it, Jane knew she was making a mistake. If this had been a man, she'd have killed him. She'd been too cautious. Too generous. Too stupid. Too weak. This wasn't finished yet. As certain as morning, the woman would return.

Up in the attic room, staring down at Swinegate, Jane ran the knife across her arm and watched the blood begin to run over her skin. A thin line, dark and rich and red, trailing over her wrist, her palm, dripping from the end of her finger. The punishment for her failure.

The pain was exquisite. But it was what she deserved.

The silver lay on the kitchen table. Rosie had eyed it with pleasure, knowing to the penny the fee it would bring when it was returned to Haigh. Jane had vanished upstairs without a word.

Why had she let the woman live? Had she hesitated because it was a female in front of her?

Who was she? Where had she come from?

A minute passed, the beauty and the agony of suffering. She let it course through her body.

'Any trouble with Barstow?' Simon asked as they left the house.

'No,' Jane replied. 'Did you expect any?'

'That bandage on your arm. I wondered—'

'I had an accident,' she told him. 'That's all.'

There was no point in asking more. Any question cast a shadow and closed a door. She'd never reveal her thoughts and feelings. Not to him, not to Rosie, maybe not to anyone on this earth. Once, he'd believed that her manner might ease after she came to live in the house, that with his wife and the boys there, a family around her, Jane might unbend a little. But it had never happened; now he was certain it never would.

'We need to find Ericsson's ring. I want you to start asking around about the girl who hocussed him.'

'Yes.'

He glanced down at Jane, but her face was blank. No expression at all, the mask that never slipped. That was her, the way she'd been as long as they'd worked together. He'd learned to accept that, to take her exactly as she was. Jane was so good at this work that she might have been made for it. She was loyal, she was dogged and ruthless. And if she chose to keep her life hidden, that was her business.

FIVE

S imon found Caleb Cross at the Mixed Cloth Hall, standing at the far end of the room, deep in conversation. His thick hands moved quickly to emphasize his points. Cross was a new kind of businessman, representing a group of millowners scattered around the West Riding. A middle man, he called himself. With his rough charm, good humour, and deep knowledge of the wool trade, he was the perfect salesman. He made extravagant promises; more than that, he kept his word. The quality of the cloth he sold was always excellent, the deliveries arrived when he promised. People trusted what he said.

He was tall man, and always wore his hat, even indoors, easy to pick out anywhere. Cross was broadly built, rushing to fat so the jacket and trousers strained at his waist. But he carried it well; in a curious way, the stoutness suited him. It made him seem more genial and believable.

Simon waited, leaning against a pillar until Cross had finished, then raised his hand in greeting. 'How's trade?'

'Fair to middling.' His usual answer. He had a deep growl of a voice, rough as gravel. That was his act, gruff, forthright. But the warmth and intelligence glowed in his eyes. 'How about yours? Catching thieves?'

'A few. I hear the government's been arresting a few Radicals out where you live.'

'Politics.' He spat the word. 'No time for it. There's only one thing that matters and that's the brass you've got in your pocket.'

'But you know about it.'

'Oh aye,' Cross admitted. 'Hard to ignore when it's on everyone's lips.'

The arrests were news out there. Strange, then, that taking

Davey Ashton had been so quiet, not even a story in the Leeds newspapers.

'Has there been any talk of a government spy up your way?'

'A few have mentioned it. No idea if it's true, mind.'

'I'm looking for a name or a description.'

Cross was curious now, rubbing his chin. He gave a searching look. 'Why, Simon? That's not your usual line of work.'

'Let's just say it is for now.'

The main raised a thick eyebrow, curious. 'Aye, well, that's your affair. Like I said, all I've heard is talk, and you know what that's worth.'

Nothing, most of the time. But sometimes a tiny nugget of gold is hidden deep in the muck.

'You know, don't you?'

Cross sighed and nodded. 'Someone did say that he was called Dodd. But that's it. I steer clear of anything awkward. It might stand in the way of profit. Life's safer that way.'

It was one thing. Maybe not even right. But it gave him a place to start.

The inns were always busy. Day and night, travellers arrived on coaches or prepared to leave. The buildings were alive with the sounds and the smells of the road, horses and dust, coachmen shouting their orders, passengers disembarking and stretching out their aches after the cramped, uncomfortable miles.

Inside, there was the promise of food and drink, rooms for those who were staying. But nobody remembered a guest named Dodd.

He stood near the market cross, staring along Briggate. The street ran down the slope all the way to the river. Teeming with people, today, every day. The rich and the desperate, and all those in between.

By now the spy had probably gone. If he'd ever existed. Davey said someone had identified him, someone he didn't know. Dodd? Maybe, maybe.

Simon turned on his heel and walked away down the Head Row.

Jane waited near the door of the Saddle Inn as Jack Harmsworth fleeced some tired travellers at cards. It was his trade, his livelihood, and every day he found fresh fools. When the hand was done, he gathered his winnings, bowed, and rose from the table.

Harmsworth was a handsome man in his early twenties, dressed in a sturdy, sober suit. With an open, reassuring smile, he looked honest. But it was all surface; scratch the skin and underneath was a man who'd slice his way through to anyone's purse without regret, then gull him for everything he carried. When Jane had first met him, he was a scrawny youth performing card tricks for coins on Briggate every market day. Back then he'd been as hungry and desperate as her. These days he'd settled into his new life.

'What is it?' Annoyance flickered in his eyes. 'There's a good game going on here. They can't wait to lose to me.'

'A ring,' Jane told him. 'Gold with an amber stone. Words inside the band in some foreign language. There's money for whoever leads us to it.'

Harmsworth nodded and returned to the table. It was enough. By the end of the night he'd have been all over town. With luck, he'd pass the word, if he didn't become too caught up in the cards. If the man did his job, greed would take care of the rest.

Finally Simon caught a hint of the spy at a rooming house in one of the courts off Vicar Lane.

'I had someone staying here who looked like that.'

Charles Eldon kept a respectable place, quieter and cheaper than the inns, sheets changed every week, the hall and stairs both neatly swept.

'What name did he give?' Simon passed him a silver coin. The man examined it for a moment, then slid it into his pocket.

'Dodd.'

Simon smiled to himself. 'How long was he here?'

'Two days. Only left yesterday. Had a woman with him. A very low type, brassy.' A frown crossed the man's face. 'But I know they're still in Leeds. I saw them on Kirkgate this morning.'

'What?' He felt his heart thudding hard in his chest. 'Are you sure it was them?'

'I'm positive. It surprised me, though. When they left, he asked me the time of the York coach. I thought he was going there.'

York. Where they would try Davey and the other men. Of course, they'd want Dodd and his evidence for that.

'Did you see where they went?'

'She took that path across the burial ground down by the parish church,' Eldon replied. 'He carried on towards Timble Bridge.'

'This woman—'

With a shake of his head, Eldon cut him off. 'I never paid her that much mind. Spoke to her once, she sounded like she was from London. Not local.'

No point in pursuing that; he'd look for her later.

'What about Dodd. How did he pay?'

'In advance,' Eldon said. 'Didn't even haggle over the price. Wanted a room where they didn't have to share, with a solid lock on the door. Not that either one of them was here much. Out first thing in the morning, not back until late.'

'What luggage did they have?'

'Only one small bag each.'

A portable life, Simon thought. A spy's life.

'Did you see Dodd talking to anyone else? Did he receive any messages?' He produced another coin to keep the man's tongue good and loose.

'No. Nothing at all.'

'If you see either one of them again, let me know.' A final coin and he was gone.

Simon walked along Vicar Lane and turned on to Kirkgate. The York coach left the Old King's Arms early each morning, long before Eldon claimed to have seen Dodd. He must still be in town. Maybe there was some hope for Davey.

Down by the church, Simon stood. To his left, the track through the burying ground led to York Street and everything beyond. The woman could be anywhere. Brassy was hardly going to help him find her.

Straight ahead, Timble Bridge and then Marsh Lane, leading away from Leeds. Buildings sprouting up all around, growing like seeds planted in the dirt. New houses for all the workers coming to the town – if they could find jobs that paid enough to afford them.

But precious few places to lodge out there, only two he could recall, and Dodd wasn't at either of them; it only took a few minutes and two pennies to learn that. Where are you, he wondered; where in God's name are you?

Evening was approaching and the mood of Leeds was beginning to shift. One or two of the shops had already shuttered their windows and closed their doors. Soon enough the rest would follow and the town would take on its night colours. A few of the prostitutes were already out, dotted along Briggate at the tiny entrances to the courts as he made his way home.

The house smelt clean. Every surface shone, all the floors mopped and glistening. Rosie stood in the kitchen, hands on her hips, sweat glowing on her face, staring at him as he entered.

'You've forgotten, haven't you?'

Frantically, he tried to remember. Finally a smile dawned. 'Richard and Amos are coming home tomorrow.'

Her gaze didn't waver. 'And you'd have been shocked to see them if I hadn't said anything.'

'I . . .' he began, but she was shaking her head. After all these years she knew him far too well.

He'd be glad to have them back. The boys had been gone for a week and he'd missed them; it felt as if part of himself had left. The house was too quiet, too ordered without them around. All their noise and chaos kept the joy in his life.

'You're right,' he admitted sheepishly.

But Davey Ashton was crowded at the front of his mind, pushing everything else away. Rosie understood that, too.

'Go on, you're forgiven,' she told him. 'Just be sure you make a fuss of them when they arrive.'

'As if I'd do anything else. I saw George Ericsson yesterday.' A change of subject might help, before she chided him again.

Ericsson meant money. That was enough to catch her interest. 'What did he want?'

He told her, watching her chuckle.

'Hocussed? For God's sake, Simon, you men are such a bunch of fools. How old was this girl?'

'Somewhere around twenty,' he said.

'And he really believed she'd be interested in him?'

'I don't know. Maybe he was prepared to pay.'

'He did,' she pointed out. 'Just more than he expected. And now he's going to give us more to get his ring back.'

'As long as it's enough,' Simon said with a grin, 'why should we care?'

Jane stood by the open window in the attic, staring out at the night. Clouds scudded across the sky, obscuring the full moon. A threat of rain in the air; she could smell it on the wind.

The girl was somewhere out there. The cut would heal, she wasn't badly hurt. But Jane had seen the hatred that flared in her eyes, the desire to kill. The next time . . .

She took out the knife and started running it over the whetstone. A preparation, a comfort. She trusted the weapon, she trusted herself. That was all she needed.

Money sat by the ewer, her share of the fee for returning Haigh's silver. She hadn't even counted it; Simon would never cheat her.

Sometimes she wondered what it would be like to not exist any more. To walk into the river, let it envelop her, to have it carry her away forever. Perhaps one or two might mourn, but they'd forget quickly enough. Their lives would move on.

Jane tested the blade against her thumb. The edge was sharp, perfect. Tenderly, she ran it once across her forearm, watching the blood appear and trickle, feeling the freedom of release. Another cut to add to the ladder of scars.

SIX

Morning, and the clouds hung low. Drizzle and dampness filled the air. Simon slipped into his coat, the old one with caped shoulders, and hurried along the streets to the Moot Hall. Down the stone steps. A coin on the gaoler's desk and he was led to the cells.

Davey was pale. He coughed, the sound wet and thick in his chest. His face wore a resigned look, as if he'd given up the fight before it had even begun.

'Are they bringing in your food?' Simon asked.

He nodded. 'It's this place. It's seeping into my lungs.'

'I'll have you free again soon.'

'Simon, please, don't promise what you can't deliver. We both know it's easy to get in here, and it's a damned sight harder to leave again.'

'You're the one who taught me the word injustice.'

'And now you can see what it means.' Davey coughed again, spat into his handkerchief and drank from a mug of water. 'It's a straight road from here to Australia, and there's nothing you can do to stop it.'

'That's not true,' Simon insisted. 'I think I've found the name of the spy. He's still in Leeds.'

He'd checked; Dodd hadn't taken that morning's coach to York.

'What about it?' Davey sighed. 'Tell me: even if you can find him, how will that help?'

'I'll drag him in front of a lawyer and make him swear that he was lying about you.'

'They'll make up something else in court. It's what they do, Simon.' He stood and placed his palms against the wall. 'They have me now. They're not going to let me go.'

'For God's sake.'

Davey Ashton had always railed against things, a man who urged fairness for everyone. For all the years Simon had known him, he'd spoken about it, written about it. And now he was going to surrender without even a protest.

He gave a wan, defeated smile. 'I appreciate everything you're doing, Simon. Believe me, I do. But you're never going to win. Do you think the government will let you?'

'We're going to find out what happens when we try. This is Curzon, not the government. He's not God.' Simon tried for some argument that might stir the man. 'What do you think it will do to Emily if they transport you?'

'People will take care of her. You, Rosie, a few others.'

'Of course we will.' Simon felt his temper starting to rise. 'But I'm not done with this yet.' A pause until Davey was looking at him. 'I didn't think you would be, either.'

'No.' Davey spoke with patient sadness. 'Nor did I. It's a

strange thing. I never believed I was a weak man. Who does? But a few days in here can change the way you look at the world. It seems I'm weaker than I ever imagined. I'm frightened, Simon. I'm scared I'll end up on the other side of the world and nothing will be able to stop it. I'm sorry.'

'Don't apologize.' He put his hand on Davey's shoulder, feeling the bones sharp and brittle under the skin. 'They haven't won yet.'

Davey Ashton breathed slowly and stayed silent.

'I told you before: I'm going to do everything I can,' Simon told him. 'You have no idea how much I owe you.'

'No,' Mudie said flatly. 'I won't do it, Simon.'

'Why not?'

He'd come to the printing shop, wanting to have posters pasted all over Leeds, asking why Davey Ashton had been arrested and demanding he was freed. No one seemed to know he'd been taken. Maybe Simon could make them care, even stir up a mob.

'Because my name has to go on anything I print. That's the law. If you start putting up something like that, I'll end up in the cell next to your friend.' He shook his head. 'I'm not prepared to risk it. I'm sorry.'

Of course; he had to look to his livelihood. In times like these, men were cautious, and who could blame them? But it was another path closed off, he thought as he walked out to Mabgate. At least he could take Emily Ashton some news of her brother.

She was restless, unable to settle, wandering around the room as he spoke, touching an ornament, a pen, a piece of paper as if they were talismans to keep her grounded and fixed in place. She looked as if she'd barely slept since her brother was dragged from the house. Deep, heavy shadows haunted her eyes. When Simon finished, she turned towards him.

'Can you save him? Be honest.'

'I'll do everything I can.' He could see the disappointment on her face. She craved certainty. But he couldn't work miracles. What he'd said was the truth.

At the door she held tight to his hand for a moment, squeezing it.

'Please,' she said. 'Please.'

'I'll try.'

Curzon was the key. But there was no chance of coming anywhere near the man now he had a bodyguard to protect him. Simon needed another way.

Dodd had answers. But first he had to find the man.

As he walked back towards Leeds, Simon sensed someone behind him. Trying to be quiet and doing a piss-poor job of it.

Close to Lady Bridge, the path curved, the bushes at the side growing thick and wild. For a handful of seconds, he'd be out of sight. That was long enough. Simon slipped the knife from his sleeve.

By the time the man appeared, head moving from side to side in confusion, Simon was hidden from view. He loosened a second knife in his boot. Give it another few moments. Long enough for the follower to grow frustrated.

Screened behind the leaves, Simon held his breath. A broad, hulking man with a vicious expression was staring this way and that. A club dangled from his belt, next to his knife. Very likely he had another weapon or two hidden about his body.

The man turned, eyes searching, then stared at the road beyond the bridge. Lady Lodge stood alone, surrounded by a field and a hedge before the hill rose towards a row of half-built houses.

Simon eased himself out from the branches, tensed then dashed forward. Just five paces, but he was moving fast enough to send the man sprawling as he caught him behind his thighs.

The man tried to turn. Before he could struggle, Simon was on him, kneeling on his back, the edge of his blade against the side of his neck as he searched him. Two knives and the club. Simon tossed them into the beck. It had only taken three seconds, and the rush of it left his breathing ragged.

'I don't like people following me.'

No response.

'Why are you doing it?'

'Orders.' The man's voice was stifled in the dirt. Simon grabbed him by the hair.

'Whose orders?'

'Curzon.'

Now he knew who this man was. The magistrate's bodyguard. Whittaker, the former government man.

'And why does Mr Curzon care what I do?'

'You've been asking questions about his case.'

'Is that a crime now?'

'It is if you try to stop justice.'

'No, Mr Whittaker.' He felt the man stir at the mention of his name. 'I'm trying to stop an *injustice*. You're going to go back and tell your master that.'

Whittaker snorted. 'Do you reckon that'll be the end of it? He'll give up and apologize because you're not happy? He's more powerful than you'll ever be.'

'That doesn't mean he'll always win. You might want to remind him of that.' He felt the man tense under him, ready to try and move. 'Don't,' Simon warned. He pressed the steel hard against Whittaker's neck. 'I'll have you dead before you even reach your knees.'

'We'll be seeing each other again.'

'I daresay we will.'

'Next time things will be different.'

'We'll find out about that, won't we?' He rose swiftly, standing back with his knife ready. 'Your weapons are in the water. The current won't have carried them far.'

Simon walked away, alert, ready for Whittaker to chase after him. But he didn't come.

Curzon had set his dog to warn Simon off. If his case was so strong, why would he need to do that?

The boys arrived, tumbling and rushing at him like a tide as he opened the door. He gathered Richard in one arm, Amos in the other, and scooped them up. Smelling fresh as the country, warm as newly cut grass, their cheeks red and healthy. Full of chatter and laughter, they brought the house to life again.

He let them slither down his body as they competed with each other to tell him about Kirkstall.

'We paddled in the river—' Amos began.

'—and climbed all over that old building,' Richard continued.

'We explored in the woods—'

'—and Mrs Burton let us help her when she fed her chickens.'

He could swear they'd grown in the week they'd been gone, taller, heavier. And now they were back, the house seemed right again, full and noisy and busy.

Simon was grinning like a fool. He knew it, he didn't care. He felt happy and complete. Then he walked into the kitchen.

The note lay on the table. Awkward letters, half-formed by a man unused to writing with his left hand.

Come and find me. I have news. Miller.

'It was pushed under the door when I came home with the boys,' Rosie said.

'It seems I need to go out again.'

'Simon, do you honestly think you can free Davey?'

'Emily asked me the exact same thing.' He pursed his lips. 'There has to be *something.*'

'It'll kill her if her brother's convicted,' Rosie said.

He knew. He'd seen the look in her eyes, lost, falling away from the world.

Miller wasn't in any of his usual places; nobody had seen him. By the eighth beershop, Simon was starting to panic. Had something happened to him? Finally, in a tumbledown building at the back of a court off Vicar Lane, he found the man. Alive, bleary-eyed, and barely sober.

'You left a note for me. Have you learned something?'

Miller looked up, struggling to focus, a vacant smile on his face.

'I don't know. Have I learned anything at all? I'm never that sure.'

'Stop it. You left me this.' He slammed the note down on the table. 'What is it, Josh? What's this news you have?' Simon grabbed the man's collar, lifted him to his feet and pushed him back against the wall. 'I don't have time for games.'

The shock of fear seemed to sober Miller a little. 'You're looking for someone.'

Simon's voice was hard. 'Unless you know where he is, you're wasting my time.'

His eyes glinted. 'I know he has a friend. A woman.'

'Who is she?'

Miller gave a soft, empty smile. 'Her name's Margaret. Margaret Wood. I saw them together this morning.'

'Where?'

'Down near Timble Bridge.'

Timble Bridge again. Simon breathed slowly until he began to feel calmer. 'This woman, who is she?'

Miller tried to shrug. 'Simon, I saw them, I heard her name. That's all.'

'What does she look like?' He could set Jane to find her.

'She had fair hair, some heft to her.' He smiled at the memory. 'Young.' He paused for a second. 'But he doesn't look that old, either.'

'Do you have any idea where they were going?'

'No.' He shook his head. Simon let go and Miller slumped back down to his seat.

'Here.' He put a silver threepence on the table. 'If you see them again . . .'

Miller was still nodding emptily as he left.

Dodd and the girl. No sign of them in any of the inns along Briggate. Not booked for the coach to York the following morning.

'I saw Curzon's bodyguard again this morning,' Jane said. She was sitting on the steps on the market cross, staring down Briggate.

'So did I,' Simon told her, and she raised her head sharply. 'Whittaker. He wanted to warn me off.'

'What did you do?'

'Took his weapons away from him.' The smile of satisfaction flickered and quickly died. 'What was he doing?'

'He was coming out of the Moot Hall. I followed him down to the coal staithe at the end of Salem Place.'

'The coal staithe?' Simon asked. 'What did he want there?'

'I don't know. He walked around, then he went over to the foundry at Holbeck. The same thing there.'

'Are you sure it was the right man?'

She stared at him. Of course she was sure. 'He came back over the bridge and stopped at the Bull and Mouth. I looked through the window. He was talking to Rob Barstow.'

'Barstow? What would he want with him?'

Seeing the two men together had troubled her. It made her think yet again about the girl who'd followed her. But she was always in her thoughts now, even in her dreams. Jane had asked questions here and there; nobody claimed to know her, no one seemed to have seen her.

She kept it all locked in her head. It was her problem, she'd discover a solution by herself.

'How long did he stay?' Simon asked.

'They were still there when I came to meet you.'

'I need to find this spy,' Simon said. 'And there's Ericsson's ring. I haven't come up with anything.'

'I told Harmsworth. He promised to spread the word.' She stood suddenly, eyes fixed on something down the street, then started to walk away without a word. The girl. A grubby bandage wrapped around the wound on her arm.

Jane lifted the shawl to cover her head, moving in the middle of groups of people, sliding from one to another, always surrounded. If the woman turned, she'd never spot her.

From Briggate to Boar Lane, then out along Wellington Road, all the way past Bean Ing Mill. There were fewer people around out here; it was harder for Jane to hide herself. But the woman never even glanced back. She kept her lumbering, constant pace, out beyond the new building by Drony Laith before she vanished into the woods.

Jane stood. The Halifax coach thundered by, raising a thick cloud of dust, but she was barely aware of it. The woods were where she'd hidden her money.

'I need to know about this spy. His name's Dodd.'

'You've already told me, Simon. Twice.' George Mudie leaned over his press, tightening a screw, then trying a lever before nodding to himself. His leather apron was stained black with ink. 'I'm not bloody deaf.'

'Where can I find him?'

'If I knew the answer to that, I'd have said.' He straightened his back and winced. 'All I've learned is what people tell me. I live my life between here and home these days. The only thing I hear is gossip.'

'There must be something. You know people all over the county.'

Mudie sighed. 'Right, do you want to listen to it all?' He

counted the rumours off on his fingers. 'He's been seen with a woman. He's on his own. He's short and dark or he's tall and fair. He's from London. He was one of the dragoons that charged the crowd at Peterloo. Can you see why I haven't passed anything on? I'm damned if I know what's true. He might as well be a creature in a book.'

'He's short and dark, and he seems to have a woman.'

'Then you know more than I do.' He reached for a bottle and poured himself a drink. 'The only thing that seems certain is that he was the one who pointed out the men in the West Riding, then he came here overnight. Why do you think finding this man will help you save Davey, anyway?'

'Because he knows he lied.'

'Fine.' Mudie stared. His eyes were hard, mouth set in a straight line. 'So you find him and make him admit that to you. What does that get you, Simon? Not a damned thing. How are you going to prove it in court?'

'If he stands up and says it—'

Mudie brought the glass down hard on the desk. 'Has something addled your brains? Don't be such a damned idiot. Use your head. They're not about to say they've used a spy. There'd be uproar. They won't have to – the evidence from Curzon and all the other magistrates will be enough.'

He was right. He understood. Davey knew that truth, too. Simon was the only one with his head in the clouds. Justice, the law – they sounded like grand ideals, but they were nothing more than words echoing through an empty room. The reality was that justice and law were anything the people in power wanted them to be. He was helpless. He was impotent. There was nothing he could do to help Davey.

'You're good at finding *things*,' Mudie continued. His voice was softer now, gentler. 'You're very good at that. I edited newspapers for years. I know about finding the *truth*. But I also know that people don't care about it, especially the ones who pull the strings. Truth is an inconvenience to them. They'd rather it stayed hidden. The only thing on their mind is keeping order and staying in power.'

'But—'

Mudie's voice rose over his. 'No buts, Simon. No exceptions.

People like you and me and Davey, we're nothing. If you've got enough money and land, then they'll listen. You can fight all you like, but you'd better realize this: you've lost the battle before it's even begun.'

'There has to be something.'

'Does there?' Mudie asked. 'Why?'

But he couldn't give an answer. Everything the man had said was right. It was ugly, it was brutal, but it was true. And yet he still wanted to think he had a chance. He *had* to believe that.

'I'm not going to stop.'

Mudie smiled. 'I know you. I never thought you would.'

Jane forced herself to keep going, one foot in front of the other until she reached the far side of the wood, fields stretching out ahead, all the way to the hills in the distance. She crept back through the undergrowth, each step cautious through the thick grass, stooping, using the bulk of the tree trunks to remain out of sight. Finally she was close enough to see the small clearing surrounding an old, broad oak. The girl was on her knees by the roots, scraping at the ground with the point of her knife.

Jane felt the breath catch in her chest. It was the right place.

A few days earlier and she'd have found a fortune.

But how could she know? Jane had never told a soul about it. Not Simon and Rosie, not Mrs Rigton, not even Catherine Shields. She'd taken care never to be followed out here.

It was impossible.

Yet the girl was right in front of her. She felt numb, scared. Someone knew her secrets.

Jane waited, hardly daring to breathe, watching as the woman dug, making the hole wider and deeper, until she tossed the knife aside and clawed at the earth in frustration. Five minutes and she'd found the tin. The girl stopped, panting heavily, looking around. She took it out, opening it reverently, then let out a shriek as she found it empty and flung it away. Birds flapped out of the branches, squawking as they flew off. The girl stood, pacing slowly, studying the ground, kicking at the dirt in frustration. Finally she stalked away.

Anger rolled from her in waves. It was there in her walk: awkward, tense, the shoulders pulled square, her back forced straight. Jane gave her a long start and kept track of her on the way into town, only slipping closer as a river of people flooded around them.

She was scared in a way she'd never felt before.

Who was this girl? How could she know so much?

Simon strode out past Timble Bridge. Despair burned inside him, anger at men who controlled everything. It had been there for most of his life. Growing up in the workhouse and seeing the absolute, blind authority of the master. Through those years when still being alive as darkness fell became a victory. It had dimmed as he'd grown older. He'd grown too comfortable, too complacent. But now it was back, as taut and bitter as if it had never gone away, a tight clutch around his belly, a fever in his blood.

He walked along Marsh Lane, where the older houses close to Leeds gave way to new, cramped streets, erected in a hurry and already looking worn, the brickwork quickly turning black from the soot in the air. A pair of children played with a whip and top at the side of the road. An infant sat in the dust and wailed. A man in his shirtsleeves stood on his front step and tried to brush a shine on to his boots, not even glancing up as Simon passed.

Jack Sorrel lived at the end of the street. He'd grown up in Hull, working on the fishing boats until he was pressed into the navy at the start of the French war. He still looked like a tar, with his bow-legged walk, the plaited queue of hair that hung down his back, and the short canvas jacket that barely reached his waist.

Jack had served on a lucky ship; it had done well for prize money. Enough for even a lowly hand who was careful with his share to buy this house along with the three next to it. He lived in one and rented the others to men who'd served at sea. Rich by the standards of this neighbourhood. And one who kept a close eye on everything in the streets around him.

'I'm searching for someone who might be staying around here,' Simon explained.

Sorrel liked to walk. Pavement or countryside, it didn't matter, as long as it was solid ground under his feet. Seven years after the wars had ended and it still remained a pleasure to him. He had a swift stride, moving as if life was an urgent matter, nodding at people he passed, stopping to talk here and there.

'What's he like?' He led the way around the streets, eyes searching, listening as Simon described Dodd, then shaking his head. 'I haven't seen anyone like that round here. What's he done?'

'He's a spy for the government.'

Sorrel turned his head and spat. 'We don't need people like that round here.'

'He's somewhere, Jack.'

'I'll ask. Like I said, though, it means nothing to me.' With that he was gone, hurrying away. If Dodd was anywhere close, Jack should know it in a few hours. But in a place the size of Leeds, where new faces appeared every day, hiding was all too easy.

Simon spent the remainder of the day moving from one part of Leeds to the next, seeking out the old women who spent their days watching and seeing everything. But they all shook their heads at Dodd's description.

By supper all he had was a sense of urgency growing like a wave behind him. Davey's time was running out and he was getting nowhere.

'Are you listening?' Simon asked.

'Yes.' Jane was staring out of the attic window. A slightly brighter morning with high, pale clouds and a teasing hint of sun. 'You want me to find someone called Margaret Wood.'

'Ask people. I know it's a poor description, but . . .'

'What do you want me to do when I find her?'

'Come and tell me.'

She nodded and gathered her shawl around her shoulders.

'Is anything wrong?' he asked as she walked to the door.

Jane turned to stare at him, face showing nothing. 'No. Why?'

Outside, she stood, looking up and down the street, all the places where someone could hide. Nobody there. How could anyone know about her money? Jane felt as if someone had burrowed into her head and examined her thoughts. What else did this woman know about her? Was she some kind of witch?

She took a breath and tried to clear the girl from her mind. To think of Margaret Wood instead.

There were people who might have seen her. The ones others rarely noticed. But they saw, and they remembered. The group of children with hard, aged faces who made their camp in an empty building behind Rockley Court. Women who walked the streets, trying to make a life selling bunches of watercress and lavender. But none of them knew the name.

The soldier who begged near Vicar's Croft did, though. He stood to attention all day, a battered tin cup dangling from his belt. One of his legs was missing, a crutch pushed into his armpit to keep him upright, and a gaze that missed nothing.

'Margaret?' he said. 'I heard that name yesterday.'

He had a soft, shy voice, full of pain. Jane always gave him a farthing when she passed. Sometimes they talked a little. Most people kept their distance from him. With a face scarred and burned, the flesh black in places, he looked forbidding, but he had a gentle soul.

'Where?'

'Right here. She was with a man, he called her Margaret.' A tiny, sorrowful hesitation. 'I remembered because I knew a girl called that once.'

'What did this one look like?'

The soldier squinted as if he could see back through the hours. 'Round. Young. Fair hair. Dressed in blue. She had a strange smile.'

'Strange?' Jane asked. 'What do you mean?'

'It wasn't real. I could see that. It only reached her mouth. There was nothing in her eyes at all. They were empty.' He turned his head awkwardly. 'I think that's why I noticed her.'

'Which way did they go?'

'Down Kirkgate.'

On the far side of Timble Bridge she stopped to see the old man who made his home in a small hut on Garland Fold. Half the slates were missing from the roof, no glass in the windows, but it was shelter for a tiny life, straw piled on the dirt for a bed.

Thaddeus Hardy had made a living by scavenging. On the riverbank, in the gutters. But that was when he was a younger man, agile enough to pick through the dirt for the little treasures people had lost. He was eighty now – that was what he claimed

– old and withered and lined, limbs twisted and painful, racked by coughs each year when the weather turned wet and cold. A few of the local women looked after him, taking him scraps, anything left from their tables.

On sunny days he sat on an old chair by his door, thin body wrapped in shawls, watching as the world passed. The rest of him might be failing but his eyes remained keen.

'Been too busy to visit me?' Hardy complained. But he smiled at her as he spoke. When Jane first met him, his voice had been firm. These days it wavered with every breath.

'I brought you something.' A pie from a street-seller's tray, the pastry still warm.

'Thee's spoiling me,' Hardy said and raised an eyebrow. 'Tha must want something.'

She told him.

'Aye, I've seen her, right enough. Alone and with a man.'

Jane jumped on the words. 'Who was she with?'

'A man. Dark hair, not as tall as her. Allus notice when I see a couple like that.'

She'd struck lucky, sooner than she'd hoped.

'Where do they live? Do you know?'

'Must be out there somewhere.' He gestured along Marsh Lane. 'You go and ask Martha Dobson. Dost tha know her?'

Jane shook her head.

'About half a mile along, once thee's past all them new houses. She has a little cottage. Spins wool for them as still weaves at home. Ask her, she's a nosy old baggage.'

The woman had hands like claws, her fingers bent and stiff. That didn't stop her working, teasing out the threads into yarn as swiftly as a young girl.

'Thaddeus sent you, did he?' Her eyes were a little cloudy, but her voice was strong and steady. 'And what did he call me this time?'

'A nosy old baggage,' Jane said. The woman had been suspicious at first, not wanting to let her through the door into the tidy room until she spoke Hardy's name. Then she returned to her stool, turning the wheel and working as she talked.

She clicked her tongue and snorted. 'Aye, that'd be him, all right. He's been like that for years, as long as I can remember, never a good word to pass about anybody. Now, you said you want to know about this lass?'

'I do. Anything you can tell me.'

'Well, if you ask me, she looks as rough and ready as they come. Seen them that way all me life. Looks like she's weighing everything and reckoning how much she could get for it.'

'Is she local?'

'Never saw her until a few days ago. Her and that man she's with, the one who looks like he's taken too much of a shine to hissen.'

'Where do they live?'

'Go another quarter of a mile along and you'll see a little track to the left. Down at the end there's a house. That's where they're staying. Near the beck. Good for watercress on the bank. I go down and pick it in the summer.'

'Thank you.'

'You'd best watch out for yourself. Keep your distance from Thaddeus. He's always had an eye for young girls, that one has, and you're a pretty little thing. He's got two of them in the family way that I know about.'

There were plenty of places to hide. Folds in the ground, a small copse caught between two low hills. Jane found a spot, pulled up her shawl and sat, watching the front door of the cottage that stood down the track.

Davey was in poor spirits. He sat in the cell with little to say for himself. He'd lost more weight, as though he was barely eating, and his clothes were smeared with dirt. After five minutes, Simon placed a hand on his friend's shoulder and quietly left.

'I followed her into town.'

'What did she do?' Simon asked.

'Went to the market,' Jane told him. 'Just wandered around, she didn't buy anything. Like she was passing time. Then she went into the Talbot. I saw her sitting with a man.'

'Describe him.'

'Small with dark hair. Half the time he looked like he was preening himself, adjusting his clothes or rubbing his cheeks.

They had a drink and walked back home. I followed them as far as Marsh Lane.'

She daren't go farther; she would have been too exposed, too *obvious*.

'They were talking and gesturing,' she continued. 'It looked like they were arguing. I was too far away to hear any words.'

She saw Simon push his lips together, thinking, calculating.

'I want to talk to her when she's on her own,' he said.

'I can watch the house and tell you.'

'Take Jem with you. He can run and find me.'

She'd met Jem two years before, a feral boy who spent his days around the churchyard at St John's. He was clever, observant, and quick on the uptake; tell him once and it stayed in his mind. Ask him and the job was done.

'I have to look for Harmsworth again, too.'

'No word on the ring yet?'

She shook her head.

'You seem distracted,' Simon said.

'No.' Her reply was sharp; Jane wondered if he could read the lie behind her eyes. Even if he did, he'd never come close to guessing the truth. This was her secret, her dilemma. Hers to solve, just hers. Alone.

And it would end in someone's death. She knew that as surely as she could feel her heart beating.

Harmsworth was standing outside the Rose and Crown, smoking a cheroot and looking pleased with himself. One hand in his pocket, jingling coins.

'Had a good win?' Jane asked

He turned, startled, a smile crossing his face.

'They never learn. Just enough time for a couple of hands while they changed the horses, so I shook them down for all I could get.'

He had his trade, he was good at it. But sooner or later someone would see through his cheating and call him out, or a man with quicker hands would come along.

'The ring,' she said.

'I've been busy.' His gaze shifted away from her.

'This is business. We're offering money.'

Harmsworth jingled the coins again and smirked. The type of man who never thought beyond today.

'I'll talk to people,' he said. 'I promise.'

Jane said nothing. She knew how little his words were worth once the cards started to run his way. She'd go searching for others, people with sharp eyes who were eager to earn a little cash. She crossed the Head Row and passed through the lychgate into St John's graveyard.

People stood, conversing in pairs or groups. A woman knelt on the grass, picking moss from a headstone with her knife. Towards the far side, close to the almshouses, she spotted Jem. Jane raised her hand, a gesture that was almost a wave. In a moment he was on his feet, dashing towards her.

'I have some work for you,' she told him. 'Come with me.'

SEVEN

Simon kicked a ball made of rags with his sons. Most of the old tenter fields by the river had gone, built over now, but a few small patches of green survived.

He made Richard and Amos run, trying to wear them out. But a week in the country air of Kirkstall had made them tireless. After an hour they were still shouting out for more as he shepherded them home.

He watched them sitting at the table, devouring bread and cheese. They'd never known what it was like to miss a meal; they'd never gone without anything. Someday perhaps they'd understand how lucky they were.

'What are you thinking?' Rosie asked. She stood beside him, an arm around his waist.

'Nothing much. Just envying their innocence.'

At their age he was in the workhouse. His parents were dead, no relatives willing to take him in. A new world, terrifying and brutal. One he was determined his sons would never experience.

'They need educating,' she said. 'They'll just grow up wild otherwise.'

Simon nodded. Put some learning in them and they could go far. He'd had to teach himself to read, then shown Rosie her letters, too. She'd taken to numbers on her own. They made sense to her; she understood them in a way beyond anything he could ever manage. The boys were bright, eager for everything; channelling it could only do them good.

'I'll talk to the master at the grammar school.'

'I'll take them to visit Emily later,' Rosie said. 'We can walk by the beck. Maybe that will distract her.'

'I saw Davey earlier. He seems to have lost all hope.'

She turned, giving him a sharp stare. 'What do you mean?'

'He seems resigned to whatever's going to happen. He's stopped fighting.' Simon tightened his mouth. 'I'd never have believed it.'

He held her close, feeling her warmth, her belief. If he could find the spy and make him admit the lies, maybe he could win. Never mind what George Mudie said, surely there had to be some justice in this country.

The hammering on the door pulled him away. He turned the key in the lock. Jem stood on the step, red-faced and out of breath.

'Jane said to tell you the girl's on her own at the house.'

Simon reached for his coat. 'Take me there,' he said.

'She's still inside,' Jane told him.

Simon stared at the small house. It was old and isolated, standing no more than twenty yards from the stream. The kind of place no one would build in Leeds any more.

'How long ago did he leave?'

'Half an hour. Maybe a little less.'

Dodd wouldn't have slipped away for just a few minutes. Simon adjusted his jacket and patted the hat down on his head. He looked presentable, amicable, not threatening.

'If you see him coming back, make a noise.' He took two pennies from his pocket and held them out for Jem. 'You've done well.'

The track was hard under the soles of his boots. Small pillows of dust rose. No other dwellings close. No cover at all, just weeds growing wild where a garden had once been.

The house was made of solid Yorkshire stone, mellowed by the years, far enough from town to be free of the soot and grime that covered so much of Leeds. Simon took a deep breath, knocked on the door and waited.

He could hear movement inside, feet shuffling around. Finally, a woman's voice, muffled by the thick wood.

'Who is it?'

'My name's Simon Westow.'

A hesitation. 'I don't know you.'

'I'd like to talk to you about your companion.'

'Why?' He could hear the small curl of doubt and suspicion.

'It would be easier if we could talk inside.'

'No.'

A heavy, final sound. She'd lowered the bar on the door. That was his answer. Simon turned and walked away, hands pushed deep in his pockets. She'd be watching him through the window, probably ducked down so he wouldn't see her if he turned his head.

He'd failed. It happened; not the first time and it wouldn't be the last. Still, each one stung. The woman would tell Dodd once he returned and he'd be on his guard. It might even push him to leave, to rush on to York and await the trials. If that happened, Simon had lost. There'd be no chance of saving Davey after that.

'What did she say?' Jane asked.

'Nothing. She wouldn't talk to me.'

Side by side they began the walk back to Leeds. Jem had long since vanished.

'What are we going to do now?'

'Find Dodd,' Simon said. 'And we need to do it quickly, before he runs.'

'Do you think he will?' Jane asked. 'I thought he had protection from Curzon.'

A word from the spy to the magistrate and Simon could find himself facing the bodyguard again. Lady Luck had been with him before. She might not smile so sweetly the next time.

'I still want to know where he is.'

'I was going to ask more people about that ring.'

'I thought Harmsworth was supposed to be telling people,' Simon said.

'That was before he hit a winning streak,' Jane replied.

He sighed. Bloody Harmsworth. He'd ignore everything else as long as fortune kept its finger on him. When it was removed and all the money in his pockets was spent, he'd be back, begging and using his charm for favours and some chance to earn enough for another game.

Soon Ericsson would start asking what they'd discovered. Simon had been too greedy taking on the job. The man deserved more than that.

'Can you look after it?'

She stared ahead. 'Yes.'

Jane found Kate Carpenter down by the water. This was one of her pitches, selling pies to the labourers who worked on the river, unloading the barges and in the warehouses. Her voice pierced like a horn as she shouted her wares, whatever was fresh from the baker that day.

She was a large woman, as tall as Simon, shoulders broad from years of carrying heavy trays, her arms and wrists heavy and fleshy, but her fingers were nimble and her gaze missed little.

Jane waited until the last customer had gone.

'About time you came by to put some meat on them bones. No man wants a lass without a few pounds on her.' Kate reached into a corner of her tray. 'Here you go, that one should still be good. Tasty bit of filling inside. I was going to save it for meself, but you need it more than I do. You're scrawny as a cat.'

The pastry was cold, but there was still a hint of warmth to the meat as Jane ate. She ambled next to Kate, going back towards Briggate. She still had a few pies left. That meant she'd be marching up and down the street, calling out until they were all sold. Any stock left and her husband would beat her. There had been times Jane had seen her in the mornings with bruises decorating her face and tears in her eyes. If any man tried to do that to her, she'd kill him. But Kate was like too many; she seemed to accept it as her due, to take it as a fact of life, a punishment for not doing her job properly.

Jane took out a penny and placed it in the tray. Then another. Kate eyed her warily.

'You don't look hungry enough to eat two of them,' she said. 'What are you after?'

'I'm looking for a ring. It's gold. The stone's amber.'

'Amber.' She looked thoughtful. 'I'll tell you who has an amber ring. Ericsson the timber merchant. I used to see it years ago. Always fancied it on me finger.' She held out a weathered hand. 'That's the only one I've ever seen.'

'It's his,' Jane told her. 'Someone stole it.'

Kate nodded. 'I heard he was back. I'll keep my eyes peeled.'

'Tell the others. There's a reward.'

Kate knew every street trader in Leeds. They looked out for each other, kept each other informed. 'Right enough.'

Jane sucked the last of the juices from her finger and brushed crumbs from her dress.

'You're growing,' Kate said. 'Taller than when I saw you last. Still need some heft, mind.' Her expression grew wistful. 'I'd have a lass near enough your age if she'd lived.'

But people died. That was the way of the world. From one day to the next, faces could disappear, and all the questions, all the hope and praying in the world would never bring them back.

'I'm sorry,' Jane said.

The woman shrugged. 'Never you mind. It was a long time ago and she was just a bairn. It's God's way.' Kate sighed. 'If someone's wearing that ring, we'll see it, don't you fret. I'll tell you.'

The day wore on. She trudged around town, catching faces she knew and asking her questions. By late in the afternoon, Jane had spun her web. From children to crones, people would be watching.

She'd added more questions of her own, asking about the girl with a bandage on her arm.

Who was she? How could she have known about the money?

At the close of the day, Jane wound her way through the streets, cutting through the courts and the ginnels, doubling back and then moving ahead again. Just in case, as if she could no longer completely trust her own instincts. Finally she found herself in the small yard behind the Green Dragon, waited a moment or two, then ducked through the hidden gap in the wall to the space beyond.

Mrs Shields was watering the wisteria, turning in alarm at the sound of boots on the flagstones.

'Heavens, child, what is it? You look like there's a ghost after you.'

That was right. That was how it felt. Something she could sense but couldn't touch.

'I don't know,' Jane said. 'Maybe there is.'

Mrs Shields sat on the rough bench in a patch of evening sunlight.

'Come on. Tell me.'

She'd promised herself that she'd say nothing, but here, with this woman, the words flowed out of her.

'You'd never seen her before all this began?' Mrs Shields asked when Jane had finished.

'No. I don't think so. I know I never noticed her. I'm scared she might come and kill you now the money's here.'

'She won't.' Mrs Shields's voice was soothing and certain, a balm to ease her fears. 'There's safety here, child.'

'But how could she know about it?' No matter which way she tugged at the idea, she couldn't understand that.

'I can't tell you, child. But I will say something – there's bound to be a simple answer. It's not magic and it's not witch-craft. Put those out of your head. They don't exist.'

Jane felt the woman stroking her hair and closed her eyes. For a moment she was a little girl again, resting by her mother's knee and feeling the simple certainty of tenderness. She let the peaceful feeling rise up through her mind. Everything would be fine.

'Your money will be safe here. I promise.'

She believed it. Everything was different in this place. Each time she visited, she felt the weight of her thoughts fall away. The darkness vanished. She was free from herself. But it scared her, too. That the comfort Catherine Shields gave her might vanish if she remained too long, and this house would become as ordinary as everywhere else.

'I wanted to . . . warn you, in case you see her,' Jane said. 'Or she comes around looking.'

'Hush, child, just let it all go for a little while. Have you told Simon about her?'

'No,' she answered quickly.

'Why on earth not? He can help you.'

'It's not his problem. He has enough to think about at the moment.'

'He cares about you.' Mrs Shields's voice was soft and insistent. 'You know that. He'd help you.'

Saying it all out loud in this place was one thing. This was separate, like stepping away from the world and into a dream. In the kitchen with Simon and Rosie it would be too real, too close to home. She'd feel the girl's breath on the back of her neck. And if Simon aided her, she'd be in his debt.

'Shhh, child,' Mrs Shields said as she kept stroking Jane's hair. 'Let the fear go.'

The frustration was rising, a growing sense of desperation as the hours ticked away. Simon dashed around town, but there was no trace of Dodd. Perhaps he'd gone to see Curzon, for instructions or payment; not any chance of getting close to the man there.

He stopped at the bookseller, choosing something to take to Davey that might occupy his long days down in the cell. He picked up a collection of essays on liberty, then replaced it. It was the last thing Davey needed when the cell walls were closing around him. Instead, he bought a novel. At the Moot Hall, he placed a coin on the gaoler's desk and kept one finger on it.

'Any word yet about when he might be moved to York?'

'Not yet, sir. Nothing.' The man eyed the money hungrily.

'If you hear anything, I want to know immediately.'

'Yes, sir.'

Simon flicked the coin towards him and strode off to the cell.

Davey had the look of the lost. He was drowning down here. Even the book couldn't rouse his spirits. He didn't want to talk, just sat and stared at the stones in the wall. Finally, Simon had to leave. It hurt his heart too much to stay. He had to free Davey while there was still something left of the man.

It was barely morning, with a chill hanging in the air, dew on the metal of the hinges and the handles. Already people were flowing up and down Briggate, men and women with their heads bent as they trudged to early shifts at the factories.

Simon waited by a coffee-seller's stall, clutching the warmth of the tin cup in his hands, hat pulled down on his head as he watched the inn. Dodd wasn't booked on the York coach. But the woman would have told him about the strange man coming to the house; it might be enough to make him run.

The coach departed exactly on time, five minutes past six, without Dodd or Margaret Wood. Simon drained his cup, placed it on the trestle and gathered his coat around him.

'He won't be leaving tomorrow, either,' a voice behind him said. 'You can sleep an hour or two longer.'

Whittaker stood with one hand resting lightly on the handle of his knife, a sneer on his lips.

'I'll keep that in mind.'

'I'll give you some better advice. It won't even cost you a penny. Leave Dodd and the girl alone.'

'You know I'm not going to do that,' Simon said.

'Your choice, but it'll end badly if you don't. It's very easy to level charges against someone.' Whittaker's lips curled into a smile. 'Anyone at all.'

'Is that a threat?' Simon could feel the blood start to surge through his veins. But the man wasn't fool enough to start anything here, with witnesses all around. Maybe words and taunts were all he needed for now.

'I have a score to settle. You'd do well to keep that in your head.' He turned his head to glare at the man approaching from the other side of Briggate. 'This is none of your business,' he called out. 'A private matter.'

'Is he bothering you, Simon?'

The deep voice seemed to rise out of the ground. He didn't need to turn around to know the owner. Henry Wise, the farrier. Six and a half feet tall, with muscles like thick rope in his arms.

'It's fine, Henry. Mr Whittaker here wants me to keep away from certain things. He used to be an agent for the government.'

Simon knew Wise had spent eight years in the army, shoeing horses and following Wellington's troops as they fought all the way from Portugal to France. It had given him plenty of time to loathe the stupidity of commanders and governments. He could almost feel the man bristle as he took a step closer.

'Is that so? I know how to deal with the likes of him.'

Henry was near enough now for Simon to smell his sweat.

Whittaker stood his ground. At least the man had a little courage; he hadn't turned tail and run as soon as Henry arrived.

'I told you: it's a private matter.'

'We'll take it up later,' Simon told him.

'That we will.' Whittaker turned and swaggered away.

'Who is he?' Henry asked.

'Do you know Curzon the magistrate? That's his bodyguard. They've locked up Davey Ashton, they're going to send him to stand trial for sedition.'

'Radical Davey?' He laughed. 'He wouldn't hurt a fly. Loves to talk, but that's it.'

'I know. I'm trying to get him out of gaol.'

'Bodyguard?' He was watching Whittaker as he moved up Briggate. 'Never a good sign when a man reckons he needs one of those.'

'No,' Simon agreed. 'How are Martha and the children?'

Henry's wife stood barely five feet in her clogs, just a button beside him, but she kept him terrorized. They had four young children, a fifth on the way.

'Making my life misery, as usual.' He gave a sour grin. 'Another month and there'll be one more mouth to feed.' Henry rolled his shoulders. 'I'd better get back to work and earning. If that one gives you any more trouble, let me know.'

'I don't think he's finished yet. But thank you.'

So Dodd had told the magistrate. Only to be expected. But why weren't they bustling the spy out of Leeds? He didn't understand that. Did they feel they couldn't trust him once he was out of their sight? Or was there something more going on? He didn't know. Dodd was here and he was staying for the moment. Now Simon had to decide the best way to disrupt their plans.

Jane looked at hands, trying to spot Ericsson's ring. In the night, she wandered through the inns and the beershops. They were busy, filled with talk, the smoke hanging thick below the ceilings. No one noticed the girl who moved silently around.

Gold glinted here and there, caught in oil lamps and candles, but no orange glow of amber.

Long after quiet had descended on Leeds, Jane was still out, wrapped in the darkness. She was strangely content, at ease with herself for once. Telling Catherine Shields made her feel as if she'd pushed off the weight that wouldn't let her rest. The problem remained, but it wasn't boring deep through her like a worm.

She was a nightwalker, at home in the dark world. It helped to keep her senses alert, honing them like a knife on a whetstone.

The girl was out there somewhere. Maybe sleeping in a bed, maybe curled in some sacking. Or perhaps she was walking on another street.

They'd meet again.

EIGHT

'Your sons might be happier somewhere else.' The master of the grammar school moved his gaze to something on the desk as he spoke.

'Might they?' Simon asked with amusement. 'And what makes you think that?'

The man had been aloof and haughty from the moment Simon had given his name.

'They'd receive a more rounded education. A more useful one. Practical.'

Something more suitable to the children of a common man. Nothing had been said, but the teacher obviously knew what he did for a living. He was good enough for the rich to seek him out and pay him to retrieve the items stolen from them, but not for his sons to be educated beside theirs.

He could feel the anger beginning to stir in his belly, but he allowed himself a smile. 'So you don't feel you offer anything useful here?'

It was an impressive building, old and solid. He could hear

the sound of young voices from the classroom, boys speaking in ragged unison as they echoed what they'd just been taught.

'Our education is more academic,' the master said.

No doubt he believed it was. But the sons of the merchants and the wealthy who came here for their schooling would grow up to become the *practical* men who ran their fathers' businesses.

'And your fees reflect that, of course.'

'They do.' The man nodded.

'The money,' Simon assured him, 'is not a worry.'

'Naturally.'

He glanced around the room, the bound books on the shelves, a huge library, one that dwarfed Davey's collection. But everything seemed stultified here, wrapped and bound in tradition. Would he really be helping Richard and Amos by sending them to a place like this? Did he want to raise a pair of young gentlemen?

Yes. They'd learn. They'd grow up with those who would become important. And they'd have discipline.

But he'd known discipline in the workhouse. Real discipline. Beaten again and again until the tears wouldn't stop. No escape. When the master was done, there were the bigger boys who stole everything he had from him until he grew tall enough to stop them.

He gazed around the study once more. No. This place was nothing more than a workhouse for rich boys. The smell that leached from the walls wasn't learning; it was fear.

Simon stood and extended his hand. 'Thank you for your time.' For a moment the master gazed at him, nonplussed. 'But you're right, this isn't the place for my sons.' Relief seeped into the man's face. 'I'd prefer somewhere they had some value. I'll bid you good day.'

The National School lay on High Court Lane, hard by the parish church. It was brash and noisy, bubbling over with life. The children looked as miserable as scholars everywhere and the teachers seemed overworked and paid too little. But at least there was a sense of hope about the place. The twins might well be happy here. With some luck, they'd thrive.

The business was easily concluded. He had money; he'd pay for the boys' education, gladly handing over the coins. Amos and Richard would start the following morning. A shock to them, but Rosie was right. They were five years old; it was time.

Down underneath the Moot Hall, he sat with Davey Ashton.

'They won't win,' Simon repeated.

Davey could only manage an empty smile. 'They already have. Anything more . . .' His words trailed away to silence.

'There's a man you should see,' Mudie said.

'Who?' Simon asked.

'Gideon Hartley.'

He'd met Hartley once before. Another of those murky figures in the cloth business who flitted between Leeds and the other parts of the West Riding.

'Why? How can he help?'

'Talk to him and find out. He's staying at the Boot and Shoe.'

The inn was tucked away in a yard off Briggate. But Hartley had left a few minutes before, the proprietor said, his bag in his hand.

Probably returning to Halifax, Simon thought; the coach was due to leave from the Old King's Arms in an hour.

Simon found him waiting in the cobbled yard with a small group of passengers – a parson, two ladies, and an army officer in uniform.

'Mr Hartley.'

The man glanced up from his newspaper, expression turning from annoyance into a smile.

'Westow.' He extended his hand. 'Good to see you again, it's been a while.'

'A quick visit?'

Hartley snorted. 'I had to come in for a business dinner last night. Hardly worth the trouble, either.'

'George Mudie told me I ought to see you.'

'He was there for the meal. We started talking about what's been going on.' He pulled out a pocket watch and squinted at it. 'Three quarters of an hour yet. We might as well sit inside. It'll be more comfortable than that damned coach.'

They rested on a bench by the window. 'What do you know about these arrests?' Simon asked.

Hartley pursed his lips in disgust. 'It's all a fabrication. Any idiot can see that. A few weavers and millhands who've talked about ideas and change. I used to know one of them. Had a loom at home, but he saw it all go. Ended up working in a factory for next to nothing when what he produced became too expensive. Machines were cheaper.' He shrugged. The same story everywhere, the old ways vanishing before their eyes.

'He has every reason to be angry.'

'Plenty of them do. You know that, Simon.' He looked around cautiously and lowered his voice. 'Sometimes I think it's a miracle we haven't had a revolution here.'

'Were they planning one in the West Riding?'

'Of course not. They'd meet in twos or threes to drink and moan about the state of the country.' He raised his eyebrows. 'Same as anyone else, really. It wasn't as if they'd ever do anything. But someone decided that because they were working men it was sedition, and ran off to find a magistrate keen to make a name for himself.'

'Sounds much like here.' Simon paused, waiting as Hartley pulled out a pipe and lit it from a spill. 'I hear there was a spy.'

'I could think of a better word for him,' he answered in disgust. 'A man appeared from London, said he was associated with the Radicals down there, promising this and that. He held meetings and got everyone worked up. A week of that and the magistrate descended and arrested the lot. Apart from the spy, of course. He stood there and pointed them all out. As soon as his work was done, he vanished again.'

'He came here,' Simon said, 'then he did much the same with Davey Ashton. Tell me, did this spy have a woman with him?'

'I've no idea. I've just heard what people were saying.' A coach rumbled into the yard, the horses flecked white with sweat. Stable boys hurried to change the team as the driver accepted a quart of beer. The guard started to toss luggage down on to the cobbles. 'That's mine. I'd better go.' He stood and tipped his hat. 'Good to see you again.'

'I've been looking for you.' Kate Carpenter stood, hands on her hips, head cocked to the side. 'I've never met anyone who's so hard to find.'

'I'm here now,' Jane told her. She'd spotted the woman on Boar Lane, crying her wares near Holy Trinity Church. 'Why, have you found something?'

'Come with me.'

She started back towards Briggate. A large, powerful figure, people parted in front of her. At the corner she put two fingers in her mouth and let out a shrieking whistle.

'Just wait,' she said.

Two minutes. Jane counted it out in heartbeats, standing in silence. Her eyes gauged the people around them, but they didn't seem to notice her; they moved to their own rhythms, their own thoughts.

She looked up as the man approached. He was tiny, reaching no higher than her elbow, dressed in old, mended clothes that hung off his frame. A child's body but a man's face, with a brash smile that tried to mask wounded eyes.

'You know Harry, don't you?' Kate asked.

Jane had seen him almost every day for the last year, standing near the top of Briggate at the old market cross. He juggled, balls, cabbages, knives, anything at all, sending impossible numbers of them spinning into the sky and always catching them, keeping them moving as he talked. He never seemed to pause for breath, she'd noticed, words pouring from him, speech and fluid movements lulling his audience into a trance.

He was skilful. He kept them entertained and they placed their money in the hat he left upturned on the ground. But behind it all she sensed something more, a kind of flailing desperation.

'You've seen the ring?'

A grave nod from the small head. 'Yesterday,' he replied. 'A girl was wearing it while I was doing me act. I was wondering how someone like her could afford something like that.'

'What did she look like?'

'Hefty,' he answered after a moment. His gaze cut across to Kate. 'Not as big as her, mind, but she still had a bit of weight on her. Dark hair. I don't know. Oh,' he added as the memory came. 'She had a bandage on her right arm, you know, between the elbow and the wrist.'

Jane said nothing. She felt her world lurch upside down.

She was the hocus girl? How had she missed the ring when she watched the girl digging in the woods?

Jane dug in her pocket. Without looking, she pulled out three coins, one for Kate, two for Harry the juggler. She wandered away, leaving them staring after her in surprise.

'Why didn't you tell us about her before?' Rosie asked. Her voice was gentle, soothing. They were sitting at the table in the kitchen, the shouts and cries of the twins playing in the yard coming through the window.

'There wasn't anything to tell. The first time I thought Robby Barstow had sent her to take back that silver.'

'Did she say that?' Simon asked. He'd been listening closely, leaning against the wall behind her. She couldn't see his expression.

'She—' Jane began, then heard the girl's words in her head once more. 'She said "he" and "him". I thought she must mean Barstow.'

'Robby wouldn't be that stupid.'

'I didn't know.' She felt awkward. Guilty, trying to push down her anger at Simon and Rosie for all their questions. At herself. She should have kept it inside, away from the light. Never sat down and spoken.

'When she was digging,' Rosie said, 'what happened then?'

She told them, from the moment she'd spotted the girl until she followed her back into town.

'It was the same spot? You're sure about that?'

'Yes. She found the tin.' Of course it was the same one. Jane knew exactly where she'd buried her money; she wasn't likely to make a mistake.

'The question is how she knew, isn't it?' Simon said.

'Nobody ever followed me.'

'Then how could she know the money was there?' he wondered. 'Have you ever told anyone about it?'

'No.'

'The same girl who hocussed Ericsson. It's a strange coincidence. I don't like it. We need to find her.'

'I'll take care of that,' Jane said. 'But I wanted you to know.'

Rosie had been staring down at the table. She looked up,

frowning. 'How long before the girl went digging did you move your money?'

'A day.'

'Is it somewhere safe now?'

'Yes.'

Jane could sense them looking at her and thinking. Judging. Quickly, she scrambled up and left the room, dashing up the stairs to the attic and closing the door. Up here, away from them, she could breathe.

'What do you think?' Rosie asked after Jane's footsteps had faded.

'I don't know,' Simon replied. 'I really don't. If Jane says nobody followed her, I believe it.'

'So do I. But then how—?'

'I've no idea.' He shook his head. 'If this girl hadn't been the one who took Ericsson's ring, she'd never have said a word, I can tell you that much.'

'What are we going to do?'

'Jane said she'd look after it,' Simon said. 'She wants to be the one to do it. For herself.'

'I hope she can.'

The door burst open and the boys roared in, grubby and noisy, bringing a smile to his face.

'Come on, you two,' he told them. 'Sit down, I have something to tell you. There are going to be a few changes starting tomorrow.'

'I'll take them to school in the morning,' Rosie said. 'I want a look at this place.'

NINE

'What in God's name have you been up to, Simon?' The banging on the door had woken him. It wouldn't stop. He stumbled into his clothes and hurried down the stairs, drawing his knife before he pulled back the bolts and flung the door wide. Dawn had scarcely broken and George Mudie was standing with a mix of fury and worry on his face.

'Up to?' He ran a hand through his hair and covered a yawn. 'What are you talking about?'

'The writing. It's all over town.'

Simon blinked the sleep from his eyes. 'George, I don't have any idea what you're talking about.'

'Then put your boots on and I'll show you.'

He felt the early chill on his face as they hurried down Swinegate. Simon pushed his hands deep in his trouser pockets and wished he'd put on a heavier coat. Mudie didn't speak, marching on ahead until he reached the corner of Boar Lane and Briggate.

'That,' he said, pointing down at the flagstones. 'Take a look at that.'

The words were scrawled in chalk on the flagstones: *Curzon will die for Ashton*. Still perfectly clear, not enough feet tramping along yet to obliterate it.

'I've seen two others,' Mudie said. 'There's one up by the market cross, another outside St John's Church.'

'They're nothing to do with me,' Simon told him. Who was responsible for this?

'You're the one who wanted me to print up posters about Davey being in prison.'

Simon shook his head. 'I told you: this is nothing to do with me.'

'Then you'd better find out who did it. It's common knowledge you want to get Davey out of gaol. People are going to start looking at you.'

Simon stared at the pavement. It wasn't Emily Ashton's doing; she'd never even think of something like this. Then who? It was hopeful to know that someone else was on Davey's side, someone who was willing to stir things up. It was heartening. But this . . . it was dangerous. Curzon wouldn't take it lightly. Simon rubbed the sole of his boot over the stone until only a smear remained.

'I'll take care of the other two,' Mudie offered. 'But there are probably more.'

He couldn't walk everywhere. And a scrawl only took a minute. Easy enough to do again and again.

'I'm sure there will be.'

'Take care of it, Simon. For your own sake.'

Jane heard the knocking. She was standing by the attic window as Simon and Mudie disappeared along the street. A few minutes later she slipped out of the house, the shawl covering her hair, another anonymous figure in the early light. Not following this time. Hunting.

The hocus girl was out there. It was time to retrieve the ring and put an end to her fears.

Emily was working in the garden, kneeling to tug at the weeds outside the cottage. She had a shawl wrapped around her shoulders to keep the chill at bay, a mob cap tied over her hair.

'You're up early,' Simon said.

'I can't sleep.' From the way her cheeks had hollowed and the cheekbones stood out sharp on her face, she looked as though she hadn't been eating much, either. Hardly a surprise when her life was in pieces. She glanced at the plants in her hand as if she was surprised to find them there. 'I thought I might as well do something useful.'

'I need your help.'

'What's happened?' Suddenly there was panic in her voice. 'Is it something to do with Davey?'

He told her. 'Can you think of anyone who'd do that?'

'There's . . .'

'Who?'

'Ciaran, maybe,' she said. 'Ciaran Regan. It's just a guess, but he can be a hothead at times.'

'I don't know him.'

'He used to be a navvy on the canals. He and Davey have been friends for a year or so. He has a temper on him once he's had a few drinks.' She paused and bit her lip, then shook her head. 'He's the only one I can think of.'

'Where will I find him?'

'He works unloading the barges. You can't miss him, he has red curly hair, and he's tall.' Another pause. 'Have you been to see Davey?'

'I have.' How could he tell her the truth when her eyes were so wide and hopeful? 'He's coping.'

'Get him out of there, Simon. Please.'

'I will,' he told her, and hoped he could make it true. 'Right now I need to find this Ciaran.'

All along Briggate, traders were setting up for the market. Old John the tinker with his neatly mended pots and pans. The women sorting old clothes on a trestle. The constant squawk of chickens crammed together in a small wooden cage. A man made a pile of last year's apples, tiny and wrinkled now, then stood back and nodded at his work. The noise was growing as customers arrived and people began to call out their wares.

A cart weaved its way through, the driver cursing as he used his whip, a coach close behind. The horses tossed their heads, as if they could smell the open road.

By the entrance of the Moot Hall, a small group had gathered, chanting out their protests at another rise in the price of corn. Jane spotted two or three worried faces inside the building. People were stopping to watch. If more came, this might turn into a mob. If not, it would fade in a moment.

She stood, half-watching, keeping one eye on the crowd milling round. The girl would come. Sooner or later she'd be here. Everyone flocked to the market. Jane stayed back in the shadows, out of sight. If need be, she could wait all day.

A fresh shout stirred her. One voice at first, then a second and a third, crying out, 'Murder!' She darted through the press of people, across the road and into Bay Horse Yard. A crowd of men stood around. She crouched to slip between bodies until she could see the corpse lying on the floor.

Jane turned and pushed her way out again, starting to run. She had to find Simon.

Down by the warehouses, Ciaran was easy enough to spot. He carried a heavy sack on his back, striding carelessly across a plank between barge and shore, then through the doorway into a warehouse. When he appeared again, he was wiping his face with his kerchief.

'You're Davey Ashton's friend,' Simon said.

The man assessed him as he carried on rubbing at the sweat away. 'And what if I am?'

The Irish accent was still there, half-buried but still recognizable. His red hair was slicked down, shiny and damp, his shirt soaked through.

'Emily gave me your name. I'm Simon Westow.'

A quick nod. 'Ciaran Regan. Davey's mentioned you.'

'I'm trying to find a way to get him out of gaol.'

'And that's a fine cause. If there's anything I can do to help you, just let me know.'

Regan was pale, his skin covered in freckles, wide, heavy scars criss-crossing the backs of his hands.

There might well come a time he'd have to count on others. For now, though, all Simon had was a question.

'Tell me, have you been leaving warnings chalked around town?'

'Warnings?' The man narrowed his eyes. 'What kind of warnings are you talking about?'

'Someone's threatening the magistrate who arrested Davey.'

Regan laughed and shook his head. 'I wish I could claim the credit, but it wasn't me.' He paused for a moment. 'Westow . . . you're the thief-taker, is that right? Davey told me what you do.'

'I am.'

'I've no idea who's been doing it. No one's said anything to me, and that's the honest truth.'

'Can you find out? And make sure they stop?'

A shout from one of the barges. Regan turned towards the sound. 'I need to go,' he said. 'I'm in the Talbot most nights.'

A cart had overturned on Swinegate, and people picked their way around the debris while the driver's lad tried to stop others stealing. A hopeless task.

The sky seemed to shimmer with smoke, tiny flecks of soot glittering in the light. This was progress, people claimed. But the ones saying it loudest were the men who made the profits. The men who built their homes in the clean air away from town.

Enough. He took a breath and tried to concentrate. Lost in his thoughts, Simon didn't hear the footsteps until they were close. He turned quickly, reaching for the knife up his sleeve, then stopped.

It was Jane, red-faced from running. 'You'd better come. There's a body.'

A prickle of fear rose up his spine. 'Who is it?' he asked.

'Henry Wise.'

They'd just turned on to Briggate, pushing and forcing their way through the people. Jane had told him what she'd seen. He knew exactly who'd done this.

Close to the market stalls, a man stepped into his path. Whittaker, with a killer's smirk on his face, thumbs hooked in his belt. Spots across the pale material of his trousers dark enough to be blood. And beside him, a pair of armed soldiers in their brilliant red coats.

'You've saved me the trouble of looking for you, Westow. Magistrate Curzon's waiting in the Moot Hall. He has a few questions to ask.'

'Find Jem,' he told Jane quickly. 'See he tells Rosie. She knows what to do. George Mudie, too.'

Then two pairs of arms reached for him and he was hauled away.

TEN

'**G**o,' she ordered. 'Now!'

Jem dashed out of the churchyard, and Jane followed, walking with the shawl over her hair.

She felt as if Leeds was stifling her, the air close and damp, smuts clogging her nostrils and her lungs.

Mudie glanced up from his work as she entered the print shop, fixing his gaze on her.

'You're the lass who works with Simon, aren't you?' He was already starting to rise from his desk.

'Curzon's arrested him.'

Mudie sighed as he ran his hands down his cheeks. 'I warned him. What reason did they give?'

'I don't know.'

She watched him give a curt nod, then reach for his coat.

'The Moot Hall?'

'Yes.'

He paused for a fraction of a second. 'Has someone told his wife?'

'Yes.'

They stood by the old stocks, close enough to see the door of the Moot Hall. All around them the market continued, crackling with the buzz of gossip and people haggling for bargains. Jane kept turning the ring on her finger. The angry crowd had dispersed, but the sense of simmering fury lingered.

Mudie looked at her. 'They're saying someone's dead.'

'Henry Wise. The farrier.' She pointed across to Bay Horse Yard. 'Back in there. Someone stabbed him.'

She was going to say more. But she caught sight of the girl, drifting between stalls, still wearing the grubby bandage on her arm. She moved again, and for a moment Jane could see the ring. A pale glow of amber and a glint of gold on her finger.

Jane closed her hand around the hilt of her knife, then stopped.

Later. She would have to wait. Simon was more important.

Curzon looked elegant, lounging against the desk. Clean and sleek, not a hair out of place. A pose, Simon thought, as the soldiers pushed him down on to the wooden chair.

'You can go,' the magistrate said. 'You, too,' he added to Whittaker. 'Westow's not that stupid. He won't start anything here.'

Silence, and Curzon was in no hurry to break it. The man had done this before. A way to intimidate, to scare. But it wouldn't work with him. Simon settled back and crossed his legs, staring.

The magistrate was still young for the job, barely into his middle thirties. A man who relished his position and his power. Someone who nurtured his ambitions lovingly.

'Someone's been threatening me,' Curzon said finally.

The messages on the paving stones. Not too surprising.

'I saw one of them,' Simon said.

'I daresay you did. After all, you wrote them.'

'Did I now?' He smiled. 'And what makes you think that?'

'You're the one trying to free your friend.'

'He was imprisoned on a lie.' Simon kept his voice low and even, trying to sound perfectly reasonable. 'But then you'd know that.'

Curzon frowned and tried to wave the thought away. 'That's not why I had you brought here.'

Interesting. The man was deflecting the idea, not boasting or defending it. He'd hit a weak spot. Maybe Curzon wasn't so certain of his case, after all. And that meant he was no longer sure about Dodd.

'It sounds as if you're worried,' Simon said.

'Of course not.' Curzon spat out the words. 'You do know that threatening authority is sedition, don't you?'

Sedition again. He seemed to have the word on his brain. First the charge against Davey and now this.

'If you're accusing me, you'd better do it in court.'

'I want to know who's behind this.'

'That makes a pair of us,' Simon told him. 'Tell me, did you see the crowd out there earlier?'

'Complaining about the price of corn.' He spoke as if it hardly mattered.

'People are bitter. Prices going up while wages stay the same or fall. Today they dispersed. Next market day, who knows? And if you start arresting people for nothing . . .'

'Is that a threat, Westow?'

'Not at all,' Simon said. The mood in the room had changed. The sheen of bravado and authority had somehow slipped away. Curzon was scared. Of Leeds? Of the future? He didn't know. 'It's a statement of fact, that's all. Why would I need to threaten?'

'Because it's how people like you work. I've heard all about you. Thief-taker?' He made it sound like an insult. 'It's an underhand job.'

'On the contrary, it's an honest living. I'll tell you now: if we go to court, you'd better know that I'll call on many of the important men around here to vouch for my character. They've been more than happy with my services.'

'I don't believe you.'

But the certainty had vanished from his voice. He was wavering. This had moved outside his control.

'Then you'll have to see, won't you? It won't look good for you, I can assure you of that.'

Jane could read the rage on Rosie's face, strong enough to hide the fear at the back of her eyes.

'How long has he been in there?'

'Almost half an hour now.'

'The lawyer is on his way. Tell me what happened.' She had her arms pressed tightly across her chest, as if she was trying to hold all her feelings down and keep them inside.

There was so little to tell.

'The writing,' Mudie said. 'I showed Simon this morning.'

Rosie was pacing, making small circles on the cobbles, stopping and raising her head hopefully whenever the door to the Moot Hall opened. Five minutes passed, then ten.

'What are they doing to him in there?'

Simon stood. Curzon backed away, mouth open, ready to shout for his bodyguard.

'Are you done with your questions?' He'd had enough of the man and his empty words.

'You can go when I say, Westow.'

But the bluster was threadbare and full of holes.

Simon smiled and placed his hands on the back of the chair. 'Fine, then. We can wait for my lawyer. Maybe you'd prefer that.'

'Your sort don't have attorneys.'

'Don't we? Would you care for a wager on that? A guinea, perhaps?' Simon let the question hang. 'No? Well, it's your choice. He should be here very soon.'

Curzon turned away. 'Go and be damned with you.'

Jane saw Pollard the lawyer move through the crowd and touched Rosie on the arm. He was an older man with coarse white hair and a long, serious face that always seemed to be considering the state of the world.

'I'm sorry,' he said. 'My clerk had to find me. Is Simon still inside?'

'He's here,' Rosie said as Simon came through the door, peering around the crowd. She rushed over to embrace him.

Jane moved quietly away. Her part here was over. If Curzon had a serious accusation, Simon would still be inside.

Out of sight, she began hunting the hocus girl.

'For the love of God, Simon. I thought Curzon was going to keep you. I came home from taking the boys to school and Jem was waiting . . .'

They were sitting in a private parlour at the Rose and Crown. Under the table, he squeezed Rosie's hand. 'I'm sure he'd have loved to, but he'd have needed to charge me with something first. And he knew he didn't have any proof.'

'Curzon's a fool, but he knows how to watch himself,' Pollard warned. He finished his glass of brandy. 'Pity, really. I'd love to destroy him in court.' A tip of his hat and he was gone.

'What happened to Jane?' Simon asked.

Rosie shrugged. 'She wandered off as soon as you came out of the Moot Hall.'

A look passed between them.

'I could use her right now. Henry the farrier's dead.'

'Dead?' Rosie craned her head to glance through the window, as if there might be something to see. 'How? When?'

'Someone murdered him in Bay Horse Yard this morning.'

'Henry?' He could hear the pain in her voice. 'His wife's due to give birth again soon, isn't she?'

Mudie placed his hands on the table. 'You know who did it, don't you?'

Simon said nothing in reply, just picked up his glass and drank.

'Simon . . .' Rosie said.

'In good time. All in good time.'

Mudie rose. 'Come by the shop at four,' he said. 'There'll be a man you might want to meet.'

'Who?'

Mudie tapped the side of his nose. 'You'll see when you get there. He's from York. Here about a printing job.'

York. The city where they'd try Davey and the other men who'd been arrested.

'Don't they have printers of their own any more?' Simon asked.

'I daresay they do, but the fools expect to make a living from their work.' He chuckled. 'No, it's something delicate, and he doesn't want word spread around before he's good and ready. Come and talk to him,' he said again.

He wasn't usually one to insist. There had to be the possibility of information at the meeting.

'I'll be there,' Simon told him.

Once Mudie had gone, Rosie turned to her husband. 'You'd better tell me what happened to Henry.'

No sign of the girl in the market. And when she returned to Bay Horse Yard, Henry's body was gone. All that remained was a dark pool on the cobbles where the flies buzzed relentlessly.

Jane knew exactly who'd killed him. The guilt, the pleasure of death, had shone across Whittaker's face. There was even a faint smear of blood remaining on the back of his hand. As clear as if he'd come out and admitted it.

Henry had been a kind man. When Jane still lived on the streets, he'd twice bought her food when she was desperate with hunger. He never expected anything for it, just an act of generosity from the goodness of his heart.

Stone-faced, Jane stood in the yard, staring down at the ground, trying to push away all the noise in her head. Then she stooped and dipped her fingertips in the small pool before rubbing it on the hilt of her knife. A promise of revenge. She'd tally up the bill for this, and make sure Whittaker knew the reason he was paying the price.

Early afternoon. The boys were strangely quiet after school, hardly any sound as they played in their room.

'They're exhausted,' Rosie told him. 'The first day of lessons. Just as well it was a half-holiday today.'

'It always worries me when they're not making noise,' Simon said with a grin. 'Makes me think they're up to something.'

'Enjoy it while you can. By the end of the week they'll be back to their usual mischief.' Her smile quickly faded as she sat at the table.

'You scared me this morning, Simon.'

He stayed silent for a while, rubbing the back of his neck.

Then, 'If you want to know the truth, I was terrified until I saw Curzon's face.'

'He was trying to warn you off, wasn't he?'

'Something like that. He looked like a man who's been preparing himself for his golden moment and sees it all falling apart in front of his eyes.'

'Why?' Rosie asked. 'He has Davey in gaol. He has his spy. What more does he need?'

'I don't know,' Simon said slowly. 'But he's definitely on edge. It must have something to do with Dodd. There's a problem with him. Maybe this man from York will have the answer.'

The silence hung, then she said, 'The woman with Dodd. Do you think it would help if I went out and tried to talk to her?'

Simon considered the idea. He hadn't managed it. God knew, Rosie couldn't do any worse; maybe this Margaret Wood wouldn't feel threatened by her.

'As long as she's alone,' he said.

Rosie gave him a look that could have crumbled rock. 'How many years did we work together, Simon?'

'Fourteen. Until the boys were born.'

'And how many mistakes did I make?'

'No more than me,' he admitted.

'That's your answer,' she told him, and tapped a finger on her head. 'I haven't forgotten.'

They'd learned the trade together, the thief-taker and his wife. Starting out young and eager, taking too many stupid risks and depending on blind luck instead of guile. But time had taught them both.

Rosie always kept herself in the background; a man had to be the face people saw. Simon answered the advertisements posted in the newspapers, dealt with the men who wanted stolen items retrieved. They could talk to him; they'd never have spoken to a woman. But the real work came after that, and that had been the pair of them together. In the brothels and the beershops, among the whores, the pickpockets and cut-throats. Those people knew her; they respected her.

Once the twins arrived, she stopped. She made the choice. By then they were successful, they'd earned a reputation. Men came to Simon with offers of work. He knew she'd had her fill of the dirt and the crime. She needed life, she needed joy, and the boys brought that.

Simon had a natural gift for it. He was born to be a thief-taker, he revelled in it. He felt at home among the thieves and the cut-throats. And Jane arrived to help with the work. Yet he knew there was some small part of his wife that missed the excitement. He understood that, the way the blood began to throb through the body, the pleasure of the chase.

'Catch her when she's out, that's the best way,' he said. 'She can't bar the door on you.'

'I'll be ready,' Rosie told him.

What was it about Dodd? Simon sat at the table in the kitchen and tried to make sense of it all. Curzon was worried; that meant his evidence was fragile, maybe not even legal. The way politics was in England, any magistrate who couldn't make a case for sedition had no place on the bench. That had to be the reason Davey was still in Leeds and not in the cells at York castle. Simon just needed the right pressure to make it all topple.

For the first time, he really believed that Davey might walk out of the gaol a free man.

How, though? There had to be something he didn't know yet, some piece of knowledge that could change it all. Something he didn't understand.

He sifted through everything he had, realizing how bare it was. Not enough facts to weigh in his hand, and he couldn't piece them all together to complete the picture. Had the other men arrested in the West Riding been transferred to York? That was something to find out. And then he needed to track down Mr Dodd . . .

Maybe Rosie would have luck with the woman. A man's touch certainly hadn't worked. But they needed to tread lightly and carefully. Too much pressure and the pair might run.

How could he do it, then?

The long-clock chimed a quarter to the hour. Time to go and meet Mudie's man.

ELEVEN

It was simple enough for her to follow Whittaker. Once again he trailed behind Curzon to the Bull and Mouth, eyes constantly moving and appraising any threat to his master. There was a taunting arrogance in the way he walked, daring people to challenge the magistrate.

But he wouldn't be expecting anyone to attack *him*. One cut was all she needed. One cut for Henry, to even up the balance sheet. But not yet, and definitely not in the middle of Briggate. Somewhere quiet, with no witnesses. Let people wonder why he'd been killed. She'd know the reason, that would be enough.

Simon would guess, but he'd know better than to ever ask her.

Curzon's carriage rumbled out, iron wheels rattling over the cobbles. Inside, the magistrate was a worried man, Jane thought, hunched and pinched by his troubles.

And then came Whittaker. She stood back, the shawl over her hair. He'd seen her once, with Simon. No need for him to spot her again.

Once the clatter of their hooves had faded, Jane moved through the streets, head down, the invisible girl. There was other work to do.

No one was following her. At Mrs Rigton's beershop she pulled the door closed behind herself.

'What is it?'

'I'm looking for someone. A girl.'

'Where is he?' Simon asked.

The man was late, half an hour by the bell at St John's Church. Mudie sat at his desk, hands steepled under his chin as he stared at a pile of papers.

'I don't know. He was supposed to arrive on the afternoon coach.'

'Maybe it was delayed.'

Mudie shrugged. 'Perhaps.'

'Who is he, George?'

The man sighed. 'The Clerk of Courts for York Assizes.'

'Then why is he coming here?'

'It's business. Some venture he's cooked up with his brother-in-law and he'd prefer people in York didn't know about yet.' Mudie shrugged. 'I don't care, as long as he's putting money in my pocket. But he'll have information about the dates for upcoming trials.'

'If he ever shows his face.'

As the hour struck five, Simon left. The coach should have arrived two hours before. It had, he discovered when he checked at the inn. The man from York hadn't been on it. He wouldn't be appearing tonight.

The Talbot was busy, all the benches full, men standing and talking as they drank. Even in the press of people, Ciaran Regan's curling red hair made him easy to spot. He was sitting at a table with four other burly men, every one of them a docker by their size, all laughing heartily, two empty jugs on the table. Simon leaned against a pillar, close enough to catch the man's eye. A nod of the head, then he left, waiting outside as evening fell.

'Did you find out who's been chalking those messages?'

'I did.' Regan pursed his lips. 'He's only a young lad, Mr Westow. You know how they are, all piss and vinegar.'

'Have you told him to stop?'

'I *suggested* it.' The man gave a worn smile. 'He means well. He just wants to let people know about Davey.'

At least others cared, Simon thought. That was something. He'd wondered if he and Emily were on their own.

'Curzon had me in today. He accused me of doing it.'

'Did he now?' Regan grinned. His eyes were laughing. 'And he got nowhere, apparently.'

'Your friend might not be so lucky.'

'I'll tell him that. It won't happen again. There are a few of us who want justice for Davey, you know.'

'I'm grateful, honestly. We're all on the same side. Just tell your friend not to make things harder.'

'I will. I'm ready to help, I told you.' Regan lifted his hands

and bunched them into a large pair of fists. 'I'm handy enough
with these if push comes to shove.'

'Let's hope it doesn't,' Simon said with a smile. 'But I'll know
who to call on.'

'I'll be there. We all will. I'd better go, they'll think I've
skipped out before my round.'

'Henry the farrier,' Jane said. 'Why would Whittaker kill him?'

They were walking across Leeds Bridge, striding briskly in
the morning air, out to Hunslet with its haze and its factories
and mills. Simon glanced across at her. Even now she could still
take him by surprise. He thought no one else had read the guilt
on Whittaker's face.

'Because Henry threatened him,' he replied. 'And it's his way
of sending a message to me.'

'Is there any chance he'll hang for it?'

'None at all.'

He watched her stare straight ahead as she spoke.

'Then we'd better do it ourselves. Henry deserves justice.'

'In time,' Simon agreed. 'Be patient. Ericsson sent me a note
this morning, wondering if we had his ring yet.'

'Today,' she promised. 'Today.'

The world was steam and smoke and sweat.

Standing in the yard, the noise a cacophony of engines rumbling
and spitting. The boiler room was twenty yards away, the big
doors open wide; even at a distance the heat was uncomfortable.
The men inside were all stripped to the waist as they shovelled
coal into the furnace, chests covered with sweat that reflected
the flames. Visions of hell on earth, Simon thought. A chimney
rose above the brick building, tiny smuts of soot showering down
like rain. The shawl Jane wore over her hair was already spotted
and black.

Finally a door opened and a man crossed the cobbles. Still
youthful, no more than Simon's age, he moved with all the poise
and confidence of money and position. His father had built the
engineering works twenty years before. Now the old man was
dead and Stephen Potter ran it all. He'd done well, expanding
the business and making himself into a rich man.

Three years earlier, a thief had broken into Potter's grand house on the hill in Armley and made off with some of his wife's jewellery. He'd placed an advertisement in the *Mercury*, offering a fee for its return. Simon had brought it back, every single piece.

Not long after that, Potter had become a magistrate, the youngest in Leeds. He still seemed embarrassed by the position, as if he wasn't certain he wanted it.

'Good to see you, Westow.' The man gave a small nod to acknowledge Jane. 'I need to go into Leeds to meet someone. Do you mind walking with me?'

'Not at all,' Simon said.

'I'll take a guess and say this is about Mr Curzon. That seems to be the only reason you'd come to see me.'

He gave a rueful smile. 'Was it that obvious?'

Their heels beat a sharp, quick tattoo on the pavement. Jane drifted along, fifty yards behind them.

'If it's Curzon, that means you're interested in Mr Ashton.'

'He's an old friend.'

'And if you're here to ask me about the case, there's nothing I can tell you. It's not my business.'

'No idea at all?'

Potter hesitated, then said, 'About the only thing I can say is that Curzon's playing his cards very close to his chest this time. Normally he'd be crowing about something like this, but he's stayed unusually quiet.'

That fitted with everything Simon knew. All Curzon had constructed was built on sand.

'What do you know about a man named Dodd?' he asked.

Potter pursed his lips and shook his head. 'I've never heard of him.'

'He's Curzon's government spy.'

'Ah.' Nothing more than that, Simon noted.

Finally Potter turned from Briggate on to Commercial Street.

'My meeting's at the Leeds Library,' he said.

'I wish you well. Thank you for your time.' He liked the man. And Potter was subtle; there'd been more in the words he hadn't spoken than anything he'd said. 'By the way, Curzon has a bodyguard these days.'

A grimace. 'I've seen him. We're magistrates, for God's sake, not the King or his family. But he won't be told.' A wave and he was gone, hurrying up the street.

'Did anyone follow?'

They were out of sight at the back of Ship Inn Yard. Simon had ducked through the small archway by the tavern. Another two minutes and Jane entered from the other end.

'Whittaker,' she said. 'From just this side of the bridge.'

'Did he see you at all?'

She lowered the shawl, rubbing soot from the wool.

'No.'

TWELVE

'Admit it, Simon, you didn't believe I could do it, did you?' Rosie had the glint of triumph in her eyes. She let out a contented sigh.

'How *did* you manage it?'

The house was quiet, the twins in their bed. They'd already been there when he arrived home, sleeping like the dead after their second day at school.

'It was simple. I watched the cottage. As soon as Margaret came out, I rushed over to Marsh Lane. I had my basket, the same as her, and we started talking as we walked into town.'

Far better than he'd managed on his visit.

'Did you tell her who you were?'

Rosie snorted. 'She thinks I'm a housewife with a pair of unruly boys.'

'That's true enough,' he said with a grin.

'And it's all she needs to know.' She paused and her expression softened. 'The poor girl's stuck out there alone most of the time. She was happy just to have someone to talk to.'

'But did she have much to say?' Simon asked.

'Well . . .' She listed the points on her fingers. 'She met Dodd in London and came up here with him. He told her it would be an adventure and they'd be rich. Margaret knows they'll be going to York, but he hasn't told her when. The date keeps getting delayed. And Dodd seems more worried by the day.'

Simon raised an eyebrow. 'All that from one conversation?'

'We're women,' Rosie told him. 'I told you, she was happy to have someone who'd listen. There's more. They had money at first, but it's been growing thin on the ground the last few days. Dodd has started acting as if she's a servant, there to cook and clean for him. She's thinking of packing up and going back to London. She even showed me the coach fare she'd kept hidden from him.'

'I'm impressed.'

'So you should be.' She preened a little. 'It's good to know I haven't lost my touch. What do you think?'

He reached out, caught her by the waist and pulled her close to kiss her deeply. 'I think I married the right woman.'

She leaned against him. 'You'd better keep remembering that. I'm going to make sure I meet her again.'

'See what else you can find out about Dodd next time.'

'If it comes up. I don't want to make her suspicious.'

'I'm sure you'll find a way.'

Jane was beginning to believe the hocus girl had vanished. She couldn't feel her anywhere in Leeds until, finally, late in the afternoon, there was a twitch of the senses. She pressed herself into a deep, shadowed space between buildings in the stink of Fish Street and waited, counting time in heartbeats. Ten, twenty, thirty and the girl passed, unaware of anything.

Jane slid out and followed, twisting the ring on her finger for luck before she reached into her pocket and took hold of the knife. Down to Kirkgate, through to Duncan Street, close to the Post Office. The girl crossed the road, jumping over a pile of horse dung, and Jane saw her chance.

A moment and she had the tip of her blade pressing against the woman's side. Pitfall Street lay just ahead of them, dark and quiet, leading to the river.

'Down there,' she hissed. 'Now.'

His name was written in precise, copperplate script. *Mr Simon Westow.* He unfolded the note as Rosie looked over his shoulder.

Sir,

You have been recommended to me as a gentleman who can find things that have been taken. I should be grateful if you could call on me at your convenience. I can be found at the premises of William Tetley & Sons on Mill Hill during business hours.

With sincere wishes,
Joshua Tetley

'Business,' she said. 'Paying work.'

'Between Davey and Ericsson's ring, we're already stretched.'

Rosie shook her head. 'It's money, Simon. If you start turning down jobs, word will spread and they'll stop asking.'

She had a clear, shrewd head for this, much better than his. Rosie always knew to the farthing how much money they possessed, in the bank and in notes and coins hidden in the secret drawer in one of the stairs.

'Do we need it?'

'We always need it. And the Tetleys are wealthy.' She tapped a fingernail against the signature. 'He's married to a Carbutt. They're rich. It's worthwhile.'

With a sigh, he read the words again. He knew he should be grateful. These days people sought him out; business came to him instead of him looking for it. He'd built an enviable name in Leeds. But Rosie was right; a reputation could break like a cobweb.

'I'll go and see him in the morning.'

'Stop here,' Jane ordered.

They were a few yards from the water, close enough to hear it lapping softly against the stones and smell the chemicals and decay and sewage.

'What do you want?' the woman asked.

'The ring.'

Her hand moved to cover it. 'It was a gift.'

'Don't lie.' Jane pushed the knife a little deeper and felt the woman flinch. 'Take it off.'

'I'll call for the watch.' But the words were all show, nothing behind them at all.

'Go ahead.' She nodded towards Ericsson's timber yard on the other side of the river. 'They can ask the owner and see what he says.'

'It's stuck.'

'Then loosen it,' Jane snapped. 'Or I'll take the finger. It doesn't matter either way to me.'

'I've done it,' the girl said hastily.

'Toss it down on the cobbles.'

The small tinkle of metal on stone. A few yards away, people were crossing Leeds Bridge. On foot, on horseback. On the carts rumbled slowly past. But down here, they were all alone.

'You can take your knife away now.'

'No,' Jane said. 'Not yet. Your name's Charlotte, isn't it?'

She felt the woman's body stiffen. 'What if it is?'

'Why were you digging out at Drony Laith the other day?'

A hesitation that stretched out into silence. Then: 'She told me. Said I could keep half—'

'Who? Who told you?'

'She'll kill me if I—'

In one movement, Jane twisted the girl's hair in her fist and pulled sharply. Charlotte fell to her knees, throat exposed, the edge of the blade resting against her skin. Jane turned the woman's head until they were staring at each other.

'And I'll kill you if you don't. Which do you prefer?'

The girl's voice was hoarse with terror. But her eyes had a mocking look as she stared upward.

'Do that and you'll never know, will you?'

At supper, Richard and Amos were subdued and orderly as Simon asked about the school and their lessons. Their replies were short, barely more than a word.

'It's not like them,' he said once they were tucked into their bed. 'They're too quiet.'

'At least they were well-mannered and attentive for once,' Rosie told him. 'Be grateful. Maybe that teacher's already doing some good.'

She was cleaning the plates, her back to him, looking out of the window into the yard. They had money to employ a servant, but when Simon bought the house they'd agreed against it; there were too many secrets in their work, and no one they could trust. It was safer to keep everything in the family.

'Possibly.' He preferred the boys raucous and wild and loud. This was too polite, as if they'd been tamed too readily.

He heard the front door open and began to rise, reaching for his knife, lowering his hand as Jane came through. She took Ericsson's ring from her pocket and placed it on the table. Pale gold and soft amber.

'Exactly as you promised.' He smiled at her. 'I'll return it tomorrow. Did she give you any trouble?'

'No.' Then she was gone again, feet clattering as she ran up the stairs.

She'd never killed a woman. She'd never imagined that she would ever need to do that. Men were the problem, violent, dangerous, grasping.

Yet as she stood there, knife trembling against the woman's throat, Jane felt the temptation. A single slice of the blade, a push, and a life would vanish into the river. So easy to do, so quick.

But Charlotte was right. Kill her and she'd never know who'd given the order, who really knew about her.

Jane tightened her grip on the woman's hair and tugged harder, pulling back until the hocus girl was staring at the sky with tears in her eyes. No words. No pleading. Just silent defiance.

She pushed, sending the woman sprawling in the dirt, picked up the ring and walked away.

Jane stood by the window in the attic. Night had fallen, distant sounds rose from the streets. She took out the knife, still with the faint stain of Henry the farrier's blood she'd smeared on the handle, and weighed it in her hand.

Had she been right? Had she been wrong?

With slow tenderness, she made a cut on her forearm to try and mute all the questions screaming in her head. One then another, watching the first drops of blood form and feeling the release from her thoughts, all the noise stilled into silence for a short while.

It would return. She knew it would return. But it was worth the pain for a few moments of peace.

Ericsson examined the ring and slipped it on to his finger, flexing the joints in his hand.

'Better,' he said finally. 'My wife didn't notice it was missing.' A pause and a rueful smile. 'Or if she did, she didn't say anything. You do good work, Mr Westow.'

Simon just offered a quiet dip of his head. Better than a lie. Or the truth, that a sixteen-year-old girl had performed the job.

A payment of twenty pounds. He slipped the notes into his waistcoat pocket and glanced around the office. Pale wood wainscoting, polished to a high shine and glimmering from the light through the windows. Outside, a yard full of lumber and the drone of the sawmill cutting boards. Beyond that, the river and a long barge being unloaded.

'If anyone needs a thief-taker, I'll recommend you, Mr Westow,' Ericsson said.

'I appreciate that. I wish you well.'

Across the bridge and through the people on Boar Lane to Mill Hill. Tetley's occupied an old shop, bow windows on either side of a varnished door. A small bell tinkled as he entered. Inside, open sacks of malt stood against the wall, the smell so overwhelming that Simon thought it might choke him.

Small casks of brandy and bottles of wine stood on the shelves by the wall. He was catching his breath as a tall man emerged from a back room.

'How might I help you, sir?' A warm, pleasant voice.

'I'm looking for Mr Tetley. Joshua Tetley.'

'I'm Joshua,' the man said.

'Simon Westow.'

'Good of you to call, sir.'

He was tall, with wispy brown hair and sideboards that started down his cheeks before fading away to nothing. Friendly, merry blue eyes.

'My apologies, I know the scent can be a little intoxicating. I've spent too long around it to notice any more. Would you care for coffee, perhaps? Or tea? It will clear the taste.'

Simon coughed. 'I'll be fine. You said you needed my services?'

Tetley glanced down at the ground for a moment before he spoke. 'I do. But a question first, if I may.'

'Of course.' Everyone had their own strange ways; he'd learned that over the years.

'I'm considering buying a brewery. Sykes's, on Salem Place.'

'Then I wish you good luck.' Most of the inns and taverns brewed their own beer, the way they always had. He'd seen any number of men try their luck as commercial brewers. Most only lasted a few months before closing their doors. Sykes was one of the very few who'd survived.

'If I said I wanted you to investigate him and his business to find any weak spots, what would you say?'

'I'd turn you down,' Simon replied, and Tetley smiled. The answer seemed to satisfy him.

'Good, very good. I wouldn't want someone willing to stoop to that. We have a problem, Mr Westow. One of our clerks has vanished and he's taken fifty pounds of our money with him.'

Quite a sum, close to a year's wages for a clerk. 'He could live for a long time on that.'

'We want it returned. Quietly, though. No need for everyone to know our business.'

'Of course.' If people learned the firm had been gulled like that, their reputation would suffer. 'And no prosecution, I take it?'

'Just the money, Mr Westow. As much of it as is left.'

'You'd better tell me about this clerk of yours . . .'

'His name is Gordon Armstrong,' Simon said. 'He had a room on the Head Row, but Tetley said he went there the day before yesterday and the landlady told him Armstrong had left.'

'If he's taken that much, he's probably already gone from Leeds,' Jane said. 'Somewhere safer.'

'I told him that, too. But he wants us to search. Armstrong's about twenty-five. Dark hair, clean-shaven, not particularly tall or short, quite thin.' He shrugged. 'At least there's one thing to help: he has a limp. His right leg is a little shorter than the left.'

Simon watched her nod slowly. At the best of times Jane never spoke much, but she'd been especially quiet lately. Something involving this hocus girl, it had to be. But if he asked, she'd

never tell him. Certainly not everything. All he could do was
wait and see if the words ever came to her.

'Do we know anything else about him?'

'That's it.'

There was little chance of finding the man. He'd been honest
with Tetley about that. Jane was right: Armstrong was probably
already in another town, living high and wide until the money
was spent.

'I'll start asking.'

As he watched her slip away, Simon felt a twinge of guilt.
Jane was doing all their work while he looked for ways to free
Davey from gaol. She didn't complain, she hardly seemed to
notice, but it wasn't fair to her.

What choice did he have? He couldn't let Davey go without
a fight.

A sigh and he strode up Briggate, crossed the Head Row and
entered Mudie's printing shop. Maybe he'd had some word from
his mysterious York visitor.

'Come on back here, Simon,' Mudie called. He was standing
by the press, papers in his hand. By his side, someone elegant
enough to pass as a gentleman. The clothes marked him out, a
dark swallowtail coat, exquisitely cut, tight, pale trousers and a
silk waistcoat, a tall beaver hat in his hand. 'This is Mr Bickerstaff.
He was delayed yesterday.'

Mudie wore an eager look. He must have smelled money as
soon as the man walked in and wondered how much extra he
could charge, Simon thought.

'Will you want these shipped to York?' he said to Bickerstaff.

'To the address I gave you.'

'I'll factor that into the cost. Let me calculate the figures.
While I do that, this is Simon Westow, the man I told you about.'

They waited until Mudie was at his desk, scribbling away with
his pen.

'George tells me you're interested in cases set to appear before
York Assizes,' Bickerstaff said.

'The ones for sedition,' Simon corrected him.

'That's valuable information.'

'Naturally.'

Simon smiled to himself. No surprise at all. Bickerstaff hadn't come by his fancy clothes completely honestly. No doubt he also had a grand house in York and a fashionably dressed wife, too. It all cost money. Simon took a sovereign from his pocket and placed it by the man's hand. Bickerstaff didn't even deign to look down until two more rested on top of it.

'I can tell you that there are no trials for sedition scheduled at the Assizes.'

Interesting. And well worth the money, if it was true.

'Could the trial be held somewhere else?'

Bickerstaff raised an eyebrow. 'It's possible,' he answered. 'But extremely unlikely. And I can assure you that I would have heard if that were the case.'

'Thank you.'

The man smiled. The money had vanished from sight. Just like a conjuror's trick.

'You're most welcome.'

No trial for Davey or any of the others who'd been arrested. The cases must be thin as gossamer. Dodd connected them all. He had to be the reason. It was definitely time to confront the man.

First, though, a visit to the cells under the Moot Hall.

THIRTEEN

'Right leg shorter than the left,' Jem repeated as he chewed the meat pie Jane had bought him.

'If you see him, I want to know about it straight away,' she said.

They were sitting in St John's churchyard, their backs against the wall of the porch. People crossed to and fro along the path, a few idling past, most hurrying as if the world was pursuing them. Jem finished the food, sucking the last crumbs from his fingers.

Jane stood and counted out ten pennies, watching his eyes widen.

'Get some of the others to help you,' she said. Two of them

couldn't cover the whole of Leeds. It was too big, too many people.

'I'm in charge, though, aren't I?' Jem asked. A hopeful question, his eyes wide.

'If that's what you want.' She placed the money in his hand, knowing it was more than he'd ever held in his life.

He was bone and skin. The wrist that poked out of his torn shirt was so thin it might snap in a strong wind, his hair lank and ragged, hanging down on to his shoulders. Ten years old now, Jane guessed. But he'd survived out here. She knew exactly what that demanded, how wearying simply staying alive each day could be. On your guard every second until the time arrived when it became too much, when all you craved was to lie down and let it end.

Jem was still here. She understood his quiet will to continue. He was quick, he was sharp and observant. Jane had been a year or two older than he was now when she started working with Simon. Small tasks at first, following someone, the responsibilities building as he came to trust her.

She'd proved herself. Made mistakes, but she was still here too.

'Off you go,' she said, and watched him run. For people like her and Jem there was no childhood at all.

Jane gave the landlady at Armstrong's lodgings a penny; she showed her his room. Empty, everything gone, no sign of him beyond a stray dark hair on the windowsill.

'He were a right good tenant,' the woman said. 'Paid prompt every week. Then he upped and flitted in the night. I thought mebbe he'd died when there were no sign of him next morning. When I came up it were like this.' Her mouth hardened. 'He must have crept out while I were sleeping.'

A quiet man, she said. Church every Sunday without fail.

'Proper Anglican, too,' she added with a note of pride. 'Not one of them strange beliefs some folk go for.'

The woman didn't understand why he'd disappear so suddenly, not even a word, as if it was an insult to her.

'I looked after him. Fed him good food in the evening, made sure his clothes were washed.' She shook her head. 'No gratitude, that's the problem with some folk.'

He spent most of his evenings alone, she said, not one to be out drinking or running after women.

Nothing there at all.

Jane walked. Mile after mile around town, on the flagstones and the cobbles, through the dust where no roads had been laid yet.

No one could disguise a limp. She saw old men who dragged a leg as they moved, men with crutches, but no one who resembled Armstrong. He'd been a clerk, a middling man, hardly rich but not ragged, either. As ordinary as anyone could be. At least on the surface.

By the end of the day, when her legs were aching and her feet were sore, she'd decided Armstrong had abandoned Leeds. Fifty pounds would take him a long way. A new life in Manchester or Liverpool. A sailing ship to America and enough capital left for a fresh start.

Jane shook the soot from her shawl and gathered it around her shoulders as she trudged up Briggate towards St John's Church. Then she felt the prickle up her spine.

Someone was following her.

'We have hope, Davey. Real hope.'

'Do we? It seems to me that you're building a house on single grain of sand.'

Davey Ashton sat on the sleeping bench, elbows resting on his knees, the thin blanket pulled tight around himself against the chill and the damp. His hair had become matted, the stubble on his cheeks quickly turning into a beard heavily seasoned with grey. He seemed even thinner than before, a perfect image of despair, Simon thought. 'All it means is I'll rot for longer down here before they do anything.'

He began to cough, and spat into the stinking bucket in the corner.

'No,' Simon said. 'It means there's a good chance I'll be able to get you out of this place.'

Davey shook his head as he looked around the cell. 'Do you know, I've had dreams about dying here.'

'I won't let that happen.'

'What can you do to prevent it? Don't tell me Curzon's

going to have a change of heart. That doesn't happen to men like him.'

Dodd. He needed Dodd, to squeeze the truth out of the man before he could slip away. Rosie had gone to watch the cottage again, to meet Margaret Wood accidentally. That might tell him more about their plans.

Simon scoured the inns. No sign of the man. But there was one place Dodd would need to go – Curzon's house. A long walk out to Potternewton and it might yield nothing at all. But it was time to admit that he was desperate, ready to follow any possibility at all.

It was a new house, the stone still the colour of honey, far from the soot and smells of Leeds. Extensive grounds, landscaped to look down the hill towards town.

Curzon had done well for himself. Name a magistrate who hadn't, Simon thought. But this one had his factory, making money the way it made smoke. He was ambitious, that was no secret, his eye on a title, some acknowledgement of the status he saw as his due.

No doubt other magistrates in the West Riding were every bit as greedy. Successful prosecutions for sedition would bring them to the notice of the government and the Regent. They'd found Dodd somewhere and made use of him. And now everything had become tenuous, on the verge of falling apart.

If Simon could discover the right lever, Davey and all the other men would go free. If.

There were few places to stand and watch the house. So much of the ground had been cleared. The best he could find was a small copse at the crest of the slope above Harehills Grove. Leeds lay on the horizon, half-hidden under its haze like a dream. On the slope behind him, the farmland of the Gledhow valley, fields and cows and silence. He settled on a pile of ferns and stretched out his legs, waiting to see if this was a fool's errand.

For a moment she froze. People bumped and pushed her, she was buffeted by the crowd. Who was behind her? The woman? Someone else?

Then the panic evaporated. She was Jane once more. In control, feet moving without thought, scurrying off along a yard off Briggate, through a passage scarcely wide enough for her scrawny body. Her senses were alert, heart pounding in her chest as she moved quickly. In two minutes she'd lost whoever was behind her. That was the easy part.

Now she had to find them again. To become the pursuer, not the pursued.

A shortcut through a stinking court and back to the street. Hand in her pocket, fingers tight around the handle of her knife. She looked around, up and down. At first there was nothing, just ordinary people passing and going about their business.

A space cleared for a second and she saw him. Whittaker the bodyguard. He was standing, stock still, eyes fixed on the court where she'd vanished, a bitter, dangerous look on his face.

It was time to see if what Simon had told her was true and she really was born for this work.

Inside, she could feel the tug of desire. To surprise Whittaker and make him pay for Henry the farrier's death. But not yet, Simon had said. The bodyguard's death would be a distraction, a chance for Curzon to open a new investigation.

Yet she wasn't going to let this opportunity lie. She couldn't simply allow it to pass. Instead, she moved up Briggate, the shawl over her shoulders, her fair hair uncovered. For once, she wanted to be visible. She needed him to follow her to the churchyard. She'd be waiting there, waiting for him.

The man was twenty paces behind her, she judged. Even in the crowd she could pick out the rhythm of his feet as he followed her. She'd have plenty of time to prepare.

Jem was over by the wall, sitting and watching. He stirred as he saw her. Jane gave him a small sign: stay there, don't move. Then she stood, as if she was slightly lost, waiting for someone. The knife was concealed in her hand.

Whittaker came up behind her. He probably thought he was quiet, but to her ears, he might as well have been an army on the move. He was close when she turned, and for the smallest moment his step faltered. Then he was on her, leering, his eyes hungry.

'So you're Westow's little slut. People tell me you're dangerous. There's nothing to you.'

His hand moved, cupping her breast, fingers squeezing so hard that the pain shot through her. It shocked, it hurt, but Jane didn't let her face betray a thing. One second, two and then three. Just long enough for him to think he had her cowed. The hilt of the knife rubbed against her gold ring as she let it slide in her fingers. Her right hand shot up and the blade carved a line down his cheek.

He jumped back as if he'd been burned, raising his hand to his face and bringing it down to stare in disbelief at the blood. 'You bitch!' he shouted.

Jane didn't move. She stood with the knife in her hand. Her voice was quiet and calm, hardly more than a whisper.

'I'm going to kill you,' she told him. 'For Henry.'

She took a step forward and Whittaker retreated, still pressing a hand to his face. Blood seeped through his fingers, dripping down his neck to stain the white of his shirt.

He kept moving, watching her until there was enough distance for him to turn his back and walk off.

She'd bested him. Humiliated him. He wouldn't let this rest. He couldn't; he was a man. Jane knew that before she began, but she didn't care. The next time, though, he'd be cautious. He'd be slow. That didn't matter. She'd do exactly as she promised.

'Did he hurt you?' Jem had run across as soon as it was safe.

'He tried.' She could still feel Whittaker's touch on her body. Her breast ached. The mark of his fingers would show in a few hours. The hurt went deeper in her, to her core. She wouldn't forget and she'd never forgive. 'But I hurt him more.' She turned to the boy. For now she'd put it out of her mind; there would be time to think about everything tonight. 'Have you found the man with the limp?'

'Daniel thinks he has,' Jem said gravely. He let out a low whistle and a boy emerged from behind a gravestone. He was a thin, tall youth with sunken cheeks and sullen eyes, dressed in mismatched clothes two sizes too small for his body. His voice was slow and hesitant, tripping over words as he told his tale.

Twice he'd seen someone with a heavy limp, he said, moving his leg in a circle to illustrate. The first time had been on the Calls, then later near the brewery on the other side of the river.

'What did he look like?' Jane asked.

A grown-up, that was all he knew. Dark hair, nothing to mark him out. Without the limp, the boy would never have noticed him. The first time he was on his own, the second he had a woman with him.

'Where did they go?'

Daniel shrugged. He'd seen them, that was all. But they were going down Salem Place, he said, by that chapel where they sometimes gave out food.

She gave him a penny, and for a second a smile bloomed on his face. As he turned to run off, Jane asked, 'The woman. Do you remember her?'

Another shrug, then he answered: 'She was bigger than him. And she had something wrapped around her arm. Here.' He placed a hand over his sleeve, just below the elbow.

The hocus girl. Charlotte Winter.

Every way Jane turned, she was there. Why?

Two hours of sitting and Simon felt close to dozing. Nobody had stirred from the house, no sign of movement inside. It was time to leave before he wasted the entire day here. He stood and stretched lazily. He'd just placed the hat on his head when he heard the crack of a gun and bark flew off a tree thirty feet away.

Simon threw himself back on the ground. Almost a minute later, another shot, a little closer this time, and hoarse laughter in the distance. Bent low, he scurried away, dodging from cover to cover until he was out of sight of the house. His breathing was ragged and his legs were shaking as he stood, looking around warily.

The whole time, someone had known he was there. Watched and waited for the chance to . . . do what? To scare him? Kill him? His heart was still thudding as he reached the main road and began walking towards Leeds. Thoughts bobbed in his mind, rising and falling.

Who'd done it? Curzon himself? Whittaker? Yes, he could imagine that. The bodyguard would relish the sport of it. Dodd? No, that seemed unlikely. But who really knew? Desperate men did dangerous things. And a magistrate could very easily cover up a murder to shield himself.

It took an hour to reach home. Halfway there he felt panic

overwhelm him, glancing over his shoulder to make sure there was no pursuit. But all he saw were coaches and carts and a few ragged souls placing one foot wearily in front of another.

'You look like death,' Rosie told him as he sat at the kitchen table and reached for the ale jug. 'What's happened?'

He looked from her to Jane as he recounted it. Rosie reached out and squeezed his wrist. So little to tell, he thought when he finished. Hours of sitting, two shots, then running. It was nothing.

'It couldn't have been Whittaker,' Jane said into the silence.

'How can you be sure?'

'Because he came after me.'

'You never told me that,' Rosie said.

Jane shrugged. There'd been no need. It was done. For now, at least. Until Whittaker returned. And when he did, she'd be prepared for him.

'I cut him.' She saw the astonishment on Simon's face. 'He was in town, so it couldn't have been him shooting.'

'What did he do?' Simon asked.

'Followed me. Grabbed me.' Even as she spoke the words she could feel the pain, on her flesh, in her head.

'Are you all right?'

Jane gave a quick, tight nod. Enough about that. She'd fight her own battles.

'That man who stole from Tetley's,' she said. 'Someone who sounds like him has been seen with the hocus girl.'

Upstairs, long after night had arrived, Jane stood by the window, honing her knife on the whetstone. Long, smooth strokes. She smiled at the memory of the cut, Whittaker's realization of what she'd done and the way he ran from her. She could have killed him without a qualm. But she remembered Simon's words. His time would come. Now she'd make certain of that.

Stroke after stroke until the edge was deadly again.

FOURTEEN

The evening had calmed. Simon sat in the kitchen, one son on each knee as they told him the things they'd learned at school.

'And Mr Ellis had to beat one of the boys,' Richard said.

'For talking in class,' Amos continued. 'And because he couldn't remember the scripture verse we'd been taught.'

'He howled all through it,' Richard said.

'I'd keep quiet.'

'Why?' Simon asked.

'So he'd never know he hurt me, of course,' Amos replied, as if it was the most obvious thing in the world. Simon recalled his days at the workhouse, in the factory, all the beatings where he'd struggled to stop the tears, not to let the men see they had power over him.

'Enough of that,' Rosie ordered. 'It's time you two were in bed.'

Later, once the house was quiet, she came and sat by him. 'Are you sure you're all right?'

'Today surprised me, that's all. I've never been shot at before.'

'I hope you don't make a habit of it, Simon.' She smiled, and her fingertips stroked his jawline, then her face grew serious. 'You weren't the only one who was busy today. I saw Margaret Wood again.'

He knew she'd never let the opportunity to work pass her by. 'What did you worm out of her this time?'

'She's doesn't like it up here – she can't understand the way we all speak.' Her eyes laughed. 'Believe it or not, she thinks Leeds is too green. Like being in the country, she said.'

All the streets of brick and stone and soot, not even a tree to be seen? Simon shook his head in astonishment.

'What else? Anything about going to York?'

'Not really. I have the impression that Dodd's chafing to leave, but Curzon wants him to stay, and he holds the purse strings.'

'Why would he keep Dodd here?' Simon asked. 'That doesn't make any sense, not when I'm going around asking questions and the whole case is like a house of cards in a gale. You'd think he'd want the man away from me.'

'Maybe he believes Dodd will bolt if he's not watched,' Rosie said. 'From what Margaret hinted at, it's possible. She's certainly ready to go.'

Maybe that was the reason, he thought; he didn't know all the tension and detail, the ins and outs. One thing was certain, though: Curzon certainly wouldn't give a tinker's curse if Margaret vanished.

'If she's that eager, why doesn't she get on a coach?'

'She's scared.' Rosie cocked her head. 'Think about it, Simon. It's not too hard to understand. She's hardly an innocent, she knows what could happen if she travels alone.'

'What about Dodd?'

'He barely has a farthing. Curzon seems to be making sure of that. Keeping him close. There's one other thing.'

'What?'

'From what Margaret told me, I'd say Dodd's about as much a professional government agent as you are. He's a crook.'

'That doesn't surprise me,' he said slowly as he sat back, thinking. 'I'd like to know how he's ended up involved in all this.'

'She hasn't told me yet. I didn't want to ask too much. It's less suspicious if I let her talk.'

'Are you going to find her again?'

Rosie nodded. 'Tomorrow.'

'See if you can steer the conversation.'

'If I can. I'm not going put her on her guard.' She yawned.

'Let's go to bed,' he said. 'It's been a tiring day.'

He took hold of her hand. For a moment, she resisted.

'What were you thinking when they fired those shots?'

'I was terrified.' He sighed and pulled Rosie to her feet. 'I thought they were going to kill me. But I'm still here.'

It was early when Simon walked along Marsh Lane, out past the track that led to Dodd's cottage. He found a thickly wooded knoll at the edge of a field that offered a good view. He didn't expect any shooting here, but this was distant enough to be safe. Today he'd find the man and press him. The truth was long overdue. It was time to get Davey out of gaol before the rest of his spirit collapsed. Once that was done, Curzon could go to the devil.

After an hour of lazing in the early sun, dappled light filtering through the trees, he saw a man emerge from the house, stop and gaze around cautiously before moving on. No glance in his direction. Simon rose and started to walk.

Salem Place. Jane stood at the entrance to the street, letting people flow around her. The staithe stood in the distance, tall black heaps of coal brought down from the pits in Middleton, dark dust rising and clouding the sky.

Closer, to her left, the smell of malt from Sykes's brewery filled the air. Across the street, Salem Chapel, its door wide open.

What would bring Armstrong and the hocus girl down here? she wondered. There was nothing else to see, just a stretch of open ground, overgrown with years of weeds.

But there had to be *something*.

The chapel was dark, hushed. Everything was plain, so different to any church she'd ever entered. Just whitewash and wood. She could hear the soft, rhythmic strokes of a brush, and in the gloom a small, bent woman working in the far corner.

'Are you looking for summat?' She'd put up her broom, resting her arms against it.

'The door was open,' Jane said.

'Usually is.' The woman had a gentle, calm smile. An air of serenity surrounded her. 'That's what the chapel's for. Everyone's welcome if they want to talk to God. Maybe you were called here.'

'No.' She shook her head. 'I'm just looking for someone.'

'We all are, lass. But some of us find Him.' She shuffled closer. Jane could pick out the woman's wheezing breath as she moved. Her hair was caught under a cap tied below her chin, her pinafore smeared with dust and dirt. 'There's something here for everyone. The word is everywhere. All you need to do is open your heart and let it in.'

But that was one thing she'd never do. She knew that life was simpler when you closed it all off, locked the door on each incident and threw away the key. Do that and there was less chance of pain and betrayal, fewer people to hurt her.

'I'll go,' Jane said and turned.

'There were two like you in here yesterday,' the woman said. 'They were young as well.'

'A man and a woman?'

'Aye, that's right.'

'Did he have a limp? She had a bandage on her arm?'

The woman's eyes narrowed. 'Came in when that shower started outside. Weren't here nobbut two minutes, talking to each other, then they scurried off soon as I tried to talk to them.'

What did they want in this place? There was nowhere to hide anything, no place to sleep without being seen.

Jane took a ha'penny from her pocket and place it in the woman's hand.

'Are you sure you can spare it, pet?'

She never gave a thought to the way she looked. An old brown cotton dress of Rosie's. Too big when she'd first worn it, becoming too small now since she'd grown. It had stains and patches. Darned stockings, scuffed boots, the woollen shawl. Just clothes. But to anyone else she'd seem a pauper, a girl who didn't possess two coins to rub together.

'Yes.' She hurried away. It had been a stupid gesture; the woman would remember her now.

Jane searched around the outside of the building. Meadow Lane was only a few yards away. Nothing. Had they really just ducked in for shelter from the rain? The question niggled in her mind. She walked on, past the iron gates of the brewery where barrels were being rolled on to the drays as shire horses waited patiently in their traces, all the way down to the entrance to the staithes. But all she spotted there was men working and steam from the funnel of the train bringing wagons full of coal from the Middleton pits.

Why here? A pair like that wouldn't wander for no reason.

She was in the shadow of the chapel when she saw him pass. Whittaker, with his swaggering walk. Staying out of sight, she watched him go down to the coal staithe, moving around as though he belonged there. Talking to the men as they worked, asking questions and listening closely to the answers. He was still there when the locomotive steamed in carrying its long load. Then the explosion of noise as the first wagon released its load into the chute. Another and another, and Whittaker watched it all. He talked to the driver, climbed on the engine.

It didn't fit. None of this had anything to do with Curzon and Dodd.

When he left, she followed at a cautious distance. Over to Holbeck, no more than five minutes' walk to Murray's engineering works. He seemed to find short shrift there, turned away by man after man. Finally he gave up, striding back towards Leeds Bridge.

From her hiding place, Jane could see the vivid red line she'd carved into his cheek. She smiled.

He knew exactly where he wanted to catch Dodd. On Timble Bridge as he crossed into Leeds. No escape there if he tried to run; Simon knew the town better than the spy ever could.

He quickened his pace, only some fifty yards behind now and gaining with each step as he walked purposefully, eyes fixed on his man. Then, suddenly, he slowed and bent to tie the laces on his boots, keeping his head down. Whittaker the bodyguard was waiting by the bridge, raising his hand in greeting to Dodd.

Simon knelt, glancing up once, twice, until the pair moved away and he could follow them up Kirkgate. The air was bad today, the haze lying thick and heavy with no breeze to thin it. He could taste it in his throat every time he breathed and feel the grit against his eyes.

It was easy to stay hidden among the people on the pavement. Lost in the middle of a crowd, he kept his distance as Dodd and Whittaker turned on to Briggate then entered the Bull and Mouth.

For half a minute Simon waited before he crept to the window, peering inside until he picked out Dodd at a table, talking with Curzon and another man he didn't know. No sign of the bodyguard.

'You're not as good as you think you are, Westow.'

He straightened slowly, hardly daring to breath as he felt the prick of a knife against his spine.

'I spotted you when I was waiting on the bridge,' Whittaker continued. 'We still have a score to settle.'

Simon turned slowly, hands away from his body, defenceless. The cut on Whittaker's face was still raw, a thin line of dried blood stretching from his hairline all the way to his chin.

Simon forced himself to smile. 'If you want your revenge here, carry on. You'll find plenty who'll watch and testify against you later.'

Whittaker snorted. 'I'm not that much of a fool, Westow. I'll have my time with you. But you've been warned to stay clear of Dodd. You'd do best to listen. Go.'

He had no choice. Shot at yesterday and now he was slinking away like a beaten dog, his pride stinging, while the bodyguard watched. Stupid, too bloody stupid. He'd underestimated the man. He wouldn't make that mistake again. Down below the anger and recrimination, a question lurked – who was the man with Dodd and Curzon?

Jane saw it all. She'd followed Whittaker across the bridge, trailed far behind on Kirkgate and seen him stop on the other side of Timble Bridge before returning with Dodd. And then she spotted Simon, trying to stay out of sight. Close to the Bull and Mouth, the bodyguard whispered something to the spy, then vanished. Jane tucked herself into the entrance of a court on the other side of Briggate. She saw Simon peer in the window, then the confrontation. But she was too far away to stop it. Even before she could have crossed the road, Simon was striding away and Whittaker stood with his self-satisfied smirk, hands on his hips.

The night before, she'd left a parcel of food on Henry Wise's doorstep. Something for the widow and children. It couldn't begin to make up for her husband's life, but it would stop the family starving for a few days. Repaying the kindness he'd once shown to her.

Another half hour by the church clock, then Curzon came out flanked by Dodd and the bodyguard. Behind them, a lean figure, tapping his hat down on a head of thick, curly hair. A few words, a nod, and they parted company.

She waited long enough for the magistrate and his party to pass, then slid out on to the street and followed the other man.

'He bested you?' Rosie asked.

'Made me looked like a damned fool. A beginner.'

The rage was ready to burst from him. Simon clenched his

fists then opened them again. In his head he could hear Whittaker's voice, mocking, triumphant.

'You're alive,' she said quietly. 'Be grateful for that.'

It was no comfort. He was furious at himself. Simon had let down his guard, allowed himself to believe he was clever and safe. He'd been arrogant enough to believe he was better than the other man, and he'd been caught out for it.

No more. It was time to be humble again, to stay alert every single second he spent outside these four walls. Whittaker was dangerous. Given half a chance, he'd be deadly.

'I saw it,' Jane told him. They walked along Swinegate in a squalling rain that had started an hour before, just as dusk fell, carried by gusts of wind. She had the shawl pulled over her hair, boots kicking through the puddles.

'Whittaker?' He turned to glance at her.

'I was too far away to do anything.'

'It doesn't matter,' he said.

She didn't believe him; the lie was there in his tone. Too light.

'You caught him well on his face.'

She shrugged. No more to say on that.

'I waited until they came out. Dodd and Curzon and another man. I followed him to an office on Boar Lane. He doesn't seem to be anyone important. Before Whittaker pulled his knife on you . . .'

'What?' She heard the bitter snap in his voice and waited a moment before describing the man's visit to the staithe and Holbeck.

'That's curious,' Simon said thoughtfully. His anger had passed like a breeze. 'Didn't you say he'd been out there once before?'

'Yes.'

'It's not a bodyguard's work. Makes me wonder what other business Mr Whittaker has.' He stayed silent for a long time, then asked: 'Have you found the man who took Tetley's money?'

'He's been seen,' she told him. 'I'll hear as soon as someone else spots him. He was down at Salem Chapel.'

'Why?'

'I don't know. He was with her.'

No doubt about who she meant. 'Are you absolutely sure it's the same girl?'

Jane nodded.

Last time they met, she'd been shocked enough to spare the girl. The next time, Jane would force her to tell her the truth. All of it. She had to know who'd given her orders, who knew the secrets she thought she'd kept to herself.

The question preyed on her, rubbing like grit in her mind. Who? *Who?* Hours might pass when she didn't think about it, then it would return, clawing and clutching in her head. Never an answer, no idea who it could be.

'Salem Place,' Simon said quietly. 'What's special about it?'

Nothing at all. It was just another street of cobble and pavement and brick. Only the coal staithe and the smell of the brewery to distinguish it from a hundred places exactly the same in Leeds. But she knew he didn't expect an answer.

'Find this Armstrong man. Let's see how much of Tetley's money we can recover.'

'Don't worry. I will.'

He'd come out intending to visit Davey. First, though, he crossed the bridge and stood at the head of Salem Place. It was full dark now, black, only a light through the chapel window and the drone of a preacher's voice gave any sense of life.

What was Whittaker doing at the staithe and then out in Holbeck? One more damned question that he couldn't answer.

Davey had a candle burning in his cell. As the wind blew outside, the flame flickered wildly, throwing shadows round the small room. At least he'd been reading the book Simon brought; it lay open next to him on the bench.

He looked a little better. The deadness had left his eyes and his face was more mobile; that had to be a good sign. Perhaps there was still some fight in him. But he was looked painfully thin, a tray of food half-eaten on the floor. His face was grubby, gaol dirt ingrained in his hands, and he stank of sweat and fear.

'It won't be much longer,' Simon said. 'I can feel it.'

'Maybe.' There was a note in his voice, half-amused and half-resigned. 'I've been thinking. I suppose the news about no trial date yet is something. But it wouldn't stop Curzon leaving me to rot down here.'

'He can't.'

Davey raised his head. 'That's the thing, Simon. He *can*. He has the power.'

'Then it's time he lost it.'

'I agree; a fine idea,' he said. 'Now tell me how you're going to achieve it?'

'Dodd. It all revolves around him. There's something very wrong.'

'You're the thief-taker.'

'Yes,' Simon told him. 'I am. So you'd better trust me.'

Davey said nothing, just stretched out on the bench and stared at the ceiling.

'I wish I could still believe in something,' he said in an empty voice.

Emily Ashton wore two shawls, one over the other, to keep the evening chill at bay. No fire in the grate, only a few pieces of wood left in the scuttle. She seemed as worn and battered as her brother. Tinier than she'd been, somehow, shrunken, too small to rattle around the house by herself.

Everything was in brisk, efficient order, the rooms tidy, swept and clean, ready for Davey to come home, as if time had been suspended while she waited for that to happen.

'I need him here,' she said as a thick splatter of rain hit the window.

'He will be,' Simon told her.

'Will he?' Her voice was full of desperation. 'Every day it's harder to hope.'

He reached out, squeezed her hand, and smiled. 'He will.'

He was beginning to feel it would really happen. Curzon's case was disappearing in front of his eyes. Simon still desperately needed to talk to Dodd, to push the man and learn the truth. Once he had that it would all be over.

'I keep praying for it. But I don't know how we'll ever pay you.'

Simon stared at her in disbelief. 'This is me paying you back,' he said. 'Both of you.'

'Who do you know on the London newspapers?'

'One or two people, I suppose. There must still be a few of them alive. Why?'

Mudie sat by the table in the rooms above his printing shop. Simon could hear the man's wife moving round in another room; as soon as he'd arrived she'd served him a mug of porter, then she vanished.

Walking back to town, he'd been in two minds about stopping here. Was it too soon for this? Counting his chickens before any eggs had even hatched. But better to have the man prepared and eager.

'I might need you to contact them soon.'

'Something's happening, isn't it?' There was a glint in his eye as he picked up the glass of cheap brandy.

'It's possible. We'll have to see.'

'But will it be a good story?' Mudie might have left the newspaper business, but it still pulsed through his veins.

'If I'm right, it'll be the best one you've ever had.'

'That's quite a claim.'

'When have I ever let you down, George?'

Mudie smiled. 'I'll make sure I'm ready, then. Did you manage to stop that chalking on the pavement?'

'There won't be any more.'

A nod of approval. 'That's wise. If this is everything you claim, we don't want any distractions.' He paused for a second. 'Would you care to give me a hint?'

'Not just yet. If the cards fall right, you'll have it all soon enough. In the next few days.'

FIFTEEN

Simon heard the click of the door latch closing and looked up from the copy of the *Intelligencer* spread over the kitchen table. Then Rosie eased herself on a chair with a sigh, and unpinned her hat.

'Dear God, all she wanted to do was talk and talk. My ears are aching.'

'Any gems in what she had to say?'

'Plenty.' With a grin, she reached for the jug of beer and poured herself a mug, drinking half of it down quickly. 'Mostly complaints. From the way she goes on, you'd think Leeds was a heathen country.'

He didn't care about Margaret Wood's views on the town. 'What did she tell you about Dodd?'

'Enough. Most of it comes from things he's told her, so I've no idea how much is real.'

'Some of it must be,' Simon said.

'Well . . .' She took another sip then began. 'According to Dodd, his family has money. But his father cut him off. Disinherited him. Mind you, he's given her three different stories so far, so who knows what's true?'

If Dodd really did come from wealth, he'd have friends with some influence, Simon thought – enough to worm his way into a job like government spy. He'd take it if he was desperate enough. It was a plausible story. But how many crooks had he met who could make the wildest ideas sound possible? They lived by the con, and Dodd was probably no different.

'Did you know they spent a week in Halifax before they came here?'

'I'd heard.'

'Dodd went round some of the mill towns; he was away overnight a few times. He talked to all sorts of groups and met people, claiming he'd been sent up from London by Radical groups to assess feelings for a different kind of government. He told them there were thousands ready to rise up down south if they had support in the North.'

'Go on.' Simon was listening intently.

'He arranged a meeting with all the men from the groups in the West Riding. By now they trusted him. He was there when the magistrate arrived with some troops, but somehow he managed to escape.' She raised her eyebrows.

'Very convenient.' It all fitted with the information Gideon Hartley had given him.

'Dodd and Margaret were rushed over here in a coach. Next morning Davey Ashton was arrested.'

'So Dodd had definitely never seen him at all when he denounced him?'

'Curzon had to point him out,' she said. The words were flat and hard.

'If all that's true . . .' Simon began. He knew it should have shocked him. It had when Joshua Miller first mentioned it. By now, though, the idea had come to appear normal in his mind. Sent to spy on Englishmen, to make sure they were arrested. To eliminate a threat. The words, the actions, had the sour ring of truth. It confirmed everything he'd learned. Sent to provoke, to lie.

'I believe her,' Rosie told him. 'I think she was relieved to finally let it all out to someone.'

'If that's published there'll be a national outcry. People will be horrified to learn the government is spying on us.' Simon's mouth curled into a smile. 'They'll have to release everyone they arrested. There'll be an uproar in Parliament. Do you think she'd tell all this to George Mudie? It might help free Davey.'

'No.' She didn't hesitate. 'She won't, and I wouldn't ask her. Not even for that, Simon. What I've told you can't go beyond these four walls. She trusted me. Don't you see, I'm as bad as Dodd? I was thinking about it as I came home. I used her. And I'm betraying her. There's something else,' Rosie continued. 'Margaret didn't say it, but she didn't have to, it was obvious. She's scared. Terrified.'

'Scared of what? Why?'

'Of Whittaker and Curzon. She kept looking around as if she thought someone was watching us.'

'Did you spot anyone?'

Rosie shook her head. 'Nothing at all. There's something else you need to know, too.'

'More?'

'Whittaker's the man who hired Dodd for this in London. According to Margaret, the pair of them have been close for a while. Before he started working for the government, Whittaker was a Bow Street Runner.'

The law. No surprise, perhaps, but still useful to know.

'She wouldn't trust him as far as she could throw him. She thinks he has something of his own going on. Some little game.'

That made sense. It would explain his visit to the staithe and the engineering works.

'What is it? Did she say?'

'She doesn't know. But she's overheard him talking to Dodd about Holbeck a couple of times, and he's mentioned a plan.' Rosie shrugged. 'That's it.'

A plan. Suddenly things clicked, and the pieces began to fall into place. The staithes and the steam train that brought the coal down from Middleton. A train that was built at the engineering works in Holbeck. They were all connected, he felt sure of that. But what did Whittaker have in mind?

Simon rubbed his chin, weighing everything he'd heard. 'Next time you see Margaret, encourage her to leave. Just gently. You know what to do.'

Rosie raised an eyebrow. 'Why? Is something going to happen?'

'Quite a lot. She'll be safer away from here. Unless she's really in this with him.'

'No.' She shook her head, adamant. 'I'm certain she's not. She liked her little spy. I think all she saw was money and some fun. She's not the type to think past that. If you're going after Dodd and Whittaker again, make sure you're very careful.'

'I intend to be.' He thought about the shots, about Whittaker's knife prodding his back. He'd been too careless, too confident. 'Every single moment.'

'I mean it, Simon. There's one last thing Margaret told me. Before they left London, Dodd went off for a day. When he came back, he told her he'd been to meet the Home Secretary.'

If *that* was true, the lies went right to the heart of the government. And they'd do anything to stop them becoming public.

Armstrong, the hocus girl. Jane wanted them both. One for the reward, the other to finally answer her questions. Today, though, they seemed to have vanished. Jem's boys hadn't been able to find them.

By afternoon, she'd walked all over Leeds, feeling the place through the soles of her feet. Wandering unnoticed, not a soul following her. Finally, she made her way past Salem Chapel, all the way down to the staithe on Kidacre Place, where the coal dust lay thick on the ground. The third time today.

Why here?

If she stared long enough the answer might come. But there was nothing at all.

As the evening began to darken, Jane stood in the churchyard at St John's waiting for Jem to return. She kept out of sight, in the shadows behind a wall, listening as the sounds of night began to blossom in Leeds.

Suddenly, her head jerked up. A sense, the feeling that someone was close, looking for her. She took the knife from her pocket and cautiously peered around.

Whittaker stood on the path, thumbs in his belt, looking around, the cut written large on his face. He wore an angry look, eyes moving as if he was searching. Another minute and he'd be gone, passing through the lychgate to the road.

She was still waiting for her heartbeat to subside when Jem arrived, running as if the dogs of hell were after him.

'They're down on the Calls. Someone seen them and told me.'

Together, they ran down Briggate, turning just before the bridge and following the street. Still just enough light to see. Hardly a soul down here, just the blank walls of warehouses and the soft wash of water against the shore. The perfect place to end all this. The ideal time. She was ready. This time she was absolutely ready.

They walked the length of the road, all the way along the river to Fearn's Island and back. No sign of Armstrong or his hocus girl. They'd gone.

'Tommy, he swore they were there,' Jem apologized. 'I gave him a farthing for telling me an' all.'

'It doesn't matter.' She felt for a coin and pressed it into his hand. He liked being the little general, she thought, having some power over the other boys. It was probably the first time in his life he'd ever tasted anything like that. A sense of being someone. 'Tomorrow,' she assured him. 'We'll find them then.'

By the corner of Swinegate, a woman was perched on a wooden box. A small crowd had gathered, ten or a dozen, no more than that. Jane listened for a moment. Another preacher, full of the word of God. She'd heard it too often. Suffer in this world and you'll have your reward in heaven. How did that help when you were starving and you had nowhere to sleep that night? The only difference was that for once it wasn't a man speaking. The woman sounded earnest and passionate, her voice a little hoarse and strained. But the words were never going to touch Jane. This life was enough; she didn't need more of it after she was dead.

She glanced at Jem. He seemed rapt, eyes wide as he listened, not even noticing as she walked away.

Mudie grinned with anticipation. 'By God, this might well be the best story I've come across in my career.'

'I thought you'd like it.' Simon had told him all that Dodd's woman had said to Rosie.

'Now bring me something to confirm it. Testimony. You do that, I'll write it and sell it to the *Mercury*. I know they'd print it.'

'Is that a promise?'

'It is. A tale like that . . . it's the kind of thing I used to dream about when I was an editor. But we need to be firm on every detail. You can't make accusations like these without evidence. Testimony.'

Simon had already been to visit Davey, to tell him, to try and bolster him, give him some hope. He listened carefully. By the end even he had a glint in his eye.

'Is it true, do you think?' he asked.

'Yes. I'm positive it is.'

'Something like that could bring the government down.'

'I know.'

Davey stared at him. 'Trying to expose it is a weight for one man to carry.'

'But worthwhile.'

'If you can do it.'

Jane was waiting in front of the Moot Hall, watching the river of people as they passed, eyes alert for a limping man or the hocus girl. She fell in beside Simon as he arrived and they started to walk towards Boar Lane. There was something about him, an eagerness, a hunger that she hadn't felt in a long time.

'You said you followed Whittaker over into Holbeck,' he said.

'Yes.'

'To Murray's works.'

'By that round foundry.'

'Did he talk to anyone there?'

'He tried,' Jane said. 'They didn't want to speak to him.'

He nodded, as if it seemed to confirm something, but he was silent for a minute until he said,

'The man you followed yesterday, the one who was with Curzon and Dodd. I want you to point out the building he went into.'

It stood across the street from Holy Trinity Church. A small entry next to a poulterer's shop, where the goods hung on display outside the window. Chickens, ducks, geese. All dead, unplucked, suspended by their necks.

'There,' she said. Simon crossed the road and read the brass plaques listing the tenants. When he returned, he was smiling.

'Good,' he said. 'Now we wait.'

It didn't take too long. Twenty minutes later a figure emerged. He was thin, his hair so dark that it seemed to absorb the light. A pale face, grey jacket and tight fawn trousers.

'That's him,' Jane said.

'Yes,' Simon told her. 'I thought it might be.' He was smiling again. 'I'll go and have a word with him. You see if you can find our friend Armstrong.'

Jem was in the churchyard, sitting on the stone bench inside the porch.

'Any sign of them yet?' Jane asked.

'No one's come and told me anything.' The boy stared down at his lap. 'You should have stayed and listened to that lady.'

'Why?'

'She was very good.' He paused, struggling to find the words for his feelings. 'She believes,' he said finally.

'I daresay she does.' She paced around the small space, boot heels ringing off the flagstones.

'I wanted to go up to her afterwards, but I didn't dare.'

'Why not?'

'She wouldn't want to talk to someone like me.'

Jane didn't reply. He was probably right. Preachers were all words, not deeds. Left it all behind when they went off to their comfortable homes. All the talk of heaven and paradise, it wasn't for the likes of her and Jem. She knew the reality: you lived, you suffered, and then you died, glad it was all over.

Jane twisted the gold ring on her finger. Armstrong and the hocus girl – where were they?

'I'm going to look for them. Any word, come and find me.'

The man turned at the sound of his name, face hardening with annoyance as he recognized Simon.

'What do you want, Westow? I'm on my way to an appointment.'

Haldane Pace was a lawyer. A shrewd tactician. Someone who could spot an opening where others only saw a blank wall. It was a skill certain men could appreciate. It made them willing to pay the fees he charged.

'Magistrate Curzon and his tame spy again?'

'No.' Pace lengthened his stride, crossing between the wagons on Briggate and continuing along Duncan Street. 'But even if it were, it's no business of yours.'

The man had arrived in Leeds ten years before. He'd quickly established himself, winning a series of cases in spectacular fashion. In the courtroom he was a showman, with an actor's presence and ability. Simon had watched him perform, impressed by his orator's wiles. Now why, he wondered, would Curzon need to consult someone like that, and with Dodd in tow? To see if he had any chance at all of making his case stick? If anyone could find a way, it was Pace.

'It's my business because a friend of mine is in gaol. All due to the men you met yesterday.'

'What about it?' Pace kept walking. 'If he's guilty, he'll be sent to Australia.'

So they had discussed Davey. And all the others who'd been arrested, no doubt. Curzon had probably spent his evening writing letters to worried magistrates across the West Riding.

'A word of advice to you.'

Pace didn't turn his head. A brief, haughty smile drifted across his face.

'And what kind of advice could you have for me?'

'I'd steer clear of the whole business. It's going to turn sour very soon. The magistrate is likely to take a fall from grace. That will tarnish the reputation of anyone involved with him.'

That was enough to make Pace pause and look. 'Is that correct?' The first hint of curiosity in his eyes. He must have seen the fragility of Curzon's evidence. 'You'll be the one to bring him down, I suppose?'

'That's right.' Simon knew he was staking everything on his belief. He was saying it, but he still had to make it work. 'I'll be the one to start it. But it will go far beyond me.'

'Bold words for a nobody.'

'Perhaps,' Simon agreed. 'But you'd be surprised what can happen.'

'Very little surprises me any more, Westow.'

'I'm sure. Just consider this a word to the wise.'

'Why?' Pace asked. 'Why should it matter to you what I do?'

'It doesn't. If you want to join a lost cause, I'm sure they'll welcome you. But it *is* lost. Make no mistake about that.'

Pace's gaze narrowed as he tried to understand and assess all the possibilities. Finally, he shrugged.

'Maybe you're right, Westow. Time will tell.'

'Indeed it will.' He doffed his hat again. 'Good day. I don't want to make you late.'

As he turned and walked away, Simon knew his words had struck home. Pace had said little, but it was in his eyes; he'd keep his distance from Curzon.

Mary Rigton's beershop was almost empty. The light through the window showed the dust motes falling through the air. The woman sat on her chair, staring into space, only stirring from her trance as Jane approached.

'I hear you've been making some bad enemies, girl.'

She had to mean Whittaker.

'His own fault. He grabbed me.'

'That's what men do. Always been that way.'

She ignored the comment. 'He murdered Henry the farrier.'

'You watch out for yourself,' Mrs Rigton told her. 'I know his type. He'll want you dead for what you did.'

Jane shrugged. He might try. She'd be prepared for him. He'd pay for what he did.

'I'm looking for a man called Gordon Armstrong. He walks with a limp.'

The woman shook her head. 'Don't know him. What's he done?'

'Took some money. He's with a woman called Charlotte Winter. She's stout, has a bandage on her arm.'

'Don't know her, neither. I'll keep my ears open.'

'There might be a little money in it. Especially for her.'

'Bad, is she?' Mrs Rigton asked.

'Not for much longer.'

'You should sit down, girl. You're pacing like you can't wait to be gone.'

But she didn't. Jane turned around and left. For a second she was tempted to tell her story about the hocus girl, but she held her tongue. She'd told it twice, and maybe even that was too much. Someone knew too much about her, things she believed she'd kept inside and locked away. Silence was a weapon now.

It took Simon an hour to find Barnaby Wade, tucked away in a corner of the Fleece on Kirkgate, deep in conversation with a man who kept smiling blankly. Finally their business seemed to be done, and Wade strode out into the light.

'Another victim?'

Wade grinned. 'A customer, Simon, grant him that much. And not yet. But he will be when I'm done with him. There won't be too much for his children to inherit by the time I've finished.'

Wade sold stocks. A few, very few, did well. Most were barely worth the cost of printing the certificates. He had charm, and a tongue like silver. Once he'd been a lawyer, a good one, too. But his ambition had overreached his ability and he'd been disbarred. Now he made his living with this, and he made it pay well. All his contracts were very cunningly worded to keep him out of court.

'And you'll be richer.'

'Money comes, money goes.' He frowned. 'What can I do for you, Simon? I hear you've been helping Davey Ashton. But you always did have a soft spot for hopeless cases.'

'He'll be out of the gaol soon. I'm not here to talk about him.'

'Oh?'

Simon laid out the pieces. Holbeck. The coal staithe. Whittaker and Dodd. Wade understood business. He might be able to understand the connections.

'What do you make of it?' he asked as he finished. 'What's going on?'

'You know other countries have tried to build railways with steam locomotives, don't you?' Wade said.

'No.'

They were on Commercial Street now, among the new buildings. Expensive dressmakers and drapers, a bookseller and the subscription library; everything elegant and tasteful, the beauty marred only by the soot and grime coating the stonework.

'None of them have succeeded. Well, they haven't managed to build anything that can haul a load,' Wade corrected himself.

'I don't follow. Why would it matter?'

'There are plenty of foreign companies that would pay good money for the full details. Governments, too, come to that.'

'Spying,' Simon said quietly. And with that, the final piece of the puzzle clicked into place. Whittaker seemed to be playing a game of his own; that was what Margaret Wood had told Rosie. Yes, he understood now. It fitted, it all fitted. A reason to be near the engineering works in Holbeck where they made the machine and at the staithe to see the locomotive in action, to study it properly.

'It all makes sense, doesn't it?' Wade said.

'Yes.' Simon rubbed his chin. 'How would they do it?'

A laugh. 'Isn't it your job to find out, Simon? Use your imagination.' Wade pulled out a silver pocket watch. 'I have to meet a man and relieve him of his fortune.' He tipped his hat. 'I wish you good luck.'

Simon stood on the pavement, jostled by the people who passed.

Spying. Yes, it made absolute sense.

He was on Briggate when he heard the news. A rumour at first, one man whispering to another to another. By the time he reached Leeds Bridge it had grown. Everyone talking. A woman's body found in the long grass off Marsh Lane.

'What was her name?' he asked the man who was passing the word.

'Someone told me she were called Margaret, but I don't rightly know.'

Simon did. Margaret Wood. Dodd's woman.

SIXTEEN

'I waited for her, but she never appeared.' Rosie's voice was blank, dulled to nothing. 'Then I came home. She must have been dead all that time.'

Simon put his arms around her, drawing her close against his body as she began to sob.

'There wasn't an ounce of harm in her, really. She saw Dodd with his money and thought she'd have some fun.'

Instead, poor Margaret would be buried in a town she didn't even like, far from anyone who might care about her.

She'd been murdered, that was the gossip he'd heard as he hurried home. Simon knew full well who'd killed her. Whittaker. Maybe Dodd was growing frightened, talking about fleeing back to London. This was the ideal way to keep him fearful and in line.

Henry Wise, Margaret Wood. Probably more in other places whose names he'd never know. Quite a butcher's bill for one man.

'I'd like to see her,' Rosie said.

'They won't let you.' Not a woman on her own. He'd seen enough of the dead in his work. So had she when she was alongside him every day.

'I want to say goodbye. We have enough to pay for a burial, Simon. The poor girl deserves that, at least.'

'Yes,' he agreed. He knew why she wanted to do it, even if he didn't agree. The woman was dead; no memorial would change that fact. 'We'll go later.'

Rosie slowly eased away from him, wiping her eyes with her sleeve.

'The boys will be home soon. I don't want them to see me crying, they'll only want to know why.'

'Enough time for that when they're older.'

She nodded sadly. 'They're not happy at school, you know.'

'They've barely started,' he said. 'It's not even a week yet. They'll get used to it.'

'The master seems to beat pupils every day.'

'That always happens at schools. It's the way of the world.' He didn't like it, but he couldn't stop it. 'Give it a chance. Let them settle in there.'

'Yes,' she agreed doubtfully. 'I know, they need to learn their letters and their numbers.'

'A better start than we ever had.'

The small cottage was empty. The door was unlocked, opening as he turned the handle. Only the cleanliness of the place – floors swept, table clean – made it apparent that someone had lived here recently. The bed had been stripped, the sheets taken. All he could find was a piece of crumpled, torn paper in the corner with the times of the London coaches on it.

Simon slipped it into his waistcoat pocket and continued his search. Outside the back door, on the worn track down to the beck, he found a tin bucket, next to it a woman's white cap. The final trace of Margaret Wood.

The round foundry. That was what people called it. Circular, three storeys high, standing out against the sky near Marshall's Mill in Holbeck. The centre of Matthew Murray's engineering works. With its curves it looked out of place among the sharp corners and steep angles of Leeds.

A series of small buildings had grown up in the square around the rotunda, smoke rising from a nest of chimneys. Men bustled about. The air was filled with the sound of hammers and machinery.

Simon stood and watched for a full minute, taking in all the activity, then strode into the throng.

'The gaffer?' a man said. 'He's probably over at Steam House.' Simon stared.

'Over there.' The man pointed, then explained. 'Where he lives.'

It could have been part of the works, it stood so close. Fairly new, he judged, but already the stonework was dirty, coated with soot. Simon straightened his coat and his neckcloth, then lifted the door knocker and let it fall, waiting for a servant to answer.

Five minutes and he was shown through to an office that over-
flowed with books and papers. The man behind the desk held up
a finger for him to wait as he finished writing. Then he was on
his feet, large, with a thick shock of hair and wild sideboards
extending down below his ears. A plump, hearty face.

'I'm Matthew Murray,' he said. 'You wanted to see me,
Mister . . .'

'Westow. Simon Westow. I'm a thief-taker.'

The title always had the same effect, a small halt in the
conversation.

'Then I don't know what I can do for you.' A faint Geordie
accent shone through the words. 'But have a seat. Some tea,
maybe? Coffee?'

Simon shook his head. 'I won't take much of your time. It's
just some information I have.'

He knew there was very little to tell, but Murray still listened
attentively. In the silence afterwards, the man sat back in his
chair.

'That's an interesting tale, Mr Westow,' he said finally.

'I know it's not much.'

'Spare on detail, I'll agree with that,' Murray said. 'But it
would hardly be the first time someone's tried to spy here.
Probably not the last either. For what it's worth, I believe you.'

'Thank you.' That was more than he'd anticipated. Half of
him had expected Murray to send him packing.

'Can you describe the man involved?'

He told Murray about Whittaker as the man made quick
notes.

'I'll tell my foreman to keep his eyes peeled. I'm in your debt.'

'No,' Simon told him. 'You're not. I want him myself.'

'Then I hope you catch him.' A brief smile. 'If you do, I'm
sure it'll be in the newspapers.' He extended his hand. A firm
shake. Murray had thick calluses on his palms and fingers. Not
a man who lived his life in this office. 'If I ever need a thief-
taker, I'll know who to contact.'

Jane felt as if she was blundering everywhere, thrashing around
helplessly. No sign of Armstrong or the hocus girl. But they were
still in Leeds; she felt them. After an hour of searching along

the Calls and Kirkgate, Boar Lane and down Commercial Street,
she returned to Briggate with its swell of noise.

She stepped between the piles of horse dung that littered the
road, glancing into every shop she passed in case they were there.
A tailor, a milliner, up towards the Shambles at the side of
the Moot Hall, where the butchers displayed carcasses and cut the
meat. Finally to the market cross, where she could stand and look
down on it all.

Just before Jem arrived, she had the sense of someone coming
close and turned, her hand on the knife in her pocket.

'Georgie saw him,' the boy said softly. 'Just a few minutes
ago, down on Vicar Lane Going towards Vicar's Croft. He was
on his own.'

A nod and she was gone, the shawl over her hair, the invisible
girl once more. She darted through the crowds, around couples.
Her eyes were wide, watching everyone.

Then she picked him out; the limp gave him a laboured, uneven
walk. Bigger than her, but thin, his clothes dusty. Jane drew
closer, just enough distance to be safe, but he hadn't spotted her;
he seemed lost in his own thoughts.

They were close to Fish Street. The market was done for the
day, but the stink lingered, as if it had been painted on the walls
and the ground. Armstrong was alone; no sign of the hocus girl.

She quickened her pace. At the entrance to the street she was
alongside Armstrong. Her knife pricked his side and he looked
at her in surprise.

'In there,' she told him.

No protest, just three awkward steps into the quiet alley. There
was a soft sadness on his face; he already knew he was defeated.

'You stole.'

His eyes were fixed on the blade. The point rested against his
belly.

'Yes.' The word came out, quiet and reluctant.

'Your employer wants the money back.'

He was silent. Jane lifted the knife towards his chin.
Armstrong was swallowing hard, his Adam's apple bobbing up
and down.

'I-I've spent some.' He stuttered out the words.

'How much do you have left?'

With his fingertips, he reached into the pocket of his waistcoat and drew old some folded bank notes and coins.

'How much?' she asked.

'Forty-two pounds.' Armstrong stared at the flagstones. 'Th-the rest has gone.'

Jane took the money from him, keeping the blade close to his flesh.

'What are you going to do now?' Armstrong asked. She could taste his terror on the end of her tongue.

'Return it,' she said.

'Is he going to prosecute me? I—'

'No.' He seemed to calm as she told him. 'Go.'

He began to move. As quickly as he could with his leg. Before he could vanish, she called: 'Tell your friend I'm coming for her next.'

Armstrong glanced over his shoulder, mouth open as if he was about to ask a question. Then he shook his head and hobbled away.

'A note came while you were gone,' Rosie said.

Simon unfolded the paper. The words were formed in an awkward, shaky hand: *News. Find me. Miller.*

'Anything important?' she asked.

Maybe it was. But there was a duty to perform first.

'It can wait an hour or two. Do you still want to see the body?'

He hated the infirmary. It stank of death and putrefaction. As they opened the doors, someone screamed at the other end of the building and Rosie shuddered.

'Are you sure?' Simon asked. 'We can leave.'

She closed her eyes, took a soft breath, then opened them again. 'No. We're here now.'

The doctor had a cold, callous manner. Too many corpses, perhaps. An endless procession of the dead.

'This is her.'

Simon knew what to expect. She was wrapped in a winding sheet. By now someone would have sold her gown and linen, pennies in the pocket, a small racket on top of their wages.

Only Margaret Wood's face and hair were on show. He'd never

seen her before, only heard her voice once, a muffled sound on the other side of a closed door.

He saw Rosie stretch out a hand and stroke the dead woman's cheek.

'How did she die?' Simon asked.

'Not here,' the doctor replied. 'With a lady present.'

'How did she die?' he repeated.

A hesitation, a clearing of the throat. 'She was stabbed in the back.' Another pause. 'Three times.'

'I see.'

'I'll see the undertaker,' Rosie said, 'and take care of the funeral.'

'Very good, Mrs . . .'

'Westow.'

'Was she a friend of yours?'

'She could have been.' Rosie took a final look and turned away.

'It's Whittaker's work, isn't it?' she said once they were outside.

'Yes. No question,'

Henry Wise, now this. He had to pay.

For once it didn't take long to find Joshua Miller. He was sitting on a bench in the third place Simon visited. The useless hand rested in his lap, an empty glass on the table in front of him. He stirred as a fresh drink was placed before him. His eyes were bleary, clearing after the first sip.

'You said you had news.'

Simon brought out a sixpence, spinning it in his fingers, knowing Miller was watching hungrily.

'Your friend. Ashton.'

'What about him?'

The clerk from York had lied, Simon thought. They'd set a date for the trial. Found a space in the court calendar. They were going to move Davey.

'He's going to be released,' Miller said. 'Tomorrow, maybe the day after.'

'Are you certain?' He couldn't believe what the man had said. Christ knew he wanted Davey free, but to hear it was happening . . .

'I'm positive. Curzon's decided. The clerk is writing the order later today. It should be signed in the morning.'

Simon added a florin. The information was worth all that and more.

SEVENTEEN

'W̲ho told you?' Emily Ashton said.

He'd wondered whether to give her the news; nothing was certain until it happened. But Miller had always been reliable in the past. And she needed the hope. The last few days had turned her gaunt; the shadows under her eyes had become craters.

'Someone who should know.'

'When?'

'Tomorrow, he told me. It could be the day after.'

She walked around the room in her cottage, stopping by the window to look out, as if Davey might come along the path at any moment.

'Remember, it's not done yet,' Simon warned. 'Nothing's certain until it happens. But I wanted you to know.'

'You beat Curzon,' Emily said. 'Thank you, Simon.'

He shook his head. The magistrate had managed this all by himself.

'I wish I had. I'll tell you when I know anything more.'

Never mind what he'd said to Emily, all the caution and humility; Simon felt victorious. Davey was going to be released. Just a few days before, he'd doubted whether they could ever win. Now it seemed definite. Curzon had reached too far, he'd tried too hard to be noticed.

He knew he should go and give Davey the news, tell him he'd won. But something held him back. In case Miller was wrong. In case the wind changed and Curzon didn't sign the order.

He turned the corner to Lady Bridge and all thoughts stopped.

Whittaker stood at the other end, elbows on the parapet as he stared down at the beck.

Simon loosened the knife in his sleeve. Whittaker turned his head and lazily stood upright. The slash to his cheek stood out, dark and red.

'You're not a difficult man to follow.' He jerked his head towards the Ashtons' cottage. 'How's the sister?'

'Well enough.'

'She'll feel better soon. Mr Curzon's decided to show some mercy and drop the charges against her brother.'

'Is that right?' Safer to pretend he hadn't heard the news.

'He'll be home tomorrow. You'll be happy now.'

Simon nodded. 'It's good that Curzon's come to his senses.'

'His decision,' Whittaker said. 'Me, I reckon we should transport all the scum. See how long they last in Australia.'

Simon didn't reply, just waited, ready, one hand resting on the knife in his belt.

'It's over now, Westow.'

'Not until Davey's out of gaol.'

'He will be. So there'll be no need for you to be on our heels all the time.'

That was the real message, Simon thought. The business was over. Time for him to ignore whatever else Whittaker was doing.

'What about your spy?'

'What about him?'

'Someone killed his woman. Margaret.'

He shrugged. 'It happens. In this business, you ought to know that.'

'But there's always a price to pay.'

'That's right,' Whittaker said. 'There is.' But Simon knew they were talking about two different things. 'And don't think I've forgotten our little matter.' He reached up and rubbed the cut on his cheek. 'Or that girl who works for you. The bill will come due.'

He turned and strode off with his swaggering gait. Simon didn't move, watching him climb the hill towards Vicar Lane. The man was right. The bill would come due. And Whittaker would be the one to pay. No money in it. Nothing more than a small measure of justice for two innocents.

*   *   *

Jane kept out of sight, waiting until Simon had moved into the distance before she emerged. She'd seen Whittaker following him out here and trailed behind, keeping herself hidden; neither of the men had any sense that she was there.

She'd watched as the bodyguard loitered by the bridge, seeing him pick up small pebbles and drop them into the water. She'd heard every word, standing ready with the knife in her hand, until the moment passed.

'Thank God for that,' Rosie said when he told her the news. 'Are you absolutely sure? It's not just a rumour?'

'It's definite. I already told Emily.' No need to mention the meeting on the way back.

'You need to let Davey know.'

'I stopped at the Moot Hall.'

In the end he'd decided to go, to tell him. The man's eyes had remained expressionless, as if the words had no meaning. He'd barely moved on the bench as he listened. No joy on his face. No relief at the idea of freedom. He was trapped in this place. In some sense, he would be here for the rest of his life. Curzon didn't know it, but he'd achieved what he wanted; he'd silenced Davey, and he hadn't even needed a judge's sentence to do it.

'I see,' Davey said finally. He didn't turn his head to look at Simon. 'I see.'

'You'll be out of here tomorrow. Home.'

'Yes. Yes.'

Some men stayed strong. Some men broke. Davey had snapped. There was no shame in it, no loss of honour. It hurt him to see the man like this, but it could never shake his friendship or his admiration. Simon placed his hand on Davey's shoulder for a moment, then left.

One debt had been paid.

Rosie was right, he thought. School seemed to have taken something from the boys. They'd only been there a few days, but they'd changed. The boisterousness had vanished, as if they'd been cowed far too readily.

They were seated, eating quietly, barely a word from them, when Jane arrived and placed a small stack of bank notes on the table.

'Armstrong,' she said. 'Most of it's there.'

'Did he give you any trouble?'

She shook her head. 'None at all.'

'What about his girl?' Rosie asked. 'Was she with him?'

'No. He was on his own.'

And she was gone, just the sound of feet climbing the stairs.

Tetley counted the notes.

'Forty-two pounds.' He nodded with approval. 'Better than I'd hoped. A pity, really, he was a good clerk when he started. I had hopes for him.'

'It happens,' Simon said, and he heard the echo of Whittaker's words in his head.

'I understand wine and spirits,' Tetley said. 'I understand beer. But I'll never comprehend people, Mr Westow. However, I thank you for your work.'

A five-pound fee. Something to add to the kitty. And goodwill in the bank. That never hurt. He had a future to think about.

Jane sat on the bed. Her hands moved, absently swiping the knife over the whetstone and pausing to feel the edge. She'd heard about the dead woman and pieced the story together from what the men had said on Lady Bridge.

Two deaths to be laid at Whittaker's door now.

After Simon's friend was out of gaol, surely it would be time to take care of everything. She wanted it. She needed it. Jane could still feel his hand on her. She still had the bruises on her skin, dark and ugly as the man who made them. She'd never forget that. Never.

There had been precious few words about Davey going into gaol. But the rumours about his release were already circulating as Simon walked through town. He'd be out that morning. No, it would be evening or perhaps tomorrow. He'd already been smuggled out and he was at home. By the time he reached the Moot Hall he'd heard every possibility.

The gaoler looked up as Simon came down the stairs. A coin landed on the table.

'When is he being released?'

'Mr Curzon is upstairs signing the order now, sir. I saw him earlier, he didn't look happy.'

'I daresay he's not. How's Mr Ashton?'

'I've been taking care of him proper. Meals in like you ordered.' He could hear the hopeful tone, craving a little more money. 'But he's not good, sir. Some people don't take to the cells, if you know what I mean.'

Davey sat on the bench, exactly the same position as his last visit, as if he hadn't moved at all.

'You're going home very soon. Less than an hour.'

'Don't give me hope, Simon. I don't want to see it dashed.'

'It won't be. I promise.'

'Words.' He lifted his head. 'They can be very cheap or they can prove to be expensive. That's something I've learned in here.'

A shuffling of feet and a small cough.

'I have the order, sir. The prisoner is free to go.'

'Thank you.' Simon passed the gaoler a shilling. 'Come on, Davey, let's get you back to Mabgate. Emily will be glad to see you.'

He walked with an old man's shuffle, standing and blinking in the light for a minute, breathing in the air.

'Ready?'

Davey had an arm threaded through his to keep himself steady. As they moved away, Simon looked back. Curzon stood at the window, glaring, Whittaker at his shoulder.

'Look at you, look at you.' Emily Ashton hugged her brother. 'It's so good to have you home again. Oh Davey, I was beginning to wonder if you'd ever come back.'

She started to fuss around, preparing food to fatten him up again, putting water on to boil so he could bathe, a razor and scissors to return him to the man she knew. Davey perched on the edge of his chair and stared.

'You're free now,' Simon said. His sense of triumph had evaporated as they walked. He felt hollow.

'I wish I were.' He had a sad half-smile on his face. 'Every time I want to open my mouth or write something on a piece of paper, I'll be back in that cell again. It might be better if they'd sent me to Australia. At least then I'd know. I'd *know*.'

'You'll feel better in a day or two.'

'No,' Davey answered and stared down at the floorboards. 'They won, Simon. They won.'

He stopped at Mudie's printing shop. The man was sitting at his desk, a flask of brandy and an empty glass in front of him.

'I hear you succeeded. Davey Ashton's a free man again.'

'He's at home with his sister. What about those other men, the ones in the West Riding?'

'No word yet.' He poured a small measure of liquor and drank it down. The colour started to rise in his cheeks. 'But it just has to be a matter of time, doesn't it? One's let out, the others will be. And I don't get my story.'

'Cheer up, George. You might have it yet.'

'If the men are free, who's going to care? The scandal's gone.'

'No, it hasn't. You think people won't want to know that the government employed someone to come here and stir people up, to lie to them, then denounce them?'

'The government lost.'

'They lost *this time*. Do you really believe they won't try again?'

'You still haven't given me the proof.'

Simon thought about Dodd. He had to find the man before he was quietly ushered back to London. Would he talk? His woman had been murdered to keep him compliant, he'd be fearful for his own life. Would he dare talk?

'I'll try.'

'You do that and I'll write it.' He poured another drink. 'I'm sick of bloody printing.'

'How is he?' Rosie asked.

'Adrift.' Simon settled at the kitchen table, running a hand through his hair. A few strands of grey in among the black; he'd seen it in the mirror that morning. Growing older and careworn and spent. 'Maybe he'll come around.'

'Emily will be happy, at least.'

'She is. She's making a fuss of him.'

'From all you said, he needs it.'

He did. More than anything, Davey needed time. That might

start to heal him. But the scars of the last week would never vanish, even if they weren't visible. No one ever wanted to realize they were weak. He'd been forced to face himself and discovered he was wanting, that he wasn't the man he'd always believed himself to be. How could anyone recover from that?

'There was another note for you.' She took it from the dresser. 'I hope it's paying work.'

After your visit, I questioned my men about strangers near the works. There has been one recently. I was curious and talked to an employee I know at the coal staithe. He reported a man of the same description there. I've written to the owner of the Middleton coalfields to report this. I feel safe in offering you a commission to stop this man before he attempts to take all our secrets. Perhaps you'd call on me to discuss it further.
M. Murray

Simon smiled. Now he had the perfect reason to go after Whittaker.

'Yes,' he told her, 'this is going to pay.'

EIGHTEEN

S
he saw the girl in the distance, down by the parish church at the bottom of Kirkgate. The bandage had gone from her arm, but there was no mistaking her size, the way she stood, how she walked. But by the time Jane had pressed through the people on the street, she'd vanished.

The girl knew the name, the one Jane needed to hear. And next time she'd make sure she spoke it.

Jane raised the shawl, covering her hair, and made her way back along the Calls. Today the smoke hung low with no breeze to push it away, so the air seemed heavy and tight around her throat.

Coming closer to the bridge, Jane picked out a strident voice rising over the noise. There, on the corner of Briggate, addressing the small group huddled on the street, was the woman who had cast a spell over Jem.

He was in the crowd, down near the front of the group, listening with an attentive smile. Face washed until it shone and dressed in clothes that weren't rags.

She slid around the back of them, hurrying away before he could notice her. He deserved his joy, however he found it. Jem wouldn't return. Once they took to religion, they rarely came back. She'd seen it before.

Still, perhaps it was better than living on the streets. It would give him a home, a family of sorts. Regular meals. He'd survive. Maybe he'd even grow up to be happy and safe.

Jane walked, thinking, letting her feet guide her until she found herself in Green Dragon Yard. She glanced around, then slipped through to Catherine Shields's cottage. The door was ajar. She tapped lightly on the wood. No answer.

Something was wrong. She could feel it, a prickling in the air, a sense of fear and pain. Jane took out her knife and pushed the door wide.

The room was a mess. Everything thrown to the floor, broken and trampled. Books, ornaments, furniture. In the next room, Catherine lay on the bed. There was blood all over her face and neck, one hand hanging at an awkward angle. Jane placed her fingers against the woman's throat. Still a pulse. Slow, but definitely there.

She placed her lips close to the woman's ear. 'It's Jane. Can you hear me?'

Mrs Shields didn't stir.

A doctor. She needed a doctor. She couldn't let Catherine die.

She tore at the loose brick, pulled it out, took a handful of the money hidden there. Her heart was pounding, her head was ready to scream with terror.

There were doctors in Park Square. She ran, not caring who saw her. She wasn't going to let Catherine die.

'This is Mr Peter Blenkinsop from the Middleton coalfield. He designed the cog system for the locomotive that allows it to pull heavy loads of coal.'

He was a burly man, with strong callused hands and a sharp

face. Like Murray, another man who spent most of his time outside the office. Dark, intelligent eyes assessed him.

'A pleasure to meet you,' Simon said.

Murray rubbed his cheeks, looking like someone who craved sleep far more than riches.

'Mr Blenkinsop has been very generous in the past, letting people sketch the details of the engine and telling them the specifications,' he said. 'So far, no one else has managed to duplicate our success.' His mouth curled into a smile. 'Of course, there might be one or two things we've chosen not to reveal.'

Blenkinsop laughed, a raw sound like a bark. 'We'd like to keep it that way,' he said. 'Hold on to our advantage. You told Matthew this man had also been at the staithe.'

'That's right,' Simon told him.

'You're sure it was him?' Blenkinsop's stare hardened. 'I know there's been someone who resembles the description.'

That was what Jane had said. He didn't doubt her. 'I'm positive.'

'As you can tell, we're taking this very seriously,' Murray said. 'I've had men here bribed to pass on secrets before. It happened a few years ago and it came close to ruining me.' Memory turned him silent for a few seconds. 'I'm not going to let that occur again.'

'What do you know about this man, Mr Westow?' Blenkinsop's turn, his rough voice loud.

'His name's Whittaker. He's the bodyguard for Curzon the magistrate.'

'Is Curzon involved?' Murray asked with alarm.

'No,' Simon answered. 'I'm sure he's not.'

'We want him gone.'

'Warned off,' Murray said.

'Gone,' Blenkinsop repeated. He'd made his hands into fists, the knuckles white. 'And we'll pay you good money to send him on his way. I don't care how you do it.'

'Peter—' Murray began, but the man waved his hand.

'I don't know what you imagine a thief-taker does,' Simon said coldly. 'But I find what's been stolen and return it. I don't kill for money.'

'Then don't. Get rid of him some other way. I just told you: I don't care. Secrets aren't worth a damned thing once they're gone.'

'Gentlemen,' Murray said quietly. He turned to Simon. 'I believe you had a hand in securing Mr Ashton's release from gaol.'

'Not as much as you might think. And that was a personal matter.'

A small nod of acknowledgement.

'We're prepared to pay you one hundred guineas if you can keep our trade secrets intact from these men and send them on their way. The method is up to you. Is that arrangement agreeable to you, Peter?'

A grunt of assent from Blenkinsop. 'Come and see me tomorrow.'

'I'll do that,' Simon said. He could imagine Rosie's eyes lighting up with greed as he told her the amount. 'My methods. But in the meantime, make sure your men turn Whittaker away from the works – and the staithe, too. That will help.'

'Of course,' Murray said. 'We'll leave you to start your work.'

It took time. Too much time. Jane had rushed into the room, seeing the people watch her with horror as she demanded a doctor. Putting her money down. She didn't know how much it was; she didn't care. It must have been enough. Eventually the man was following her, wheezing as he hurried from Park Square and up the Head Row, through to the small cottage.

'Who did this?' the doctor asked as he started to examine Catherine.

'I don't know.' A lie. She knew exactly who was responsible. 'That's how I found her.'

'Are you a relative?'

'I'm a friend.'

She paced while the man worked. In the living room, out in the small yard. She watered the flowers in their pots; doing anything was better than nothing at all. She twisted the gold ring as she worked.

Finally the doctor emerged from the bedroom.

'She's awake now, but she's very drowsy. Someone beat her badly. Enough to break her nose. Her wrist, too. I've set that. How old is she?'

Jane shook her head. She'd never asked. Why would it matter?

'Things like this, they . . .' He didn't finish the thought, looking at the damage in the room. 'Whoever did this . . .'

'They'll pay.' Something in her tone made him take a small pace back.

'She'll need someone to look after her for now.'

'I'll do that.'

'Good.' He lifted his hat. 'You know where to find me, Miss . . .'

Jane didn't bother to reply.

The doctor had cleaned up Catherine's face. At least the blood had gone and her nose was straight again. But bruises were already beginning to form. The woman looked so old and fragile, her arms so thin that they couldn't have any weight to them.

Jane took her hand and stroked it lightly. 'What do you need?'

'Cordial.' The word was dry and swollen, as if she could barely form it.

She removed the lace covering the top of the jug and poured a cup, tipping it to Mrs Shield's lips as she took one tiny sip, then another and another, lapping at the liquid like a bird until the mug was empty.

'Is that better?' Jane asked and the woman gave a small nod. The skin had already swollen around her eyes, making them into thin slits.

'Yes.' Her voice was clearer now, a little stronger.

'Who did this?' She knew. But she still needed to hear it.

It took a long time for Mrs Shields to answer. And when it came, her tears flowed with it.

'The girl. She wanted to know where I'd hidden your money.' She paused, swallowed. 'I wouldn't tell her.'

'I know you didn't. I'm going to stay here until you're well.'

Mrs Shields tried to shake her head, but the pain made her wince. 'I'll be fine, child. It will all pass in time.'

'Your wrist.' The doctor had splinted and bandaged the break. It rested in a sling against her chest.

Catherine raised her arm a few inches from the bed, grimacing with the pain. 'This will mend, too.'

The woman stayed silent for a long time. Slowly her breathing eased into the rhythm of sleep. Jane stood, watching, then quietly began to clear things in the other room. She stopped often, pausing to glance in at the woman. Still sleeping.

She'd remain here. Look after Catherine, as best she could. And she'd find the hocus girl and kill her for what she'd done.

First, though, she needed to tell Simon and Rosie. No Jem to carry a message now he was trailing after the preacher. It would only take a few minutes, she told herself. A final glance, then she pulled the door of the cottage closed and began to run.

'A hundred guineas,' Simon began, but Rosie interrupted him, her voice tense and urgent.

'Jane was here, you just missed her. Someone beat that friend of hers, the old woman who lives behind the Green Dragon. She's going to stay there if you need her.'

'Who'd do something like that?' he asked.

'The same one who hocussed Ericsson and was going around with that man who stole from Tetley's.'

He tried to make sense of it, but nothing came. 'Why? Do you know?'

'She didn't say. But I've never seen Jane like that before, Simon.' Rosie bit her lip. 'She was on the verge of tears.'

It was impossible for him to picture. Jane never let the world see anything. Her face was always blank. Always. No trace of emotion at all.

'I'll . . .' he began, but he didn't know how to continue.

'Leave her for today,' Rosie advised. 'Let her take care of it.'

'Yes,' he agreed after a moment. 'You're right.'

'Now, you said something about a hundred guineas.'

Catherine was still sleeping. She looked peaceful with her sparse white hair spread on the pillow.

Jane swept the floor in the other room, cleaning until the only signs of damage were the empty spaces where the broken keepsakes had once stood. Catherine's history had been split open and smashed into fragments. All of Jane's money couldn't replace that.

The hatred was like a knot in her stomach. The hocus girl. She'd have the name, make her beg, and only after that would she let her die.

* * *

Later, after evening had arrived, Jane sat on the bed, feeding Mrs Shields gruel with a spoon. It all seemed wrong, somehow, upside down. Yet she never doubted what she was doing.

'I have a will,' Catherine said finally.

'You're going to be fine,' Jane told her. 'You said so yourself.'

'It's with my solicitor. Davis in Park Square. Can you remember that?'

'Yes. But you won't need it for years yet.'

The woman turned her head. 'Do you promise you'll remember it?'

'I will.'

A little more food, a drink of the cordial, a silence that seemed to stretch out into the darkness. She thought Catherine had fallen asleep again, and started to rise.

'The will. I've left you this house. I know what it means to you, and there's no one else.'

'Please,' Jane said. She didn't want to hear any of this, to have it in her head. 'Please.'

'I've known you for a long time.'

'Five years, since I brought you that cordial from Mrs Rigton.'

'No,' the woman told her. 'Longer than that. Since you were little.'

Jane couldn't speak. Catherine's mind had to be wandering, the attack must have done something to her.

'I used to see you in the market with your mother. I always thought you were such a bonny little girl.'

It couldn't be. All that was gone. It vanished the day her mother came home and saw her father in his daughter's bed and heard Jane's screams. The day she threw the girl from the house.

'Jane Truscott.'

The first time in years that she'd heard her full name. She'd forgotten it, erased it, scrubbed at it until it there was nothing left. All she could do was sit and stare at the emptiness.

'When you came back into my life, child, it seemed like fate. God's will.'

'I don't need anything. I don't want anything.' She could hear her voice. But it seemed to come from a distance, to belong to someone else.

Mrs Shields started to doze, head propped on the pillow. Jane took the dishes and washed them, then sat by the empty hearth.

Truscott. The name tumbled through her brain, falling and falling and falling . . .

For the first years she was on her own, Jane believed her mother would come looking. She'd apologize and cry, kneel and sob before taking her by the hand and leading her home again. But, inside, she always knew it was just a forlorn dream. Her childhood had ended that day the door slammed behind her.

This house was the closest she'd come to ever finding peace, the battered woman in the bed as near to a real mother as she'd known. And now this, this line connecting to the past.

Jane took out her knife and felt the edge. It was sharp. She rolled up her sleeve and drew the blade tenderly across her skin, trying to find the meaning in it all. If the blood flowed, maybe she would.

NINETEEN

Jane heard the rough sound of boots on stone. Quickly, she rose, the knife already in her hand, and moved close to the door.

Mrs Shields was still sleeping. For hours now, the only sound had been her low, steady breathing. Jane had moved through the cottage all night, restless in the darkness, waiting for first light. Too many thoughts. Too many questions she didn't want to ask, that she couldn't begin to answer.

After a moment, she recognized the footsteps, the rhythm of the walk. Simon. As soon as he knocked, she pulled the door open and slipped outside to stare up at him.

'I thought I knew Leeds, but this place is tricky to find.'

'Someone found it,' Jane said.

Simon nodded towards the cottage. 'How is she?'

'Asleep.'

'The hocus girl did it?'

'Yes.'

She watched him draw in breath and nod slowly. He walked around the small yard, touching the plants, looking up at the sky without speaking.

'What are you going to do?' he asked finally.

'Kill her.'

'We have work,' he said. 'Paying work.'

'I need to look after Catherine.'

Simon pursed his lips. 'Whittaker. We're being paid to see him off.'

'He won't leave just because you tell him.' She knew. She'd understood that in his eyes that day in the churchyard. Words would never be enough with him. Only force.

'He will.' Simon's voice was flat. 'And I'm not going to forget the deaths. But I'll need you.'

She relished the work, being good at something, doing more than simply surviving. It gave her life a purpose.

'Catherine . . .' she began.

'I know. But when you can. As much as you can.'

'All right,' she agreed. 'It won't be today.'

He hid his disappointment well, she thought. Just a brief flicker on his face, then he was nodding again.

'You look after her. I'll come again in the morning.'

She picked up a jug, filled it from the butt and started to water the plants, exactly the way she'd seen Mrs Shields do it. Doing this, heating the gruel last night, being domestic – it was all new to her. She felt awkward, unnatural.

Inside, she hurried through to the bedroom as Catherine began to stir.

'Child,' the woman said as she opened her eyes. 'I thought I'd dreamed you were here.'

'No,' Jane told her. 'It wasn't a dream. I'm real.'

Strange, Simon thought as he walked along the Head Row. He'd never known that house existed. It seemed set apart, hushed. He could understand why Jane liked the place.

He'd needed to see her, to judge how everything stood. She looked different. Older, somehow. For the first time since he'd met her, she appeared to care about someone.

He'd never met Catherine Shields, only ever heard of her because

Jane had taken the boys to visit once when they were younger. But whatever bond existed had to be strong.

At the corner of Briggate, Simon stopped to think. If he were Curzon, what would he do? Slip Dodd out of Leeds. The magistrate would want the man gone before he became an embarrassment. Send him back to London where he could be anonymous.

Down at the New King's Arms, Simon had to press himself against the wall as a coach came flying out of the yard, the driver flicking his whip to urge the horses out on to the road. The two outside passengers were holding their hats, looking nervous, ducking as they went under the arch.

To London, twice each day, the printed notice on the wall announced. *Express and Union Service. Depart at nine o'clock in the morning and three of the afternoon, sharp.*

A few quick questions, a couple of coins dropped on the table. Dodd was booked to leave the next morning. His name was written right there in the book, no attempt at disguise. Before the spy went, though, Simon wanted his testimony. Every word. He was going to bring it all crashing down.

On Salem Place, the smell of malt and hops filled the air, tangy and sweet. Tiny flecks of soot, from the factories, from the staithe, floated down to coat everything.

Simon stood near the chapel, watching as the locomotive juddered to a halt in the distance. It edged forward, stopping to allow a wagon to shed its load into the coal chutes, then forward again. Each time he felt the ground shake and watched the cloud of dust rise and settle.

He followed a worn track out of town, up the slope towards Middleton. The ground was thickly wooded, the air clearer and fresher as the hillside rose away from town. Sun came through the branches and dappled patches of light on the ground. He heard the engine labouring back up the track to the coalfields.

An hour's walk and he was there. Up on a ridge, a large steam engine thudded, powering a hoist. A single stone chimney rose, belching out its smoke. No grass anywhere. The land seemed desolate and wasted, peopled by miners in pale trousers and waistcoats, blue kerchiefs knotted at the neck. Women and children bent over heaps of coal, breaking up big black chunks with hammers as they sorted them.

This was progress, Simon thought as he watched. It looked like a vision of hell on earth.

He was close to a shaft when someone challenged him, a man who held a pickaxe so lightly it might have been a twig.

'I'm looking for Mr Blenkinsop,' he answered.

'Right there.' He pointed to a house off to the west. 'And mind yourself. There's old bell pits sunk all over. Fall in one of them and you'll be gone forever.'

He crossed carefully, saw two of the pits as he picked his way to the house. Small openings in the earth that widened underground; the light didn't reach to the bottom.

Blenkinsop was standing by the window in his office, no jacket, the sleeves of his shirt rolled up to show thick, matted hair on brawny forearms.

'The bell pits go down a fair way,' he explained. 'But they're mostly worked out these days.' He pointed to the hoist with its large winding wheel. 'That's what keeps the men busy now. A deeper shaft.'

'Has Whittaker been up here?'

'I asked. He was here once, talking to the locomotive driver and the stoker. They reported it afterwards. By then your man had gone, of course.'

'Did he learn much?'

Blenkinsop pushed a hand through his hair. 'A little, perhaps. The real expertise is down at Murray's.'

An engraving of the first engine hung on the wall. Not a beautiful sight, but it did the work efficiently, hauling ton after ton of coal. Blenkinsop had been involved with the design, coming up with the cog rail system that was the real trick of it, allowing the train to haul so much weight. A man with an inventive brain, Simon thought.

'There's nothing to keep people off the coalfield,' Blenkinsop continued. 'No fence around it, and there's the track up from the staithe.'

'That's how I came.'

'How are you going to keep him away without killing him, Mr Westow? After all, that's why we're paying you.'

'The simplest way is to stop him coming back.'

The man raised an eyebrow. 'Do you think you can do that?'

'Yes,' Simon told him. 'I do.'

'Achieve that and I'll say Murray made the right choice in hiring you. Now,' he said, rolling down his sleeves, 'I have a meeting with the mine owners.'

A slow walk to Leeds, back down the track. The train passed, moving barely faster than a man could walk, noisy and dirty, the steam pluming into the sky as it rose. The age of the machine, Simon thought. How long before people weren't needed at all?

He had a long day ahead. Plenty of plans to make. And without Jane to help him.

By the end of the afternoon he was drained. Things were in place. Not all of them, but enough. Two more people to see before he went home.

Emily Ashton was bright, full of life and joy as she opened the door. And why not? Her ordeal was over, her brother was home. Davey sat in his chair, a book open on his lap, the same as ever. But he hadn't been reading, simply staring, empty-eyed. At least he managed a weak smile.

'He's starting to recover,' Emily said. 'His appetite's back.'

'That's good news,' Simon said. But food wasn't the problem. The man's spirit had been broken. That might never return.

He left after a few minutes. Davey was home and settled, but Simon couldn't feel much satisfaction, not when all that had come home was a husk.

Up Lady Lane, along the Head Row, into the yard behind the Green Dragon and through the small gap in the wall. He tapped on the door and stood back.

Jane appeared, wary, the knife in her hand.

'How is she?' Simon asked.

'A little better.'

'I could do with you tomorrow.' He saw the hesitation in her eyes. 'Not for long, an hour, perhaps a little more.' He dangled the bait. 'I need you to distract Whittaker.'

'Distract?' she asked. 'What do you mean?'

* * *

'Who was that, child? I heard a man's voice.'

'Simon.'

Jane saw Catherine Shields wince as she shifted slightly in the bed. The bruises were bursting into bloom, on her face, all over her body, but the sparkle was beginning to return to her eyes.

'Does he want you?'

'In the morning.'

'Then you must do it.'

'But—'

'I shall be fine,' the woman said, as if the matter was settled.

Jane sat on the edge of the bed, staring at her. There was too much on her mind. Even last night's cutting had brought no peace. All it achieved was to quieten the voices for a short while. Not long enough. Keeping busy had helped. Cleaning up the house, trying to cook, looking after Catherine, tidying around the plants. She'd never done any of it before, and fumbled her way through tasks most girls could manage without thinking. But all the questions, the images, wouldn't leave her alone. They hammered and echoed inside her skull.

One screamed louder than all the others.

'You said you knew my mother,' Jane said. She could hear the waver in her voice and tried to calm her heart. 'What was she like?'

'You saw it, Simon,' Rosie said. 'What are we going to do?'

Yes, he'd seen it, the welts on Richard's arse where the teacher had beaten him with a birch branch. He'd kept the anger inside until his son had vanished upstairs again.

'I'll go to the school tomorrow.'

'I'll come with you,' she said, then shook her head. No man in authority would take a woman seriously. 'Are all teachers like that?'

'Probably.'

He hated to see his boys so cowed. He wanted their wildness back. Give it time; that was what he'd said before. He'd been wrong.

'A tutor,' she suggested, and he stared at her questioningly. After they'd moved into the house, they'd agreed: no one else here. No maid or servant. There were too many secrets in this place, all tempting to an outsider. Jane had been the exception. 'He could come in for a few hours each day. I'd be here. You can see they're not happy at the school. Why do they need to learn the scriptures? What good will that do them?'

She was right. In his heart, he knew it. It might be the answer.

'I'll ask for some names,' he said, and she held him tight.

Darkness outside. The door was locked tight, the shutters closed, the only light from a candle at the side of the hearth. Catherine Shields was asleep.

The woman had made up a draught to aid her rest. Jane had supported her as she shuffled slowly from the bed to the cupboard where she kept her herbs, shocked at how little she weighed, how light and fragile she seemed. Mrs Shields studied the labels, selected three, measured out amounts with a trembling hand, then added water.

A mystery, Jane thought. Magic. She couldn't read the words; she'd never learned her letters. But it had worked. In just a few minutes, Catherine was settled back among the pillows, eyes closed, peaceful.

Tomorrow she'd have another chance at Whittaker. She drew out the knife, sliding the blade over the whetstone as she thought about the things Mrs Shields had told her earlier.

TWENTY

'Will it work?' Mudie asked.

'I don't know,' Simon answered. This was all he had; there was no alternative. Whittaker would come down to the coach with Dodd; he was absolutely certain of that. To make sure the spy left.

He was banking on them arriving early; that was the only way to ensure a good seat by the window. From there . . . it was all hazy, and down to chance.

'If you can make him talk, we'll be fine.'

Simon grinned. 'Then we'd better hope I'm good enough.'

They were sitting upstairs at the New King's Arms, in a private parlour that overlooked the street. Simon kept his gaze on Briggate, watching for the men to approach. A little more than an hour until the coach left. Soon, he thought, be here soon.

Jane seemed to appear from nowhere; suddenly she was standing by the table. 'They're on their way. Here in five minutes.'

Simon's heart began to beat harder. At this rate it would be rattling in his chest. 'Just the two of them?'

'Yes. The man with Whittaker is carrying a small valise.'

'You know what to do?'

She nodded, but there was a look in her eye, as if part of her was elsewhere. Worried about the old woman, he decided.

'Right,' he said. Then she was gone again. He turned to Mudie. 'I hope you have your questions ready, George. We won't have long.'

Jane waited in plain sight. She needed Whittaker to see her, to boil with revenge.

She'd barely slept again, everything that Catherine had told her still ringing loud in her ears. Her mother had been weak, that's what the woman had said. Mrs Shields had reached out and stroked the back of her hand as she spoke, as if that might make the words easier to take.

'I don't know what happened to you, child, but I can guess. I knew *something* had. I could see it in her face at the market after you disappeared. I tried to talk to her, but she walked away. After that I hardly ever saw her again.'

There was more. Little details that sparked memories she believed she'd hewed away to nothing. Things she'd wanted to leave behind forever. But here they were, whole once more.

She'd asked; she'd wanted to know. And now she did. It was her own fault that the answers hurt.

From the corner of her eye, she saw Whittaker and the other man approach. She took a step towards them.

She saw him hesitate as he saw her; then he said something to the other man, and pointed. Jane began to run. Not fast, just enough not to lose him as she moved up Briggate. Past Boar Lane. Beyond the Moot Hall and the meat and blood of the Shambles.

She could hear him, the pounding of his boots on the cobbles, and speeded up a little. At the market cross she glimpsed the woman preacher, and Jem, attentive and listening. Two members of the watch stood by, not sure what to do.

Jane ducked and slid between carts on the Head Row, glancing over her shoulder as she reached the other side. Whittaker was still behind her, trying to cut across the road. The gash on his face was starting to heal, but the line stood out red and angry against his skin.

She caught her breath. As he started to move again, she darted through the lychgate into St John's churchyard.

Simon stood by the window. He watched as Jane began to run, and saw Whittaker follow. Dodd stood for a moment, confused, then trudged under the arch into the yard, the bag weighing heavy in his hand.

'You'd better wish me luck,' Simon said, and Mudie raised his eyebrows.

Dodd stood by himself, the bag at his feet. It was the first time Simon had been close to him. People had said that he looked like a rat, and it was true. He was small, with a sharp nose and prominent front teeth, a low-crowned hat covering sleek dark hair.

'I was sorry to hear about Margaret.'

Dodd looked up in alarm. 'What? Who are you?'

Simon smiled. 'There's no need to worry, Mr Dodd. My name's Simon Westow. I'm not going to hurt you. You know Whittaker murdered her, don't you?'

'Yes,' he admitted, glancing around fearfully to check if anyone was listening. 'He never said anything, but I knew.'

'It's all right, you don't need to worry about him,' Simon said, watching the man's expression turn hopeful. 'He's going to be occupied for a while. I have a friend I'd like you to meet. He wants to ask you a few questions, that's all.'

'But—'

'You'll still be on that coach. If you want some advice, though, disappear as soon as you reach London. You know Whittaker has friends there.'

'He used to be a Bow Street Runner,' Dodd said.

'That's what I'd heard. Like I said, he knows people there.'

Simon paused. 'And he's not a man who likes loose ends. I'm sure you follow my meaning.' A gentle nudge. 'Come and meet Mr Mudie.'

'I . . .' the man began.

'Come on, Mr Dodd.' He put steel behind the words, enough to bend a weak man. 'Time's wasting.'

Jane knew the churchyard. All the places to hide, to watch. She chose a large stone on the far side of an old oak tree, squatting out of sight as Whittaker entered, head moving around, as he searched for her.

She rose as he turned away, knowing she'd catch his attention, and vanished around the far side of the church. The knife was in her hand, ready. Don't kill him, Simon had said. She'd do what he wanted. Unless she had no choice. Then she'd relish every moment.

Jane taunted him, vanishing then appearing, leading him back around the church, seeing his face redden with anger. She was behind one of the headstones when she heard a man call out: 'Looking for someone?'

Slowly, gracefully, she stood and began to walk.

He left Dodd with Mudie, then ran from the inn, hoping Jane had been able to lead Whittaker to St John's. If not . . .

He saw him. Simon took one knife from his belt, a second from his boot. 'Looking for someone?'

Whittaker's face was twisted, angry. He turned suddenly as Jane rose from the grass.

'Two of you. Think you can take me, do you?' He sounded cocksure. But it was bluff. 'About time I paid you both back.'

'You've got blood on your hands,' Simon said.

'Prove it.'

Simon shook his head. 'This isn't a court. I don't have to prove anything at all.' He took a pace forward.

Jane was circling, step by step, slowly moving around behind the man.

'You kill me and Curzon will come for you.' He could hear a faint tremor of desperation under the words.

'No, I don't believe he will. Not after he learns what else

you've been doing on his time. Curzon won't take kindly to anyone using him. You've been out to the coalfields, and to the engineering works in Holbeck. Mr Murray and Mr Blenkinsop will vouch for that. But you won't be getting within a hundred yards of either place again. You've failed. Still, you've been busy, Mr Whittaker, I'll grant you that. Serving two masters. Someone must have offered you very good money.'

He saw the man try to hide his astonishment. Good, but not good enough; if only for one small moment, the mask slipped. Just the way he'd hoped. He'd read Whittaker well. Now he needed to keep him occupied until the coach left, and hope Mudie's newspaper skills were still sharp.

Whittaker kept glancing worriedly over his shoulder. Jane stood ten feet behind him, the sun glinting on her blade. He was a murderer, a spy; he liked to believe he was a hard man. But he wasn't a fool. He knew he had no chance of winning today. He'd cut his losses while he still could.

'What do you want?'

'For you to leave Leeds. Tell Curzon whatever you like, say you've had enough of being among the heathens if you want.' The magistrate would probably be relieved to see him go. His power had been broken when he let Davey out of the gaol. To continue strutting around with a bodyguard would make him a figure of fun. 'Go on back to London. Anywhere you want.'

'Is that all?' He was suspicious.

'And before you walk away from here, you put your weapons on the ground. *All* of them.'

'Why should I trust you?' Whittaker asked.

Simon smiled. 'You can't. But I don't kill in cold blood. I'm not going to speak for Jane. She may decide to cut you again.' That was enough to make him look back at her. 'But it seems to me that you don't have any choice.'

Two knives and a cudgel landed on the grass. He stood, hands hanging by his sides.

'Now you go to Potternewton and tell the magistrate you're done here. Gone from Leeds by tomorrow.'

Whittaker snorted. 'Or else?' One small last act of defiance. Let him leave with his pride, Simon thought.

'Or else I'll find you and make you pay.' He stood aside. Jane

took a step forward and Whittaker began to walk, a bitter fury
in his eyes. Outside the gate he turned away from town.

'Is that it?' Jane asked. 'We just let him go?'

'It's not done yet,' he told her. 'We won today, but you know
his type as well as I do. He's not going to be satisfied until he
tries to kill us both.'

The coach was nosing out of the New King's Arms as Simon
strolled down Briggate. He spotted Dodd in the far corner, a
worried man peering anxiously out of the window.

Mudie was still up in the parlour, going through his notes,
adding a little more here and there.

'Did you get what you needed, George?' Simon asked.

'More than enough.' He took a sip of brandy and sat back,
satisfied. 'The way it poured out, the poor bastard must have
been desperate to tell it.'

'Good stuff?'

'Incendiary,' Mudie replied with pleasure. 'Everything rings
true. There might even be questions in Parliament over this.' He
rubbed his hands in glee. 'How about you? Did you deal with
this bodyguard?'

'For now.'

'I'll start turning this into an article. With luck, the first part
should be in the *Mercury* the day after tomorrow.'

'First part?'

Mudie's eyes were alive. He held up a finger. 'The rules of
this business, Simon: if you have something good, stretch it out.
Keep them coming back for more.'

When was the last time he'd seen George look so happy, Simon
wondered as he walked down Briggate? Certainly not since his
own newspaper went out of business.

The timing of publication would be good. Whittaker would leave
on a coach in the morning. He would make a show of it. But he'd
return after a day, maybe two. Simon had seen how the hatred
glittered in the man's eyes, almost heard his mind working, calculating his way out alive. He wasn't the type who could ever admit
he was beaten. He'd be back to salvage what passed for honour in
his mind. Men like Whittaker lived on that. They had nothing else.

*   *   *

Jane hurried past the people on the Head Row, invisible to them all. Across the street and through to Mrs Shields's house. She'd been gone for two hours.

The woman was up, sitting in her chair, reading a book. She turned with a sweet smile as Jane came in.

'Child, what is it?' she asked. 'You look like you've been running.'

'I was worried about you. Are you all right?'

Catherine was still wearing her night linen; with her wrist it would have been difficult to dress. She still seemed so frail that she might break, but slowly she was coming back to herself. The bruises stood out in a rainbow of colours across her body. Her face was still swollen, her eyes almost shut, but her serenity had returned.

'A little better. Perhaps a bit weary now,' she added after a moment. 'I know I upset you yesterday, when I talked about your mother.'

Jane didn't reply. What could she say? It was true. Even in the churchyard with Whittaker, her mother had still hovered at the back of her mind. Still, she'd asked the question. And now the woman lingered around her like a ghost.

It was easier to do things than to think. Safer. She helped Catherine stand and guided her slow shuffle back to the bed, pulling the blanket over her.

'I'm going to sleep for a while, I think. How was your business, child? Successful?'

'Yes,' Jane answered after a moment. But she hadn't given Whittaker another thought once she left the churchyard. That was over, done – for now, at least. If Simon was right, if he returned . . . she'd consider that when it happened. Too many things were crowding her mind to worry about it.

Catherine looked so peaceful. She stood for a moment, trying to let everything wash away. But it was no use. Whatever doors she tried close again, they remained ajar; however much she attempted to ignore things, they were out in the light now.

'It's done, then?' Rosie asked.

'Not yet,' Simon said, and the disappointment showed on her face.

'I was hoping that would be the easiest hundred guineas we'd ever earned.'

'We should be so lucky,' he replied. 'I'll watch him leave tomorrow, but he'll slide back. I could smell it on him.'

'Then you'd better stay alert.'

'I will,' he said seriously, then he relaxed. 'I'll go and have a word with this schoolmaster. And after that we'll need a tutor before the boys become too wild again.'

'I was out shopping today and I saw Mr Ericsson. He was full of praise for you.'

Simon grinned. 'Satisfied clients are good. Especially if they tell other people.'

'He gave me the name of a tutor. I've sent him a letter.'

As if it was all meant to be. He nodded. 'Maybe it's for the best,' he said.

TWENTY-ONE

He waited at the New King's Arms, the second morning in a row. Simon stood in a shaded alcove, tucked out of sight, but with a good view of the passengers as they climbed on board the London coach. Whittaker was at the front of the queue, thrusting his small bag into a guard's hand.

No Curzon to see him off. No love lost between those two now, Simon guessed.

He sidled through the stable and into the inn. The coach driver stood talking to the owner, taking a long draught of beer before the journey.

'You've a man on board,' Simon began.

'We've plenty of them,' the driver answered. Half his teeth were missing, the others brown and rotting. 'It's almost full.'

'He's big, looks dangerous. A wound healing on his cheek.'

'Oh, aye? What about him?'

Simon produced a few coins. 'If he gets off before London, send a note to me. Westow, care of here.'

The driver eyed him suspiciously. 'Why?'

As if by magic, two more coins appeared. 'Because I'd like to know.'

'All right,' the man agreed. 'I suppose I can do that.'

One final, shiny coin dropped into his palm to seal the bargain.

'Your boys aren't at school today,' the master said. They stood outside the classroom, the noise growing on the other side of the door.

'No,' Simon agreed, 'and they won't be again.'

'I see.'

'You don't.' He stood with his arms folded, staring down at the man. 'But that doesn't really matter.'

'They've only been here a few days. And they're still very young.'

'We've decided that it's been long enough. We've engaged a man to teach them at home.'

A brief, bland nod. 'That's your choice, of course.'

'Yes, it is.' His voice became darker. 'I'll tell you this. I don't appreciate anyone beating my sons black and blue just because he can.'

'We need discipline in the classroom. You must understand that.'

The noise reached a crescendo. 'Then maybe you should employ someone who can enforce it without using the birch so much.' He raised his hat. 'I'll wish you good day.'

The next morning Simon strolled over to the inn. A short message was waiting for him: *Your man left the coach at Wakefield.*

It was what'd he expected. The only stop the express made before London. Whittaker probably thought he'd been sly. Did he really believe Simon was that stupid? Very likely he was back in Leeds now, trying to stay out of sight, thinking he was about to become the stalker. It was time to pass word around and turn the tables on him.

Simon crumpled the note, thinking of Henry the farrier and Dodd's woman, Margaret.

A quiet day. Jane made up drinks as Mrs Shields directed, with this herb and that one. She opened a small jar of pungent ointment and rubbed it lightly on the woman's skin. Little talk today. But she needed the silence, a chance to let everything she'd heard settle, and slowly quieten in her mind.

Catherine slept in the late afternoon and Jane sat outside in a patch of sunlight. The town was just a few yards away on the other side of a wall, but it could have been miles. Every sound was muffled and distant.

Nothing brought comfort. She'd beckoned the past and it had come crawling with a monster's face. All the things she'd pushed away for years. The fear and the rage and the sorrow. The feel of her father on top of her that night. The smell of his sweat. Begging him to stop. Her sobs and pleading. The way her mother refused to look as her as she dragged her from the bed, pulled a dress over her head and pushed her out of the door, locking it behind her.

'After a while I didn't see your mother at the market any more,' Mrs Shields had said. 'A few months later someone mentioned that the family had gone, moved to another town. I didn't know what had happened, I thought all of you went. Then when Mrs Rigton sent you here to deliver the cordial, I knew your face . . .'

Away, gone away. Her mother had fled from the guilt and the shame to a place where she'd never have to see her daughter again.

She felt something on her cheek and rubbed it. A tear. Don't, Jane thought. It wasn't worth that. Nothing was.

Later she slept, troubled by dreams that left her glad to see daylight. Half the morning had passed when she heard footsteps crossing the Green Dragon Yard. Simon. But she still drew her knife, prepared.

'Whittaker's probably back by now,' he told her. 'If anyone sees him, they'll let me know. Be alert. Remember, he's after you, too.'

Jane nodded. This place felt apart from the world, as if nothing beyond the walls was quite real. But it was all out there, waiting, and soon she'd need to return to it, to deal with Whittaker, to find the hocus girl, make her talk and make her pay. The monsters didn't only live in her head.

Simon was out as the town was waking, talking to more people, knowing word would spread like ripples across Leeds.

Barnaby Wade was writing, papers scattered around him on the table of the coffee house. A few words, a pause, then scribble a little more and stop to read it. He didn't look up until Simon was sitting on the other side of the table.

'Business?'

'The hazards of it,' Wade replied with a frown. 'I sold a man some shares and he wasn't happy with the way they performed. He's suing me.' He raised an eyebrow. 'I'm composing a letter to his solicitor, pointing out exactly what was in his contract.' He put down the nib and pushed everything aside. 'You must be pleased with today's *Mercury*.'

He'd completely forgotten. Mudie's story about Dodd.

'I haven't seen it yet,' he admitted.

'George did a good job. It's explosive.' Wade raised an eyebrow. 'I hear you're looking for someone.'

'That's right.' The man already knew; that was good.

'I haven't seen him, but I'll keep my eyes open.'

'Do that.' Simon stood. 'And good luck with . . .' He nodded at the papers.

'It's nothing more than an annoyance. Remember, I was a lawyer once.' Until he'd been disbarred. 'I know how to write a contract.'

Outside the Moot Hall, the ragged seller with a phlegmy voice hawked copies of the *Leeds Mercury*. The story took up the entire front page. Wade was right: George Mudie had done his work superbly. No mention of Dodd or Curzon by name, nothing to drag him through the courts for libel, but it was hardly necessary. This was an indictment of the government, of the way they used spies to entrap their own citizens.

Slowly, he walked home, opening the door to the sounds of his sons laughing and shouting. Better than school, Simon thought; he'd been wrong to insist on sending them. They needed to learn, but not the regimentation of a classroom.

Rosie looked hot and harassed. She brushed back a lock of hair. 'The tutor will be here for his interview in an hour,' she said.

'You'll have time to read this, then.' He placed the newspaper in front of her.

'That's going to cause ructions,' she said after a few minutes.

'I hope so,' Simon told her. 'I sincerely hope so.'

Mr Meecham the tutor was a young man with a ready smile, wearing old clothes that had been delicately mended. He wanted to meet the boys, calling them by their Christian names and asking questions to draw them out.

'I can certainly teach them reading, writing and numbers,' he said after Rosie had sent Amos and Richard out to the yard. 'Much more than that, if that's what you want.'

'As much as they can take,' Simon told him.

'It doesn't happen overnight,' Meecham said nervously. 'Please, don't expect them to know everything in a week. Not even in a year or two.'

'We understand that,' Rosie told him. 'Little by little is the best way.'

The man seemed relieved, then tried to hide his pleasure at the money Simon offered. Far more than he'd expected, obviously.

'Five mornings a week, from nine until noon,' the tutor explained. 'At their age, that's a good way to begin. It doesn't tax them too much.'

'The boys seemed to take to him,' Rosie said after Meecham had gone.

'Yes.' He was still uncertain about an outsider in the house. But his wife was happy; that was enough. He pulled the watch from his waistcoat. Almost eleven. 'I need to be working.'

Back to the inns and the beershops, exchanging quiet words with familiar faces. No one had spotted Whittaker. Sooner or later, though, he'd show his face and someone would see it.

People were talking about Mudie's article. Simon had seen it pasted to the chimney breast in the White Hart and the Talbot, there for everyone to read. He heard the outrage, disgust, the anger at what the government was doing, and he smiled with satisfaction.

The pall hung low over Leeds today. Every breath tasted of soot. When he glanced up he could see the smoke rising from the manufactory chimneys. Industry was king in this town.

Mudie was sitting at his desk in the printing shop, a full glass of brandy by his side as he read through a small pile of papers.

'The second part?' Simon asked as he took off his hat and sat down.

'Third. The second runs tomorrow.' He was grinning with satisfaction too. 'What did you think of the first?'

'It won't help Curzon, will it? And if people read it in London, there will be questions.'

'They'll see it. The publisher's made certain of that. One hundred copies have gone to Parliament.' He sat back and took a sip of his drink. 'I wouldn't be too surprised if we hear that our friend the magistrate has decided to resign from the bench. His career's destroyed now. I can't say I'm sorry.'

'Pleased to have played a part?'

Mudie gave a broad grin and raised his glass in a toast. 'Delighted. This is the kind of story that a writer comes across once in a lifetime. Twice if you're very lucky. I'm grateful to you.'

'Curzon's bodyguard left Leeds yesterday.'

'Superfluous to requirements now?'

'Something like that.' It was better to ignore the man's other work; Murray and Blenkinsop wouldn't appreciate the attention. 'Boarded the London coach. But a little bird told me he alighted in Wakefield.'

Mudie's forehead creased. 'Why would he do that?'

'Because he wants to kill me. And Jane. He has a score to settle.'

For a long moment the man was silent, staring. 'What's going to happen?'

'He thinks he's been very clever, that I won't expect him back. But I'll be waiting.'

'I hope you are. I saw him a couple of times. He's big, Simon. He looks dangerous.'

'He is. But he's not going to win.'

'Don't be too cocky.'

'Believe me, I'm not.' Whittaker had fooled him before. It wouldn't happen again. 'I know he's impressive at his job, and I have some very good reasons to stay alive.'

'I've looked after myself for a long time, child,' Mrs Shields said gently. 'And I've had broken bones before.'

Jane had been pacing around the house and the small yard since Simon's visit. 'But . . .' she began.

Catherine Shields took hold of her hand and stroked it. 'You're restless. Don't tell me you're not.'

'You're not well . . .'

'No,' the woman agreed. 'But I'm starting to get better.'

The bruises still wore their brilliant colours, yet Catherine had managed to wash and dress herself. Slowly, awkwardly, but she'd refused help, quietly determined to do everything on her own.

'What if the hocus girl comes back?'

'She won't.' The woman said it as if it was fact. 'She's done her worst, she won't return.'

Jane wanted to believe her.

'Trust me,' Catherine said with a calm smile. 'I'm safe from her now.' She put a fingertip on the gold ring she'd given to Jane. 'So are you.'

'I'll only be gone for a few hours.'

'Take all the time you need, child. I'll still be here.'

Jane came out on to the Head Row, overwhelmed by the noise and the people. She had to stand for a moment, to stare around. Then she gathered the shawl over her hair and began to walk.

Mrs Rigton glanced up and gave a small nod as Jane settled on the stool next to her, eyes moving over the customers in the beershop. All of them had gone back to their drinks.

'Someone came and hurt Catherine.'

'How badly?' the woman asked.

'Broke her wrist and her nose. She was bruised and beaten. I've been staying with her.'

Mary Rigton picked a clay pipe off the trestle, lit a spill from an oil lamp and began to smoke. 'Who did it? Do you know?'

'The girl I've been looking for. The one who was hocussing.'

'I remember. But I've not seen hide nor hair of her. What are you going to do?'

'What I should have done before.'

'Before?' Mrs Rigton asked sharply. 'When?'

'I could have killed her, but I didn't.' Jane heard herself, full of regret.

'You made a mistake. That's not like you, girl.'

'I wanted a name. She wouldn't give it to me, said if I killed her I'd never know.'

'Did you get it in the end?'

'No.' Her face hardened. 'But I will.'

'Maybe she's gone,' Mrs Rigton said.

'If she's here, I'll find her.'

'If I hear anything, I'll make sure you know.' She tapped out her pipe against the leg of her stool. 'Did you hear about this spy? It was in the newspaper. Everybody's talking about it.'

She'd heard them as she came down Briggate, men standing with their newspapers, talking, voices buzzing like wasps. 'He's gone.'

'Has he?' The woman cocked her head. 'Well, happen you'd know. I'll tell you something, it's made Curzon a laughing stock. He won't dare show his face in town for a while. Not if he has any sense.'

'Curzon had a bodyguard,' Jane said.

'I know. Big man, face like he'd kill you.'

'If you see him, I want to know.'

'Why, girl?'

'Simon's looking for him.'

For a moment, Mrs Rigton looked as if she was about to speak. Then she shrugged. 'All right.'

Jane left the beershop and prowled around Leeds, senses alert, eyes sharp. But there was no sign of the hocus girl. None of the people she asked had seen her.

But she was still in town. Jane could feel that.

By evening, after she climbed the hill of the Head Row, she was grateful to slip through the gap in the wall behind the Green Dragon.

There, on the bench outside the cottage, Mrs Shields sat with Simon. He had his hat perched awkwardly on his lap, a mug in his hand.

'I was looking for you,' he began. 'Catherine said I should wait.'

'He was telling me about his sons. I remember when you brought them here.'

She wanted to turn and run off, not return until he'd left. She didn't want him here. Bringing a brief message was one thing. But to sit and talk, to be a guest, that was different. This was her special place, where she could come to feel whole again. *Hers.*

He stood, putting down the mug. 'Jane's here now. I just need a word with her and then I have to go.' A small bow. 'Thank you for the company.'

They waited until Catherine was inside, the door closed.

'I can see why you love her.' His gaze moved admiringly around the small yard. 'There's something about this place, isn't there?'

She cut him off. 'What do you need?'

'The girl who attacked Catherine. I saw her a few hours ago.'

Jane could feel her heart starting to race.

'Out at Drony Laith,' he continued. 'Past where they're building that new factory.'

'Where did she go?' She held her breath.

'Into the woods. I waited a few minutes, but she didn't come out.'

Where Jane had kept her money. She'd never thought to search out there again, hadn't imagined that the girl would ever go back. Stupid. She should have been thorough. It would be dark very soon, too late to look out there now.

'I'll go in the morning.'

'Whittaker,' Simon said.

'I haven't seen him.'

'No one has,' he told her. 'I checked at the engineering works in Holbeck. He hasn't been there.'

She nodded. Her knife was sharp.

TWENTY-TWO

'What's wrong, child?'

'Nothing,' Jane answered. She closed and barred the shutters, keeping out the night.

'You've been like a scalded cat since Simon left.'

'It's just work.'

She knew Catherine was watching her. She didn't want to lie, but she couldn't say the things on her mind, either.

'Drink this.' She held out a mug. 'It will calm you.'

Jane could taste honey on her tongue, light and sweet, and so much more she couldn't begin to identify. But after a few minutes she could feel the tension starting to leave her body and a sense of drowsiness rising in her head.

'You settle down now,' Mrs Shields said. She stroked Jane's hair. 'Rest. We're both tired. It'll do us good.'

She slept, and was gone from the house with the sunrise. A quick glance into the bedroom to see that Catherine was sleeping comfortably, then Jane was out in the chill early air, gathering the shawl around her shoulders.

People were already about, making their way to the morning shift at the manufactories. After she passed Gott's mill at Bean Ing, the road was almost empty. A few carts straggling into town. An early coach galloped along, enjoying the freedom of the highway.

The woods were thick and green and peaceful. But soon enough they'd be gone and all this would become another factory or two. She followed a thin track for ten paces then stopped. A chance for her ears to adjust to the soft noises of the place. Birdsong, rustling, tiny scraps of sound from all over.

She knew this ground and all the paths the animals had made across it. With the shawl over her head Jane drifted silently, one more dark shape among the trees. Around and along, the knife in her hand, wary of any clearing where someone might make a camp, stopping to watch, to breathe it in. No other person was moving here.

Cautiously, she circled the area where she'd kept her money hidden, staying out of sight among the deep shadows and the oaks. Someone had been in this place; there was charred wood where a fire had burned.

But it was all empty now. Dew on the grass, the embers cold to her touch, no sign that anyone had walked there this morning.

The hocus girl had been here, though. More ground around the trees had been dug up, the earth scattered everywhere. It was easy to piece the picture together. She'd failed to find the money at Mrs Shields's house, so she'd come back here, desperate, digging again. Jane felt some of the clods; still dampness in the soil.

The girl must have stayed long into the evening, a fire to keep her warm and give some light as she dug. But she hadn't spent the night. Where had she slept?

The light changed as she walked back into town. Hazy, muted. Dulled. The air was sharper, soot and dirt bitter on her tongue.

Catherine Shields was up, dressed as well as her broken wrist would allow. With her good hand, she stirred a pot of porridge. Her bruises were vivid now, at their height. But there was more life about her, and the swelling around her eyes had lessened. She moved more easily too; the stiffness and the injuries were starting to heal.

'Did you find her?'

'No.'

The woman put down the wooden spoon. 'Please think, child. I know what you intend to do when you find her. Do you really believe that will help?'

'I need a name from her,' Jane answered after a moment. 'This time I'll make her tell me.'

'What if she won't?'

'She will,' Jane said with certainty.

'Child.' Mrs Shields stroked her hair and laid the good hand on her arm. The woman was stronger than she looked, her grip sturdy. 'I don't know the things that have made you who you are now. Even if you told me, I could never *really* know. I haven't lived your life. But it hurts me to see you so hard when I know you have so much love inside you.'

Love? She didn't want to love anyone, to give them that power to hurt her. She'd learned too much in the last few days. The nearest she'd come to love was right here, with this woman. And now? She didn't want to watch Catherine turn against her, too, to hate her for something she had to do. It was easier to leave before that could happen.

'I have to go,' Jane said. 'I'm glad you're recovering. I'll come back soon, I promise.'

She let the latch fall as she closed the door. A quick touch on the stone as she eased through the wall and back into the world. She had work to do.

Simon was beginning to doubt his certainty. Nobody claimed to have seen Whittaker after he left on the coach. Yet the note from the driver proved he'd alighted in Wakefield. There was nothing in that town for the man.

He paced around the kitchen, trying to force it all into some kind of shape.

'If you're going to be this restless, walk it off outside,' Rosie told him. 'The tutor starts today. I want the boys to be able to concentrate.'

He stopped and stared at his sons. They were sitting at the table, faces and hands scrubbed, as presentable as he'd ever seen them. Their clothes were clean, hair neatly combed as they wolfed down the bread and cheese.

'You're right,' he said.

'I always am.' Rosie grinned. 'And you know it.'

Mudie might have heard something. A morning whisper. He bought a copy of the newspaper from the rheumy old seller, glancing at the front page as he walked. The final part of the interview with Dodd, and one final, huge revelation, that the spy had met with the Home Secretary and his spying had been approved.

'You saved the best for last, George,' Simon said as he walked into the print shop with its raw tang of ink. The man was sitting at his desk with the paper in front him, staring at his work with a contented smile.

'Leave them with something they'll remember. And I don't think they'll forget that, do you?'

'Questions in Parliament?'

'Bound to be. Very embarrassing ones, too. I wouldn't be astonished if the Home Secretary is forced to resign. Speaking of that, Curzon's stepped down. Very quietly, but that's what I heard last night. And those men over near Dewsbury have all been released. Charges dropped.'

The articles had achieved a great deal, and maybe more to come. 'Well done.'

'I'd love to claim the credit, but they managed to cock it all up without my help, as usual.' He sighed, but there was deep pleasure behind it. 'Enough of that. What can I do for you?'

'Whittaker. Has anyone mentioned seeing him back in Leeds?'

'Not to me. Why?'

'Keep your eyes peeled, that's all.'

Mudie nodded. 'I will; I owe you that. You brought me the best story I've ever had.'

'Davey's out of gaol and he won't be going back. That was all I ever really wanted.'

'He's safe now. No one would dare touch him after this.'

He was in the garden of the cottage, kneeling in the dirt and pulling out weeds between the flowers.

Davey Ashton glanced up, forehead creased with worry as he heard the footsteps approach. Then he started to smile as he stood.

'Come to visit the invalid, Simon?'

'It looks as if Emily's keeping you busy.'

'Fresh air and simple work. It's good medicine for the soul.'

The gaol pallor had left his cheeks. There was colour in his face again and a hint of playfulness in his expression. He was filling out, regaining most of the weight he'd lost in his cell.

'You heard that Curzon resigned?'

'No.' It seemed to take him by surprise. He was silent for a moment, then nodded. 'I can't say I'll miss him. I've been reading the *Mercury*.'

'Interesting stuff, isn't it? The men in the West Riding are free, too.'

'Now that's heartening news.' He sighed. 'Come inside, Simon. Have a drink, we ought to celebrate. Emily's in the middle of cooking.'

'I can't stay. Another time.'

'I don't think I've told you how grateful I am for . . . well, everything you did.'

'Not that much. I told you before: I was repaying what you did for me.'

'All those days, sitting there. It gave me time to think, to understand myself a little more.' He looked down at his hands, then pushed them into his trouser pockets. 'I broke very easily, didn't I?'

'No more than many, Davey.'

'I . . .' he began, then shut his mouth and shook his head. 'Maybe it doesn't matter. I still have a great deal to consider.'

'You'll find some answers.'

'In time, perhaps. I don't know what I'd do without Emily.'

'She's a good woman.'

Davey smiled. 'She chivvies me to this and that, but it all helps. I feel I'm being useful for a change.'

'You've always been useful.' He looked at his pocket watch. 'I need to go. I'll come back again soon.'

'Bring Rosie and the boys next time.'

'I will. I promise.'

At least the man seemed to be content, Simon thought as he walked down Mabgate. Maybe something good had come out of it all.

The arrest felt like history now. Hard to believe it was only a few days ago. So much had happened since then. Ericsson and the hocus girl. Tetley and his thief. Murray and Blenkinsop and Whittaker. The business that still had to be resolved.

On Salem Place, the smell of hops and malt caught at his throat as he passed the brewery. The coal staithe was busy, men loading wagons to deliver around Leeds. Off in the distance a steam whistle shrieked as the locomotive rattled slowly into view.

No sign of Whittaker. Simon walked over to the engineering works. Not there either. Murray had put his men on their guard. Twice in the space of two minutes, Simon was challenged about his business and no one would let him in any of the buildings. Simple precautions they should have taken long ago.

He ambled back towards Leeds Bridge, alert for any hint of Whittaker. Then his hand moved to his knife. Someone was behind him. Thirty or forty yards, as near as he could judge, keeping the same slow pace.

Simon didn't stop or turn, nothing to make the follower aware. Instead he crossed over the river like a man lost in thought and turned the corner on to Swinegate. A few yards along, a low passageway led though to an old court by the river. He ducked in. It would buy him a few seconds, long enough to see if it was friend of foe trailing him.

Neither. It was a stranger who stopped, then straightened as Simon appeared behind him, hissing into his ear.

'I have a knife against your back and I can kill you before you move. Do you understand?' No reply. 'Do you?'

The man nodded dumbly.

'Who sent you?'

'I was told to give you a message.' He stammered and tripped over the words. Simon could see him almost shaking with fear.

'What is it?'

Trying to collect himself, the man took a deep breath. 'He said he'd see you tomorrow.'

'Where? Who said it?'

'Sunset. At the staithe. He said you'd know who he was.'

He did. A meeting? But not to talk, and only one of them would walk away from it.

'Where is he now? How are you supposed to tell him you delivered the message?' He grabbed the man's collar, lifting him on to his toes. 'How?'

'He said he'd find me today. I have to walk up and down Kirkgate for an hour this afternoon and he'd see me.'

Simon let him drop. Clever. A long street, and from the right place, Whittaker would be able to spot if the man was being followed.

'Go and tell him you passed on the message.'

'Yes, sir.' He scurried away.

A day and a half and this would be over. Now he needed to find Jane and make his preparations.

TWENTY-THREE

'She's upstairs,' Rosie told him. 'Came in an hour ago and went straight to the attic.'

Simon could hear the drone of a voice from the front room. Meecham the tutor with the twins.

'Whittaker sent me a message.'

'What?' she asked in amazement. 'What does he want?'

He told her and watched her face harden. 'No, Simon. You're not going. He'll have some trick planned. A trap.'

'I've no doubt he will. I plan on having a few of my own.'

'Simon . . . don't meet him. You don't have to prove anything.'

'You liked that girl he murdered.'

'Yes, I did,' she replied. 'But I'm not going to lose my husband over it.'

'There's Henry – who knows how many others he's killed?'

'It's not your job.'

He opened his arms. Rosie hesitated, then came to him and he held her close. 'I'll be prepared. I promise. Not just Jane. I'll have others with me.'

'Don't, Simon. Please. There's no need.'

But he felt the pull, the challenge. And being a thief-taker was all risk. He had scars that proved it. Rosie had lived the life with him. She knew.

'I'll be as careful as I can.'

He knocked on the attic door. No answer. Simon turned the handle. The room could have been empty, just a bed, dresser, jug and ewer, except for the girl staring out of the window. She had a hand clasped tight around her forearm, a tiny trickle of blood seeping through her fingers.

He coughed and she turned, her eyes slowly focusing like someone emerging from a dream.

'I knocked.'

'It doesn't matter.' She kept her hand in place, pressing down so hard on the flesh that it turned white.

'Whittaker. Tomorrow at sunset, down by the coal staithe.'

Jane nodded.

'I want more than the two of us there,' he said.

She looked at him curiously. 'Why?'

'Because I'd trust him as far as I can throw him. I'm going to hire a couple of Robert Allston's men.'

'Are you going to kill him?'

'Not unless I have to.' Simon stared down at the floorboards.

'I'll do it,' Jane told him.

He tried to read the look in her eyes, but there was nothing for him to see. No anger, no hatred, no grief. The same as ever, a steady, even gaze that kept everything inside. Shutting herself away so perfectly. Except for the blood. But he knew about that, he had for a long time. All the scars and the bandages, the small excuses that never seemed to fit.

That was her way, it was how she coped with a world that was too big for her. He didn't understand it, but it wasn't his business.

'Why?'

'For Henry. He was kind to me once.'

As simple, as plain as that.

Allston sat in the scullery of his small house, arms folded in front of his chest. Only one of his men with him today. He listened as Simon explained what he wanted.

'Can't do it, Westow.'

'Why not? I'm offering good money.'

'The men are already busy. Booked up, that's what we are.' He gave a toothless smirk. 'Popular.'

'Whittaker.' The man had been here before him.

'You know me better than that, Westow. I never reveal the names of my clients.'

'How many are busy?'

Allston wavered for a moment, then answered. 'Four.'

'I see. And a higher offer?'

The man chuckled. 'You could go double or triple and it wouldn't change a damned thing. I keep the bargains I make.'

A nod and Simon was gone, trying to think as he strode up towards the bridge. Whittaker and four big, brutal men against him and Jane. That wasn't a battle; it was slaughter.

He needed another way. To find Whittaker before any of this could happen.

Simon stood, looking down at the water but barely noticing it. He slammed his palm down on the parapet.

After Simon left, Jane stayed in the attic. Through the window, she saw him walk down Swinegate. Off somewhere to make his preparations.

She pressed a piece of cotton against the cut in her arm, watching it turn red, then a rusted brown as the blood began to dry. One more rung. Her punishment for all the things she'd felt. For failing herself. For allowing Catherine Shields to be hurt.

She was nothing more than a stupid girl who couldn't think properly. A girl who'd asked a question and learned too much.

She wanted to cry, to feel the release, but she'd left tears behind when her mother locked the door on her. All the things she'd done and seen. No, she thought. That single tear she'd shed at Mrs Shields's was the last she'd allow herself.

Without thinking, she turned the ring on her finger. As she noticed what she was doing, she eased it off and slid it into her pocket. The gift to keep her safe. It was a sham, an illusion. Magic that didn't work. There was no safety in this world. Only different degrees of pain, and you had to keep your mouth closed and never let it show.

As she came down the stairs, a young man ushered the twins out of the front room and through to the kitchen. Richard and Amos looked happy, smiling as bright as day. The man saw her, bowed his head and continued.

She waited until they'd gone then closed the front door quietly behind herself. Whittaker was tomorrow. She had business of her own today.

Back to Mrs Rigton's beershop. More drinkers today, a table crowded with young men, their heads close together as they planned something. A laugh, a raised voice that quieted swiftly. The woman saw her, shook her head, and Jane left again.

At the top of Briggate she spotted Jem. He was still in the good clothes he'd been wearing the last time she saw him. In a high, earnest voice he urged people to the Lord, handing out tracts to anyone who'd take them, avoiding the blows from men who tried to cuff him.

'The preacher has you doing this now?' Jane asked.

'Her name's Miss Carr. And I wanted to,' he replied with thin, childish defiance. He pushed one of the papers towards her.

'Don't waste your time. You know I can't read. Is she treating you well?'

Jem nodded. 'I have somewhere to sleep and I eat with her and the others. She's promised she'll teach me my letters and numbers. It feels . . .' He struggled to find the words and failed.

'I'm pleased for you.'

'She showed me God. Just listening to her talk that first day.' His eyes widened as he spoke.

'Maybe it was what you needed.' A part of her envied him such simple, open faith. To be found. To belong.

'You might see Him, too, you know, if you listened to her. She has the gift.'

'No,' Jane said. 'Not me. Do you remember the woman with the bandage on her arm? Big, dark hair. I'm trying to find her.'

'I can't,' Jem replied. 'I've left all that behind. Miss Carr showed me how it was hurting my spirit. Please come and listen to her sometime.'

'Maybe.' She owed the boy more than outright refusal. But even as she said the word, Jane knew she'd never go. So did he. Jem had taken his path. He'd survive. Maybe he'd even prosper. Jane had heard about Ann Carr. The woman did some good, that was true, and Jem was young enough to be saved. Even religion was better than sleeping in a churchyard and stealing scraps to survive.

He was squirming, eager to be away from her. She was part of the skin he was trying hard to shed, something to be forgotten and put away out of reach.

'Look after yourself,' she said and walked down towards Vicar Lane.

Whittaker was going a fine job of keeping himself hidden. But the man had been a Bow Street Runner, he knew the porous line between the lawful and the lawless and how to move from one side to the other and back again. How money and threats could purchase silence.

At least he knew the man's plan now. But that wasn't going to help flush him out. There were a few Simon could call on. Big men, hard men, like Ciaran Regan the stevedore. But none of this had anything to do with them. It wasn't their battle. Involve them, and some would be hurt or die. He couldn't do that.

Curzon.

The thought arrived and the world seemed to stand still.

The magistrate might know something useful about Whittaker. He'd employed the man, he'd seen him every day.

But Simon had ruined the glittering career Curzon had planned for himself. He'd been forced to release Davey Ashton, then to resign from the bench. He wasn't likely to welcome the thief-taker into his house.

He gazed down at the water, moving sluggish and dark, the stench rising, as he weighed things. A trip to Curzon's home might well be a wasted journey. The man probably wouldn't even see him.

But he was simply thrashing around helplessly in town. Whittaker had a crook's mind. He'd made his arrangements, he might even have planned everything before he left. Someone knew where he was, but so far no one had whispered a word.

Three miles out to Potternewton. Less than an hour. He had nothing to lose.

The grounds were carefully sculpted to seem as if they ran on forever, all the way down towards Leeds, that Curzon owned everything he could see. In the distance, low, pale clouds rested over the town. Out here the air was clean, fresh and sweet in his lungs.

At the head of the drive, Simon took a breath and walked to the house. Not the back door; no servants' entrance for him here. He brought the knocker down hard on the wood and waited, looking up to see the hill where he'd waited on his last visit. Where the shots from a gun had come close to hitting him.

Eventually he heard footsteps and the large door glided open.

'I'm here to see Mr Curzon. Tell him it's Simon Westow, the thief-taker.'

He waited, nervous, pacing up and down on the step. He'd been turned away from grand houses often enough in the past; another instance would hardly be a new experience. But when the servant returned, he asked Simon to follow.

Inside, the place was smaller than he'd imagined, less impressive than it seemed from the road. A parlour looked out over the terrace. Curzon sat in a chair by the empty fireplace, a newspaper on his lap. He waved away the servant. Simon heard the soft closing of the door.

'I'm surprised you have the nerve to show yourself here.' The man's voice was cold, his eyes dark and hard. 'You did me a great deal of damage.'

'You arrested a friend of mine on false evidence. That's not the law.'

'Your *friend* Ashton . . .' he began, then halted and let the thought vanish. 'Did you walk out or ride?'

'I walked.' It seemed an odd question.

'Do you ride at all?'

Simon shook his head. 'Only Shanks's mare.'

Curzon leaned back and rested his head on the back of his chair, rubbing his chin.

'It must be important, then. Well?'

'Whittaker. Your—'

'I know full well who he was.' The man's voice boomed around the room.

'Then you'll also know he's a murderer and a spy.' Simon kept his tone low and even, his gaze fixed on Curzon.

'What?' The man's hand fell to his lap.

'Perhaps he forgot to tell you. When Dodd's woman wanted to leave, Whittaker killed her. It was a good way to keep your spy in line.'

'No. I didn't know he'd done that.' He sounded chastened. 'What's this about him being a spy?'

'He's been hunting for details about the Middleton coal loco-motive. It's not because he's interested for himself. He was asking questions at the works in Holbeck and at the staithe. He even went up to the coalfield.'

'He left two days ago.'

'I know. I saw him board the coach myself,' Simon said, then paused for a second. 'A funny thing, though. He alighted in Wakefield and made his way back here.'

'Are you sure? How do you know?'

'I've had a message from him. He wants to meet me tomorrow. He's after revenge.'

'Really?' Curzon raised an eyebrow. He sounded doubtful. 'Revenge for what?'

'I disarmed him once. And for that cut he received on his cheek.'

'You did that?'

Simon didn't reply. No need to mention Jane, so much easier to keep it simple.

'You know what Whittaker used to do?' Curzon asked.

'I'm told he was a Runner.'

'Yes. A good one, too, until he became greedy. That's what his captain said. After they dismissed him, he began performing small tasks for the Home Office. This and that.'

Simon could imagine what was involved. Dirty work, easily denied if he was caught.

'Why did you employ him?'

'Pride,' Curzon admitted after a little thought. 'And I'd been putting a plan together with some of the magistrates in the West Riding. Whittaker recommended Dodd, said he'd known him in London and he could be convincing. They intended to use him to teach some of their Radicals a lesson. I thought I could do the same thing here.'

'And Davey was an easy target for you.'

The man shrugged. 'Whittaker seemed a good man to stop any trouble. Some friends in London suggested him; they thought he might do a fair job up here.'

'They didn't know him well enough.'

Curzon gave a wry, defeated smile. 'So it seems. But I still don't see why you need to come out here and tell me this.' He cocked his head. 'Or is this simply to rub my nose in the disgrace?'

'I'm simply trying to find him before this meeting.'

'Afraid, Westow?'

'Yes.' The truth seemed to surprise Curzon. 'He's bought the services of four men. I don't mind a fair fight, but I'm not about to sacrifice myself for anyone.'

'What do you want from me?'

'He worked for you. Do you have any idea where in Leeds he might be? I haven't heard a peep.'

'Not as good at your job as you believed?'

Let him have his dig, Simon thought. Words weren't going to hurt. 'Perhaps I'm not. Did he make any friends that you know about?'

'If what you've told me is true—'

'It is.'

'Then I didn't really know him at all. He was gone on business for several hours at a time. Only when I was at home, so it didn't matter. I didn't think much of it.'

'No idea at all?'

Curzon shook his head. 'None. You've had a wasted journey.'

It had been a gamble. He'd thrown the dice and lost. At the door, Simon turned.

'I was out here once before. Watching from a hill. Someone shot at me. Who was it?'

'That was me, Westow. There was never any need to worry for your life. I intended to scare, not to kill. I don't like people spying on me.'

Of course not. That cut too close to home. But it was fine to have someone do it *for* you, he thought as he began the long walk back to town.

TWENTY-FOUR

Twice, Jane imagined she had a glimpse of Charlotte Winter. But as she drew closer, the shape changed. Not the hocus girl at all. She stopped and leaned against a wall, not caring that it was covered in soot and dirt.

Her gift for this work seemed to have deserted her, was mocking her. She walked and walked, asked people, but she found absolutely nothing. The girl hadn't left Leeds. Jane could feel it. Or perhaps she was simply fooling herself, letting hope ride over the truth.

She stood and let people move around her. They jostled her, pushed her, but she was barely aware of it. Inside, she felt empty. Hollow, as if words and thoughts could ring endlessly, echoing around.

Jane wasn't even looking, staring at nothing, when she caught a movement at the edge of her vision. Someone moving away into the distance. A man. She knew his shape. Whittaker. She pulled the shawl over her hair and followed. The hocus girl vanished from her mind for now.

He had no idea she was there. He walked too easily, freely, never glancing round or making sudden turns. Not like a man in hiding at all, but someone about to own the world.

Down Kirkgate and over Timble Bridge, past the butcher's shop, the undertaker, and then striding out along Marsh Lane. She lingered. There were fewer people on the road here; if he turned she'd be easy to spot.

Whittaker was almost out of sight when she began to walk, her finger clutching the knife in her pocket. The man was clever. He might be leading her into a trap. But when she reached the top of the small rise, there he was, still far ahead. And now she knew exactly where he was going.

Jane retraced her steps, past two cottages, before knocking on the door of a third. Martha Dobson's home. She'd been here before, sent by old Thaddeus Hardy, when she was hunting Dodd and his girl. His dead girl.

'You must have heard about him, then,' the woman said wearily, settling back on her stool. 'Daft old fool.'

'Who?' Jane asked, confused. 'Thaddeus?'

The woman nodded.

'What happened to him?'

'You mean you don't know?'

'No.'

'He found an old fowling piece somewhere and thought he'd have himself a pigeon for his dinner. When he tried to fire it, the whole thing exploded in his face. Poor soul.'

'He's dead?' Jane asked.

'Went in the ground two days ago. Unmarked. Just me and a couple of the others from round here by his grave.' She sighed. Her fingers never stopped moving as she spoke, twisting and spinning the wool. A second nature born of years. 'Happen it's for the best. He was in a bad way.'

Jane didn't reply. She'd never known the old man well, never seen him healthy. She tried to imagine Thaddeus young and vital, but it was too great a leap.

'At least he's got hissen some peace now,' Mrs Dobson said.

'Has he?' Jane asked.

'With the Lord,' the woman replied with certainty. 'If you're not here about him, you must be after summat else.'

'The cottage. The one you told me about last time I was here.'

'Ah.' There was a gleam in her eye. 'They've gone. Someone killed the woman.' Her voice tightened and she pursed her mouth. 'All very dark. No one knows who did it, but the young man left right after.'

'I heard,' Jane said. 'Do you know if anyone else is living there now?'

Mrs Dobson gestured towards the window without losing her rhythm. 'Seen someone going out that way a couple of times. A man. He can't have been there long, mind. A day or two, that's all.'

'Thank you.'

No need to go any closer and risk being seen. She knew now. On the way back to town she paused by Garland Fold and thought of Thaddeus Hardy for a minute. Everyone died, and he'd lived longer than most. At least his end had been quick.

'He's living *there*?' Simon said, cursing himself for never thinking of the place. It seemed so obvious now, empty, isolated. And safe, with open ground all around. They had little chance of creeping up on the house and taking him by surprise.

He sat back and rubbed his eyes with his fists. They were in the kitchen, Rosie and Jane sitting across from him. Early evening, and the boys were playing in the yard, hitting a ball with a pair of sticks and shouting. The wildness he cherished in them.

Over supper they'd been full of everything they'd learned from their tutor, eager to tell it all. He and Rosie had listened, bemused, until they ran out of words. She'd fed them and sent them outside to play just before Jane arrived.

'I didn't follow him all the way,' she said. 'Someone's in the house, though. A woman who lives nearby told me.'

'He never knew you were behind him?'

'No.' Her body stiffened and her face became thoughtful. 'He never showed it.'

It was unlike her to show any uncertainty. She'd changed in the last few days. Simon tried to peer at her, but she was staring down at the wood, tracing the pattern of the grain with her fingertips.

He needed to think, to plan. Whittaker wasn't someone to be underestimated. Simon hadn't forgotten that the man had taken him by surprise, could have killed him so very easily. He'd take no chances.

'We still have a day until this meeting he wants.' He felt the pressure as Rosie placed a hand on his arm and pushed down hard against the muscle. 'But we're not going to that.'

Jane raised her head. 'Why not?'

'Because he's hired some men to accompany him. We wouldn't have a chance.'

'What are you going to do?' Rosie asked.

'Stop him before any meeting can happen.' He could hear the finality in his voice.

'How?'

He didn't have an answer for that. Not yet.

She tapped lightly on the door. A light shone through a small gap in the shutters. Almost dark, the shadows long and deep and tempting.

'I'm sorry,' she said as the small woman appeared. 'I was stupid.'

'Come in,' Mrs Shields said with a gentle smile. 'I'm glad you're back.'

Her bruises were still vivid, the colours slowly beginning to fade, the edges shifting through shades of yellow. She moved slowly, hesitantly, as if she wasn't quite certain of her balance, then lowered herself in her chair with a contented sigh.

'I was angry,' Jane said. 'Childish.'

'It doesn't matter. You were upset because Simon was here?'

'Yes. I . . .'

Catherine smiled. 'You want to keep this house apart from the rest of your life, don't you?'

'Yes.' She nodded. 'That's it. That's what I want.'

'There's nothing wrong with that, you know. We all need our special places. Our secrets.'

'But I was upset when I saw him with you.'

'Everyone gets angry, child. We're human.'

'You're never like that.'

'Oh, I am,' the woman replied with a small laugh. She leaned forward, smiled and whispered. 'Inside.'

Jane felt easy again. She was still welcome here. Mrs Shields wasn't going to turn her away.

'I have some more money. Can I put it with the rest? Do you mind?' Her share of the Tetley's fee. Work that happened a lifetime ago.

'You help yourself. It'll save my old knees trying to bend.'

Simple enough to do, now she had the knack of removing the

stone. The last time, she'd been fumbling and scrambling, rushing to fetch a doctor to see to Catherine. Now she folded the notes in with the rest, tucked it all away and hid it again.

By the time she returned to the living room, Mrs Shields's eyes were closed and her breathing had the soft rhythm of sleep. Jane took a blanket off the bed and wrapped it around the woman, then silently let herself out and drifted through the streets.

Simon turned over again in the bed.

'You might as well get up,' Rosie said in a groggy voice. 'All you're doing is keeping us both awake.'

He slid out from the covers and dressed, carrying his boots downstairs. A hat, a long dark coat to cover him and he was ready. Swinegate, the Calls, past the parish church and over Timble Bridge, letting the darkness carry him.

Off in the distance, pinpricks of light showed where people were still awake in their houses. There was nothing to guide him except memory. Tricked by the night, he took two wrong turnings, blundering through grass and low bog before he found the right track.

The cottage was down there somewhere. A hundred yards away, maybe less. In the blackness it might not have existed at all.

Simon settled with his back against a tree. Sitting, thinking. Time was running out.

He was home long before first light arrived, waiting in the kitchen as Jane came downstairs.

'I need you to watch the place where Whittaker's staying. Can you find Jem?'

'He won't help now. He's taken up with one of the preachers,' she told him. 'Found religion.'

Damn it. 'Is there anyone else?'

'No one I'd trust,' Jane said. 'Why?'

'It doesn't matter.' Simon pushed his lips together and grimaced. 'We need a way to lure Whittaker out of the house.'

'Fire,' she said.

Slowly, he turned his head to look at her. 'How would we get close enough to start one without him seeing us?'

'Do it quickly.'

It might work. The images were already beginning to form in his mind.

'Come on,' Simon said, standing up.

The cooper was at work, shaping staves for his barrels. Simon selected two, dipping them in a bucket of pitch before paying the man. Jane matched him stride for stride as he walked out along Marsh Lane.

At the entrance to the track, he stopped. 'We need to be quiet. Attack him from the front and back of the house. I'll light these. We each break a window and throw them in. That will have him outside.'

Jane was silent for a moment. 'And once we have him?'

'We'll see from there.'

The man needed to die, but Simon had never been a killer. He didn't want the dark dreams that would haunt his nights.

'You take the back,' he continued. 'Be ready for him.'

Jane showed him her hand. The blade was already there, reflecting the spring sun.

'I don't know which door he'll use. If he comes out towards you, shout. I'll do the same.'

With his tinder, he lit some cotton. Seconds later, the staves were burning bright and hot. He gave her one.

'Ready?' he asked. She nodded, and they began to march.

As they drew closer, Simon felt exposed. If Whittaker had a gun . . . he pushed the thought from his head. The man used knives and cudgels, not firearms. Fifty yards, forty, thirty, twenty. The ground was dry and rutted; they hardly made any noise as they moved.

He leaned his head towards Jane. 'Run,' he whispered, and she was gone.

Simon stood in front of the house, listening for the sound of breaking glass. He had a rock in his hand.

A shattering. He stood, waiting, counting down in his head, then throwing the stone. He pushed the brand through and moved away, drawing two knives.

The flames began to take hold, flames licking and leaping. But their crackling was the only sound. Whittaker couldn't still be inside. There was too much smoke, he'd be coughing and choking.

Nothing. No shout from Jane.

Finally, Simon crept forward, lifted his foot and kicked down the door. The lock gave and it swung wide, crashing against the wall. Smoke billowed out into his face. He retched and covered his face before dashing in. The blaze covered the floor, creeping up the far wall, edging across the ceiling.

Heat pushed against his face, searing, hard as iron.

The house was empty. Whittaker had gone.

Simon ran back out and stood, gulping down the fresh air, three or four deep, sweet breaths to clear his lungs before he walked around to the back of the place. Jane was alert, turning as soon as she spotted his shadow emerging.

'We missed him,' Simon said, surprised at how dry and parched his voice sounded. Nothing would stop the blaze now. Soon only ash and cinders and crusted black beams would remain. 'It's time to go.'

At the end of the track he glanced back. Flames had made holes in the roof. The sky shimmered above the cottage. He'd thought the plan was inspired. It had been another waste of valuable time.

'What are we going to do now?' Jane asked once they were back in Leeds.

'I don't know,' he said. It had all come to nothing.

'Do you still need me?' He heard the plea under the words and shook his head.

'Not until dinner time. I have to come up with something else.'

By the time he looked again, she'd vanished.

Just a glimpse, a flash of a movement that she thought she recognized. The hocus girl? She couldn't trust herself enough to be certain. But she needed to follow, to *see*. As soon as she left Simon, she let the crowd swallow her, the shawl covering her hair as her eyes searched in the gaps between people.

Ten more paces and she felt something. The familiar crawl up her spine, a prickle. Jane pressed herself against a wall, out of the way. She needed to strip away all the noise of voices and feet and machines until they became a soft hum she could ignore and let her other senses take over. To let herself *feel*.

That way. She knew it. Up ahead that way.

No rush, nothing to make her stand out. She was at the top of Kirkgate, close to Briggate with its roar of traffic and people. She found the gaps, crossing with a few others then along Commercial Street. Just another invisible girl in the crowd.

Her heart was beating in her chest, but she felt calm, composed. Farther along, beyond Albion Street, the press of people thinned and she saw her. The hocus girl. Now she just needed the right place to ask her question.

And this time she'd make certain of an answer.

TWENTY-FIVE

Simon stood by the coal staithe, oblivious to the thunder as each wagon dropped its load into a chute.

Too many places to hide, he decided. Whittaker would have the men he'd hired scattered around the place. Every move would be another trap. There could only be one winner in a rigged game.

Hands in his pockets, he started back towards town, past the brewery. Salem Chapel stood, its door open. He ducked inside. It would be somewhere to sit for a moment and try to gather his thoughts.

A woman was cleaning, on her knees with a brush and a bucket of water, scrubbing at the floor near the altar. He sat at the back, resting against the unforgiving wood of a pew.

The cottage had been his chance to surprise Whittaker, to confront him somewhere out in the open. But that had gone. Anything else was going to be pure chance, and that was always in short supply.

Five minutes and he rose. No great idea had come to him. No divine inspiration. After the gloom inside Simon blinked as he looked into the distance. Then he pressed himself hard against the door frame.

The distant figure striding towards town from the staithe looked like Whittaker. Simon glanced back into the chapel. Luck couldn't be that generous.

*   *   *

The girl seemed to be going nowhere, to have no destination. She wandered from one street to the next. At first Jane thought she was going back to Mrs Shields's house, but she changed direction once more.

No reason to it that she could make out, unless she believed she was being followed and wanted to be certain. Fine. She'd make sure the hocus girl knew someone was behind her. She quickened her pace, drawing closer, watching the girl tense a little, then speed up.

But she could never know these streets, the courts, the yards the way Jane did. They were in her blood.

Just ten yards separated them. The hocus girl kept to the roads, where people were always passing and moving. Jane needed somewhere quieter, where no one would see or hear. Out here, a simple scream would bring people running.

She put her hand in the pocket of her dress, searching for her knife. But her fingers found the gold ring Catherine had given her. Nothing could hurt her when she was wearing it, the old woman had promised. Jane smiled. Superstition and wishes. But it couldn't hurt to put it on.

She saw her chance. The girl had strayed too far down the Head Row, beyond Vicar Lane and along Nelson Street. Millgarth lay at the bottom of the hill. No more than a handful of people on the pavement and a couple of carts with weary-looking old nags to pull them. A few more yards and they'd reach the entrance to a court with plenty of open ground beyond. Around here a cry wouldn't even make people stir.

Jane needed to time it perfectly, to make sure the hocus girl did exactly what she wanted. She judged the distance, moving a hair faster so she'd be close as they reached the opening. Her knife was out, glinting in the dull light, her boots sounding a rapid rhythm on the flagstones.

The girl started to run, but she was large and graceless, lumbering like an ox. She wasn't quick enough.

Jane's hand moved like quicksilver, slashing through skirt and stocking, slicing into Charlotte Winter's thigh. As the girl stopped, clutching at her leg, Jane caught her off-balance and tumbled her down to the ground. She stamped on the woman's hand, feeling the bones crunch and snap as a knife fell away.

It had all happened in a heartbeat; no one had even noticed. Jane brought her knife close to Charlotte Winter's cheek, close enough to shave the pale down from her skin.

'Try to scream and I'll kill you.'

The hocus girl nodded. With her left hand she cradled and pressed her broken fingers, trying to ease the pain. A low moan came from her mouth. There was blood down her dress from the cut.

Jane took hold of the girl's collar and dragged her out of sight. Just a few yards, but it still took all her strength; she was heavy. Finally they were lost in the shadows, removed from sight.

A quick search. Another knife in the girl's boot. A sock in her pocket, knotted and weighted with sand. She tossed them aside and stood, gazing down and breathing hard. The hocus girl might look defeated, but Jane wasn't fooled. She might have a trick or two left yet.

'What do you want?' Her eyes were wet with tears and her voice croaked with pain.

'The same thing I wanted before,' Jane told her. She stayed just out of reach of any sudden movement. 'But if you don't tell me, I'll kill you anyway, for what you did to Mrs Shields.'

The girl stared up at her, defiant. 'I never found your money. She wouldn't tell me where it was.'

So she wasn't completely cowed yet. Jane had to take care of that, to make her crave to give up the name of the person who'd sent her hunting for the money. She had time. She'd break the hocus girl.

'I know.' She weighed the knife in her hand then spoke slowly. 'I've never had to kill a woman before.'

'You won't this time.' The woman tried to spit at her, but it just dribbled over her lips.

'You're wagering your life on that. It's a very foolish thing to do.' She took a pace closer, seeing the doubt begin to cloud the girl's eyes. Good.

No, luck could never be that kind. As the man drew closer, Simon realized it wasn't Whittaker, just someone with a similar size and shape. Still, he waited inside the chapel until the man had passed, breathing slowly and letting his heartbeat settle.

He wanted to confront Whittaker, but he knew he was scared of doing it. The man was clever, sly. And he was brutal; he'd already proved that. Someone who killed without compunction.

Simon walked over to Holbeck, trying to piece together all the fragments of his thoughts. Two or three pieces would fit, then he'd add a fourth and everything would fall apart.

The works boomed with the metallic clang of hammers and men shouting. He stood for a moment. A furnace roared as its door swung opened. A bare-chested man shovelled in coal as the flames fought and rose.

Fire. Hard to believe that no more than a few hours had passed since he'd started the blaze at Whittaker's cottage.

'Who are you?' A hand grabbed his arm and turned him. Simon started to reach for his knife then stopped himself.

'I'm working for Mr Murray,' he yelled over the din.

'Prove it.' He had a powerful grip, squeezing hard, and a face ruined by smallpox, pitted and raw.

'Let's go and see him.'

The man kept firm hold as they marched over to the office. Murray wasn't there. At least his assistant recognized Simon, giving him the nod. The workman reddened. Before he left, Simon asked, 'Have you seen a large man here today? A stranger?'

But he simply shook his head.

No, of course not. It would be too dangerous for Whittaker to show his face again in this place. He was hidden away somewhere, biding his time until the shadows started to lengthen.

'I heard about the fire,' Rosie said. She ladled food into a bowl, steam rising, and placed it on the table. 'It was the talk of the market. No one knows how it happened.'

'He'd already gone.'

'Pity. It was a good idea.'

High, sweet laughter came from the front room. Richard's voice. Simon smiled. 'They seem happy with the tutor.'

'They haven't spent much time with him yet,' she warned, but there was a glow on her face as she spoke. 'Are you any closer to finding Whittaker?'

'No.' He ate, but he hardly noticed the taste of the food.

It was simply something to keep him going for the rest of the day. 'Has Jane been back? I told her dinner time.'

'It's early yet,' Rosie told him. 'She'll be here.'

If he lived to be a hundred he'd never understand Jane. Yet still he trusted her with his life. Her and Rosie. The only two he could rely on for anything. But waiting wasn't easy. He wanted her here, to try and plan, to do *something*.

The only certainty was that he wouldn't be at the coal staithe at sunset. The best thing would be if Whittaker never showed his face there, either.

He paged through the *Mercury*. The Dodd affair still held the front page, but the focus had shifted. Now it was all in London, as members of Parliament began asking questions about the conduct of the Home Office. Why were they spying on Englishmen? Why were they using agents to try and incite an uprising? The wars were over, and they were demanding answers. So far, they'd heard none.

The tendrils had stretched so far and so high that it seemed impossible to believe he was the cause of it. All because he wanted to free Davey Ashton. Now, according to one writer, it was possible that the government might fall. One small action with some mighty ripples. It stunned him. He'd pursued one thing, never imagining what else it might bring. Was he so blinkered in the way he saw the world? Was his view too narrow and parochial? But Leeds was what he knew, and he couldn't change that. Even Curzon's resignation from the bench had seemed like huge power toppling to the ground.

His questions, his actions. And Mudie's words. George would be satisfied. His articles had pulled the trigger and caused the blast. He'd written a story that might yet change England; he'd proved the power of the page.

The squeak of the old hinges on the front door brought him back to the here and now, then the tread of boots in the hall before Jane entered. There was a flush across her face. Not from running, this was something else, something deeper. A young man? No. Jane was someone who'd always keep her distance. Her heart would stay locked for the whole of her life. The nearest he'd glimpsed of tenderness and caring in Jane was when he saw her at Mrs Shields's house.

'What is it?' he asked. 'Have you found anything?'

She simply blinked and shook her head, reaching to tear off a hunk of bread.

'How do we find him?' Simon said. 'He's somewhere in Leeds. He's close. He has to be.'

'Who does he know, apart from Curzon?' Rosie asked.

'Nobody I can think of,' he replied after a moment. 'That's the problem. There's Allston and his men, but I can't see him waiting there. They'd believe he was worried.'

She stirred the pot, watching the food shift under the spoon, before raising her head again. 'Where's the place he's least likely to go? Somewhere no one would expect.'

'I don't know.' A thought struck him. 'Davey and Emily's house?'

'It has to be worth trying,' Rosie said. 'What else do you have?'

'Nothing at all,' he agreed as he stood. 'Absolutely nothing.'

And it would be better than sitting here with thoughts falling around him.

'If he's there . . .' Briggate teemed with people and carts and horses, the creaking sound of wheels turning. Simon tasted soot on his tongue as he walked. The sky was thick with it. 'If he's there, I don't want them hurt.'

'He'll kill them without thinking,' Jane said. 'You know that.'

That was the problem. *If* Whittaker was even there. It was one more desperate gamble, probably pointless. But this was what it had come to. Simon glanced around. The man could be watching them right now, gazing through a window and smiling at Simon's stupidity.

They crossed the Head Row.

'Wait a minute,' Simon said and ducked in to Mudie's printing shop. A minute later, the two of them came out.

'I don't know what I can do,' Mudie complained. His face was taut and wary.

'It's simple, George. You just knock on the door and announce yourself,' Simon told him. 'That's all.'

'What if—?'

'After that, just stand back. Stay out of harm's way.'

'If I didn't owe you for the Dodd story . . .' the man said.

'But you do. And the odds are there's nothing wrong here.'

Across Lady Bridge, out along Mabgate. Simon walked in silence, trying to find a plan. If Whittaker was there. *If. If.* Probably Emily would open the door, stare at them in surprise and invite them in. Davey would be sitting in his chair, reading. Everything the way it used to be.

Jane trailed ten paces behind. He knew her eyes would be searching for any familiar face, any sudden movement.

A few yards ahead the road turned. Simon stopped. From there, anyone in the Ashtons' cottage could see them. He turned to Jane.

'Go through the woods. Stay out of sight behind the house. You know what to do. If it's clear, I'll whistle.'

She nodded, pulled the shawl over her hair and vanished into the undergrowth.

'What about me?' Mudie asked.

'Give me a minute, then walk along. Go to the door and knock,' Simon told him. 'After that, you stand back.'

For a moment he thought Mudie might refuse.

'All right,' he agreed.

Simon grinned and clapped him on the shoulder. 'Don't worry, George. You'll be safe enough. Remember, one minute.'

He drew two of his knives and started moving into the shadows. Time to start hoping.

She moved unseen. A tangle of trees, thickets of bushes to hide her. An old, beaten track that animals used. Soon she found a place where she could watch, tucked out of sight.

The knife waited in her hand, ready.

The hocus girl had given her the name. She lay in the dirt, blood seeping from the cut in her leg, trying to ease her broken fingers. Jane stood over her, caressing the woman's cheek with the flat of her blade. The tiniest prick of the point at the edge of the eye, lightly tracing down her cheek. So sharp, so soft she didn't even feel it until the sting of the blood began. Then she howled.

Then she believed.

But still she hesitated. Her eyes were filled with fear. Scared of what would happen if she spoke, terrified of how it might end if she didn't. All the bravado she'd displayed the last time withered to nothing.

Now she realized that Jane really would kill her, that her life could end here in the dirt and mud of this place. And she knew her secret wasn't worth that. In the end she'd given up the name. She whispered it so softly that Jane wasn't even sure she'd heard it. Yet it hung there in the air between them.

'If you're lying . . .' She brought the knife close enough to touch the hocus girl's eyelashes.

'I'm not.' She hardly dared to speak, not even breathing, holding herself rigid until Jane stood.

'You're going to leave Leeds today.'

'Yes, yes.' But by then she'd have agreed to anything.

Jane watched her scuttle away, crawling, turning her head. At the entrance to the street she pushed herself up, tested the weight on her leg and limped off, cradling her fingers. She'd never see Charlotte Winter again, she knew that. The girl was broken, she'd given up the name and she didn't dare stay.

The name. It was impossible to believe. But inside, she knew it was true.

How, though? She'd never told anyone where she'd hidden her money. She'd kept the knowledge locked away. But somehow . . .

She'd been betrayed. For greed. And the person who'd done it knew the price for that.

She wasn't sure how long she stood there. She sensed the pattern of light and shade shift around her. Inside, though, the blackness was rising and her heart felt as if it was made of lead.

Her eyes blurred and she brushed at them angrily with the back of her hand. Then she began to walk.

Somewhere close by, a bird sang in a tree. She tightened her grip on the knife. Not from fear of Whittaker. He was just a man, and one died as well as the next. She listened; it was quiet enough for her to hear the footsteps on the gravel of the path and the hollow knock on the door.

She tensed, watching the back door of the cottage, ready to run towards it. But for long seconds there was nothing. No one yelling. Then Simon's low whistle. Jane put the knife away and walked to the front of the cottage.

*   *   *

'I don't understand,' Emily said. First she looked at Jane, then Mudie, and finally Simon. 'Why would you think he was here, of all places?'

'Because I've run out of anywhere else to look,' Simon told her, 'and this was so unlikely, it was worth trying.' He stared at Davey. The man hadn't moved from his chair, but he wore a wry smile. 'How are you feeling?'

'Stronger by the day,' he answered. 'Different, but I've told you that before.' He waved at the shelves full of books. 'Maybe it's time to clear out the past, for all the good it's managed to do.'

'You taught me. You made me think.'

'There are other things I can do. Something useful for a change.'

Simon opened his mouth to speak, then thought better of it. Davey had to find his own way now. He'd done what he could to help. He tipped his hat to Emily.

'I'm sorry. We shouldn't have frightened you. You're safe. No need to worry. He won't be coming out here.'

TWENTY-SIX

Wrong. Wrong. The word pounded in his skull. Wrong. He'd wasted time going to the house when he could have been searching in better places.

Where, though? They didn't exist.

Mudie had lingered at the cottage to talk to Davey. He probably sensed another newspaper article in the conversation. But Simon hurried back into Leeds, Jane by his side.

There was nowhere else left to try. Even his wildest shot had gone wide. And now he had no idea where to find Whittaker. The man would have heard about the fire. He'd stay out of sight, not showing himself until evening arrived.

Simon knew he couldn't go down to the staithe tonight. He might as well ask the man to kill him. But the pull of it, the chance to settle things . . . he shook his head to dislodge the idea.

Jane hadn't spoken since they left the Ashtons' house. She kept pace with him, but she was far away in her own thoughts.

'Where is he?' Simon asked and she turned her head to him.

'I don't know.' But she sounded as if it barely mattered to her. Her mind was elsewhere.

As soon as he opened the door he could hear the boys playing upstairs. High, raucous voices at odds with each other. This was what he lived for, his sons alive, spirited. It was what he needed to remind himself not to take pointless chances.

Rosie picked up the note on the table. 'It came a little while after you left.'

The man you want has been wandering around up here.
Blenkinsop

'Who brought it?'

'A man,' Rosie answered. 'I've never seen him before.'

'Whittaker was up at the coalfield.' He glanced at Jane. 'We need to go.'

'Simon, he's probably gone again by now,' Rosie told him. 'That arrived almost an hour ago.'

'Then maybe we'll find him on his way back.'

Jane followed, through the crunching dust of the coal staithe and up along the track by the railway. Somewhere in the distance the train was running; she could feel the vibration through the soles of her boots.

Simon led the way, pushing branches aside, moving swiftly up the hillside. She followed, eyes watching everything. It was impossible to be quiet here. Twigs crackled and broke underfoot as they walked.

She had no feeling that Whittaker was anywhere close, but that didn't mean a thing. Jane felt as if all her senses were broken. The name the hocus girl spoke had shaken her. It had upended her world. Simon wanted Whittaker. She needed answers to the questions reeling in her head.

Jane turned the gold ring on her finger as she walked, her hand moving without thought. She felt as if it kept her from floating away, that it helped her retain some small control of herself even as she ached to scream.

She placed one foot in front of the other, stopping as the train passed on the other side of an embankment. The noise deafened her, continuing as wagon after wagon rolled by, an endless procession of sound, louder and darker than anything in her nightmares.

Simon had carried on, relentless; she had to hurry to catch up, cresting a hill to see a dark, pitted plain ahead. It stretched all the way out to the horizon. Sheds stood in the distance, and smoke rose from a tall chimney. Men moved around, some with axes, others pulling small carts.

'Be careful,' Simon said. 'They told me last time. You need to watch where you step.'

She stood outside the office. A girl invisible as people carried on their work. She saw men and children going underground, disappearing as if the earth was eating them. Down into absolute blackness. A girl cried and a man smacked her hard and dragged her along with him.

Jane stirred as Simon returned. He looked haggard, the skin tight around his mouth.

'They chased him off. We've wasted our time again.' He sighed. 'Not that we had anywhere else to try.'

By the time they reached the path she felt as if she was coated in coal. The fine, dark dust itched against her skin and fouled her mouth. All from no more than a few minutes. What was it like for those who worked here? And the ones who went down to mine the coal and haul it through the tunnels? How could they ever escape it?

She glanced towards Leeds. From here, the thin haze that covered the town seemed to hang suspended in the air. Above it was a clear sky with a few high clouds. Around three in the afternoon, she judged. The day was wasting away.

She wanted to be back down there, to march through the streets, to open the door and have her reckoning. She'd have her truth. Her hand moved towards the knife, feeling her ring rub against the hilt. It was comfort, security. It was revenge.

Every way he turned he ended up against a wall. Simon's arms swung by his sides and he sweated inside the heavy wool suit.

Not from the heat but . . . what? Fear? No doubt about that. He needed to make an end to this. To complete the job he'd undertaken for Murray and Blenkinsop.

The mine manager had been blunt. 'My men have better things to do than chase him away from here. He was snooping around the locomotive again with his bloody notebook in his hand. We're paying you to take care of this.'

'He left. He took the London coach, got off in Wakefield and came back.'

'Then make sure he leaves again.' Blenkinsop glared at him. 'And I don't want him to return. Ever. Understood?'

A simple enough message. Now he just had to make sure it happened.

He'd been an hour too late in Middleton. Ample time for Whittaker to return to Leeds, to hide himself away once more. But in town with thousands of people, you could lose yourself in the middle of a crowd.

'We might as well go home,' Simon said. He felt weary. It had all come to nothing. Chasing around town, hunting a shadow.

'Are we going to this meeting he wants?' Jane asked.

'Not unless you have an urge to sacrifice yourself. Let him wait all night if he wants.'

'He'll come again tomorrow.'

'I hope he does. As long as he doesn't bring the hired men.' He rubbed a hand down his face.

'He might put word around that you're a coward.'

Simon shrugged. 'Let him. It doesn't matter.' He meant it. People would think what they wanted. He wasn't going to be a martyr to please them. 'Give them a few days and they'll forget, anyway.'

'Do you need me again today?'

Where else could they look? he wondered. 'No,' he said finally. 'I don't. Why?'

'There's something I have to do,' Jane said.

'What?' he asked, but she didn't answer. Her face was set, determined. Her thoughts had already left him behind. Whatever it was, she'd face it alone. He wanted to help, but she'd never allow him close enough for that.

They crossed the staithe. Simon stayed alert in case Whittaker and his men had arrived early. But it was empty. Noise and smoke came from Sykes's brewery, the smells of hops and malt and soot all mingling as he breathed.

Across the bridge, to the corner of Swinegate.

'Watch out,' he reminded her. 'Whittaker wants you dead, too.'

'I haven't forgotten.'

'The hocus girl, what was her name?' he asked suddenly. 'Did you ever find her?'

'Charlotte Winter.' Jane's voice was flat. She looked up at him. Her eyes were empty, her expression bland. 'Don't worry, we won't see her again.'

'All done, then?'

But she'd turned away, pulling up the shawl and turning into the invisible girl.

She'd already forgotten the ruined earth of the coalfield, put it out of her mind. All that existed was this moment and the hatred and anger she'd tamped down all afternoon. Now she could bring it back to the boil.

The door was locked. She rapped on the wood, kicked it, but it wasn't going to yield for her. Jane heard an old man laugh and turned.

'What?' The knife was in her hand and he backed away a pace, fear pulling at his face.

'Not heard, have you?' he said.

'Heard what?'

'Way I was told, someone came about noon and told her summat. She kicked everyone out, then she locked and barred the door.'

'She's still inside?'

'Mebbe.'

She turned to stare at the place. Mrs Rigton's alehouse. Mary Rigton, the woman who'd let her sleep on a bench before the embers of the fire when she was younger. Who'd given her scraps of food and helped her stay alive.

The same woman who somehow knew her secrets, who'd wanted to steal her money. The woman who'd had Catherine Shields beaten.

Why? She didn't understand it. Jane would have given her the money if she'd asked and never questioned why. But this . . . this was betrayal.

The back entrance was locked, not giving an inch as she put her shoulder against it. But there was a small window. It was too narrow for a man, but she'd be able to squeeze through.

Her knife blade rasped against the catch, then slipped. Again and again. Jane wiped her palm against her dress and tried once more. Finally it stayed. Pressing down, she could feel the old lock starting to ease and give. Just a small amount, a start, then it stuck.

She paused, never letting go of the hilt as she breathed deeply and rested her muscles. Another effort and it gave a little more. A judder as it moved and she held her breath. It caught. She twisted and turned the knife in the opening, trying for some kind of purchase to finish the job. Sweat cascaded down her forehead and ran into her eyes.

So close. So near. Jane moved her arms to ease out the cramp.

One final effort. All her strength and the catch popped open with a dull sound. She reached for the window, tugging at it. The wood was old and stiff, warped in its frame. She took out the knife again, sliding it into the gap, using all her strength to try and tease it open.

The woman inside must know. Jane hoped she did. She wanted Mary Rigton to understand that she was coming.

Finally the window released, springing wide with a thin waft of air as it passed her face. She pulled herself up, twisting to the side, gripping the frame to steady herself. Her head was through. Her breasts pushed against the frame and she bit her lip hard and ignored the pressure and the pain. Then she was inside, lowering herself slowly, standing and dusting herself down as she let her eyes adjust to the gloom.

A storeroom, unused, with empty boxes and cobwebs. She heard something move across the floor, the scraping of claws on dirt. A rat. Arms out, she felt her way across the small space until she touched the door, feeling for the latch.

At first it didn't want to move. She tugged hard and it lifted. Slowly, Jane pulled the door back, waiting for the hinge to squeak, but it opened silently and she was in the empty bar. A fug of smoke and smell of stale beer filled the room.

It was warm, shutters closed and barred, door locked. Exactly the way she remembered it from all those winter nights she'd slept here, back when it felt like security. Without a sound, she moved around, touching tables and benches. So familiar, but so strange now. This would be the last time she'd ever come here.

Jane reached the stairs, looked up, and hesitated. How had kindness become hatred? However much she tried, she'd never understand that. Was she too stupid? Was that it?

With the knife in her hand, she placed her foot on the first step and started to climb.

In the hallway, Simon closed his eyes and let out a slow breath as he locked the door. Home. Safety. But he'd managed nothing today. Nothing at all. Then voices clamoured in the kitchen, a scramble of feet, and his sons rushed out to meet him. He knelt, arms encircling them, tickling and wrestling with them until they squirmed away, laughing and squealing.

Rosie stood at the entrance to the kitchen, a look of pure relief on her face. With her hair tucked under a cap, and wearing an old cotton dress, she could have been a servant. He stood and embraced her.

'No luck in Middleton?' she asked.

'We missed him again.' He guided her back into the kitchen and poured himself a mug of beer, washing the frustrations of the day away as he drank.

'You're not . . .' she began, and he could hear the fear in her voice.

Simon shook his head. He wasn't going to meet Whittaker and his men tonight. Not for pride, not for honour or any of the foolish ideas that poisoned men's minds. Not with all he possessed here.

'He can wait until tomorrow.'

'I was terrified you'd changed your mind.'

'I was tempted for a while. But I'm not going anywhere.'

Still during the evening, he wandered upstairs time after time, peering out at Swinegate through the darkened bedroom window. In their room, Richard and Amos snuffled and coughed as they slept.

The street was quiet. Darkness had come. Whittaker would

have left the coal staithe. Where was he now? Sleeping? Satisfied? Something would happen in the morning. The man still wanted his revenge. By now it would be raging inside him.

'Come to bed, Simon,' Rosie said. 'It's late.'

'I know.' Finally he sighed and slid under the blanket. He knew he wouldn't sleep. But lying here with his wife by his side was much better than gazing into the empty darkness.

TWENTY-SEVEN

'**Y**ou found a way in, girl.' The voice was like a rook's caw. 'That old window in the storeroom?'

'Yes,' Jane said. The shutters were open upstairs, letting in the night, just enough to heighten the shadows and glint on the knife in Mrs Rigton's lap. She was sitting in the far corner of the room, utterly still and composed.

'The girl told you.' It wasn't a question, not quite a statement.

'I didn't give her any choice.' She took a step closer, still ten feet away from the woman. 'How did you know about the money?'

'Do you remember one night when you came here, soaked right through? It wasn't long after you started working for Westow.'

She'd forgotten that. It happened before she started living with Simon and Rosie. Rain had fallen all day, so much that the streets were awash with it, a river flowing down the middle of Briggate. She was cold all the way to her bones, shivering with it. Water dripped from her dress and her hair. Mary Rigton had fed her hot broth, banked up the fire to keep her warm during the night and sat with her into the small hours as she shuddered and her teeth chattered, her body beyond control.

'I do.'

'You had a fever, started saying all sorts of things. About your mother. About a man.' She paused. 'About the place you hid your money.'

Now she understood. She'd said it without knowing, released everything and the woman had heard it all. Jane tightened her grip on the knife.

'You waited a long time.'

'I've kept my eye on you. I knew you'd do well. You've been earning plenty. It must be a pretty penny by now. And I needed the right person to do it for me.'

'The hocus girl.'

'Hocus girl?' Mrs Rigton cocked her head, then shrugged. 'She was obedient and she was greedy.'

'And when it wasn't there?'

'I thought about where else you might have hidden it. You trust Catherine Shields. More than you ever trusted me.' She spat the words bitterly.

'So you sent the girl there.'

'For all the good it did.'

'The money was in the house. Not ten feet from her.' It could do no harm to say it now. The words would never leave this room.

'It was?' Mary Rigton's eyes narrowed as her head jerked up. 'How much is there?'

'Enough.' That was the only answer she was going to give. Another step towards her.

'What did you do to the girl?'

'You'll never see her again.' Let her feel the fear rise. But Mrs Rigton's face showed no emotion at all.

'What are you going to do now?'

'Stand up,' Jane ordered.

The woman shook her head. 'If you're going to kill me, you'll have to do it while I sit here.'

'Put the knife on the floor.'

Mrs Rigton let it clatter on the boards. Her fingers were bony, and the way the light caught her face she looked like a crone. Ancient, past her time to die.

'There,' she said as she rested her hands on the arms of the chair. 'Now, how are you going to do it? Fast or slow? Are you going to make me pay? That's what you came for, isn't it?'

'Why did you do it?' That was the question she'd come to ask. But the only answer was the woman's slow smirk. 'Why?'

But she might as well have talked to the air.

'Stand up.'

The woman didn't move. Jane grabbed her by the front of her

dress, feeling the fabric tear as the dragged Mrs Rigton to her
feet. A body so light that she seemed no more than bones inside
a sack of skin.

But sly. The woman let herself slide down, then rose back up
quickly, the top of her skull crashing into Jane's chin. She went
spinning back, tasting the blood that was filling her mouth.

'You're a stupid girl. You always were.'

Jane had dropped her knife. Tears ran from her eyes, blurring
her sight until she could barely see. Mary Rigton ran at her,
sending her crashing into the plaster wall.

'I was doing this before you were born, girl. You don't come
here threatening me. I'll have you under the ground before
morning.'

Simon felt an arm around his waist, then warmth as Rosie pressed
against his back.

'How long have you been standing there?' she asked.

'I don't know,' he answered. It was a lie. He'd spent most of
the night by the window, watching, wondering.

'You've been thinking about Whittaker.'

No answer was needed.

'Simon . . .' she said.

He put his hand over hers. 'It's not regret,' he told her. 'Nothing
like that.' It was mostly true.

'It's Saturday today, the tutor won't be coming.'

Was it? He'd lost track of the days somehow, they blended
into one another. 'I don't understand.'

'Richard and Amos can play with Mrs Fulton's boys down the
street.'

'No,' he said, but she continued as if he hadn't spoken.

'I can work with you. He won't be expecting me.'

Rosie knew this job. And she was deadly, she'd proved that;
she had killed a man once, someone who would have murdered
her. But she'd never encountered someone like Whittaker.

'I—'

'With three of us, he won't have a chance,' she said.

'I don't know where Jane is. I didn't hear her come home.'

'She'll be here,' Rosie said with certainty. 'She won't let you
down.'

He hoped she was right. Unless . . . Whittaker could have found her. Or the business she had might have proved too much for her. Even with her skills, all her concentration, she was still young. She could be foolish. She wasn't as strong as she believed.

The light was growing, gauzy under the haze that glowered over Leeds. He could see men and women starting to move along the street, slow and insubstantial as ghosts.

He dressed, watching Rosie as she slid a cotton dress over her linen. He still loved her after all these years. No once could ever know him so well, understand him and forgive him. From the first time he'd seen her, sitting by the side of the road and staring at the signpost she couldn't read, he'd never wanted anyone else. Without trying, she'd captured him completely. And then Richard and Amos arrived. Between the three of them, he had everything a man could desire.

She pinned up her hair and tucked it under a cap, assessing her appearance in the mirror, then smiled at her reflection.

The boys ran like dogs let off the lead, roaring into the Fulton house. Simon grinned. The pleasure of other boys for company. They'd be safe there.

As they walked towards Briggate, Rosie asked, 'Search together or apart?'

'Apart. We can cover more ground.' He turned and faced her. 'If you see him, keep your distance. Watch where he goes. Don't confront him. Please.'

'And will you do the same?'

'Yes.' He dragged the word out of himself. 'Let's meet in front of the Moot Hall in' – he took out his pocket watch – 'an hour. At nine.'

'What about Jane?' Rosie asked. 'Where is she?'

All he could do was shake his head. This wasn't like her. He was worried now. She'd been so quiet lately, so withdrawn since she told them about the money and the way Mrs Shields had been beaten.

He'd go and see Catherine Shields. She might have some answers. He needed Jane.

'Let's hope she's fine.'

*　　*　　*

The woman had the strength of desperation, battering and clawing at Jane's face. All she could do was try to defend herself, pushed back tight against the wall. With a knife . . . but that was on the ground, out of her reach. It might as well have been on the other side of the world.

She blinked once more and her sight cleared. Mary Rigton's small fist caught the corner of her mouth and she tasted more blood. If she stayed still she was going to die. The woman's eyes were narrow with fury. Years of it. She came again, nails out this time, raking down the inside of Jane's arm. She pushed, putting all her strength behind it, sending Mrs Rigton spinning back until her boots finally gripped.

The woman lowered her head and came rushing again. Jane was ready this time, standing her ground. She tensed, grabbed the woman's neck, twisted it hard and used her momentum to throw her down to the wooden floor. She sprawled, her dress ridden up to show pale calves like sticks, the breath knocked out of her for a moment. Long enough for Jane to duck down and pick up her knife. Her fingers tightened around the hilt. She had to spit out blood before she could speak. 'Is this what you really want?'

The woman was too full of anger. She'd never surrender. Her right arm moved, inching away towards something out of sight. 'How it's got to be,' she said. 'You or me.'

Jane nodded. There were knots of pain across her face, she couldn't breathe through her nose. She opened her mouth and gulped in air.

'Get up,' she said. 'Now.'

Mary Rigton had listened to her secrets. She'd used them. But she'd used people her entire life, everyone she'd ever known. Coldness and violence ran in her blood. Yet she'd shown something else once, letting a girl sleep by the drying fire every night for a winter, giving her the leftover scraps of food to help her stay alive.

The woman scrambled to her feet. Her grey hair hung loose and wild. For a second she looked withered, powerless. And then, from somewhere, a blade appeared in her hand and her mouth curled into a hateful smile.

'Yes,' she said, her voice cracked. 'Yes.'

Jane didn't give the woman chance to strike. She felt flesh

yield as she drove her knife in all the way to the hilt then twisted it inside. She watched as Mary Rigton's eyes sprang wide and her mouth opened. Heard the empty sound as the woman let her weapon fall. Held her as she started to slump. Jane pulled her blade out.

'I'd have let you live,' she whispered. 'All you had to do was ask.'

But it was too late for words now. Too late for anything.

The daylight through the windows fell on her shoulders. She sat on the top step, staring at the corpse on the floor. Flies were gathering, dozens of them buzzing around. She needed to leave, but for a long time she couldn't bring herself to move.

'Goodness, child. Goodness.'

Jane had come here, running through the early morning streets, keeping her head bowed so no one could see her. She felt as if a hand was squeezing her heart so it might burst at any moment. She rushed through Green Dragon Yard, then the space in the wall until she was standing at Catherine Shields's door and believed she could begin to breathe again.

A feeble knock, and then the woman's good arm was around her, drawing her inside, cradling her and inspecting her face.

'I . . .' Jane started to speak, then the words froze inside her.

'Hush now. It doesn't matter.' For a woman with one arm in a sling, she moved deftly. Put some liquid on a cloth, then wiped the wounds. It stung, but Jane never flinched. She closed her eyes, letting herself drift on a river of darkness and forgetting. Then the woman was putting something in her hands. A mug.

'Drink it,' Catherine told her. 'You have blood on your dress.'

Dark spots and splatters across the faded cotton. Jane brushed at them with the back of her hand.

'What happened, child? Your face, your arms.'

It came out in short bursts and long silences, as if she was living the night once again.

'Finally I climbed back out of the window and tried to close it again, but it wouldn't push all the way in. Then I ran here.' Another silence. Helplessly, she stared at Mrs Shields. 'Why did she do it? She wouldn't tell me.'

'Greed, child.' The woman's voice was soft and calming.

She drew Jane close, arm around her shoulders. 'I've known Mary Rigton for a long time. Before she was married, although that was over quick enough. She always had a grasping heart.'

'But . . . the things she did for me. I don't understand.'

'People are made of many different shades.' She paused for a second. 'We're all a mixture. Even her.'

'But she told that girl to come and beat you and try to get my money.'

'That's all over now. I'm mending.' Jane felt the hand stroking her hair. 'You will, too.'

She started as she heard the boots on the flagstones outside, then the urgent fist hammering on the wood. Jane stood, pulling out the knife as she shrank towards the corner. Mrs Shields moved softly and gracefully, opening the door a hair's breadth, then wider. Simon.

'I—' He spotted Jane, taking in everything at a glance. 'I was worried about you.'

'She'll be fine,' Catherine said. 'Give her time. She's strong.'

He nodded, then turned to her. 'We're hunting for Whittaker,' he said. 'Rosie's there, too. We have to finish this. But . . .' She felt his eyes on her. 'Are you strong enough?'

'I'm coming,' Jane told him.

Through the pain in her body she could still feel Whittaker's touch, the hand squeezing her breast until it hurt. The viciousness in his eyes.

At the door, she turned. 'I'll come back later.'

'See you do, child.' Mrs Shields smiled. 'And make sure you wear the ring.'

She searched the area from Vicar Lane down to Sheepscar Beck. Walking, looking at faces. Trying not to feel, to keep it all at bay, locked up and out of sight and memory. Catherine was right; the wounds on her flesh would heal. None of them were bad. It was the ones insides that might fester. She'd never killed a woman before. Even the hocus girl, she'd hurt her, terrified her, but she'd let her live and crawl away.

Someone who'd saved her once, and then betrayed her . . . she couldn't understand. How could anyone do that?

Jane felt a prickling up her spine, not even sure why. She pulled the shawl closer over her hair, stopping and letting her eyes rove across the people on the street. There, fifty yards ahead. He moved with his usual swagger, pushing through the crowd. Whittaker.

She was careful to keep her distance, far enough to vanish in a heartbeat if he suspected anything. Somewhere, a shrill steam whistle sounded. The man kept moving, along and along, on to Duncan Street, between the women gazing in the shop windows near the Bottom of Briggate and crossed the bridge.

Jane stood, watching as he strode down Salem Place, beyond the chapel and brewery. Towards the coal staithe.

'She looked . . .'

'What?' Rosie asked. As she spoke, her gaze moved over the crowd passing the Moot Hall. 'Looked like what?'

'She's been hurt. Cuts on her face and arms.'

'Is she all right? Who did it?'

'I don't know. But it isn't that. It's how she seemed . . . as if she could have shattered into pieces on the floor.'

That was the only way he could describe it. Not just the wounds or the blood on her dress. Those were bad enough. She'd been in a brutal fight, most probably a deadly one. But her face showed shock and sorrow, as if it was only sheer will that held her together. She hadn't said a word as Simon explained what he needed from her. She listened, then walked off as soon as he finished.

'We'll need to take care of her,' he said.

'Do you think she'll let us?' Rosie asked.

No. Of course she wouldn't. Because that would mean letting someone inside, being fragile and open. He could only hope that Catherine Shields would find a way beyond the wall Jane had built.

She appeared out of nowhere. Not a sign of her on Briggate, then she was next to them, panting, out of breath.

'I saw him. Going down to the staithe.'

Simon glanced at his wife. 'Then we know where to go.'

They walked together, the three of them abreast, not speaking, each of them locked inside their own thoughts. Simon became aware of smaller footsteps hurrying to keep pace.

'Where are you going?'

Jem. Wearing clothes that almost fitted and shoes only a size too big. Washed and scrubbed until his face shone, hair brushed and neat. A little more to him, as if someone had been feeding him regularly. And a stack of tracts clutched in his arms.

'Business,' Simon told him. 'Nothing for you today. You're safer out of it.'

The boy was torn between duty and curiosity, he could see that. But after a few yards he dropped back. Just a look, the smallest encouragement, and he'd come running, Simon knew. But he was careful not to glance over his shoulder. This was going to be no place for bruised innocence.

TWENTY-EIGHT

Whittaker would still be at the staithe. Simon felt it in his core. Back to visit last night's triumph when Simon Westow had been too petrified to show his face. The man would relish the opportunity to gloat once more.

He watched Jane. She tried to hold her body taut, to ignore the pain. The wounds on her face stood out in sharp relief. What had she done? Her eyes stared straight ahead as they walked down Salem Place. The chapel door was open to those wanting to find God, the brewery scents wafted and rose up to the skies.

'We're going to have to spread out.' His mouth was dry. He swallowed. 'Jane, you go to the left. You to the right,' he told Rosie. God knew that he would have loved to send her back, to ask her to think of their sons and not take any risks. But he'd never say it. She missed all this, the excitement. The hunt. At least there was a shimmer of fear on her face. What worried him was the hunger in her eyes.

'What do we do when we find him?' she asked.

'We try to keep pushing him back. There's a path.'

He'd said it, but Simon didn't believe it would work. Whittaker wanted this confrontation. He'd stand his ground. He had something to prove.

'Ready?' he asked. He took the knife from his belt, a second from his boot, and began to walk.

He was aware of them, moving wide like a fan. But he kept a straight path, boots crushing the coal dust. Men were working, shovelling coal on to waiting carts. They paid him no mind, as if he wasn't there at all.

At the far side of the staithe, a figure turned. Broad, tall, the bright light picking out the thin, raw line of the healing wound on his face. He pushed back his coat, took a cudgel and a knife from his belt, weighing them lightly in his hands.

No need for words. Simon kept moving, one foot then the other, staring at Whittaker. The man was smiling as if he'd already won.

Simon halted and let out a high whistle. From the corner of his eyes he saw Jane edging closer. Then, appearing on the other side, Rosie.

Simon began to walk again, slowly, as the women moved forward. Whittaker was looking from one to the other to the next, gauging the danger.

'A woman and a girl?' He laughed. 'That's the best you can do?'

Simon didn't reply. He kept his steady pace, tightening his grip on the knives, until he stood six feet away from Whittaker.

'One final chance.'

The man snorted. 'To do what? Run off?'

'There's no shame in retreating from a battle you can't win.'

'What makes you think I can't beat you?' Whittaker said with a grin.

'Because I know these two.' The words came easily, calmly. 'Once it starts, they won't let you live.'

'Is that right?' He feinted towards Rosie, blade slicing through air. She didn't flinch, didn't move. But Jane took a step closer. Whittaker turned sharply to face her. Rosie edged two short paces to the side until she was behind him.

As he moved his head to keep an eye on Rosie, Jane darted forward, burying her knife deep in his arm and pulling back before he could react.

Blood began to seep through the man's coat, the dull, dark patch growing on the cloth.

'I warned you.' Another step forward, close enough to see the sweat appear on Whittaker's forehead. His eyes moved frantically as the blood seeped down his sleeve. 'It's your choice. You can give up or you can die.'

The man turned and bolted.

At first Simon was too stunned to move. It was wrong. Whittaker was supposed to be a fighter. But at the very first wound, he'd turned tail. The bully was nothing more than a coward as soon as the advantage was torn from him.

He looked at Rosie, then Jane, smiled as he shook his head in astonishment and disgust, and began to follow Whittaker. Steady, no rush. Let him wear himself out while they pursued.

Single file up the trail, Simon in front, Rosie at the back, keeping close watch in case Whittaker had hidden himself, trying to surprise them.

But the man was running for his life. A branch cracked as the man blundered up the hill. Simon felt the pounding of boots on the dry, packed earth. Let him run all the way back to London.

She'd drawn blood. Jane had seen her chance, slid forward and away again before he realized what had happened.

But she hadn't done it. It wasn't her in this place, walking along the pale dirt of the track. That was another person. She was still in Mary Rigton's beershop, sitting on the stair and gazing at the woman's corpse. Or she was with Catherine Shields, trying to push away the weight pressing down so hard on her head.

The girl here was an imposter, someone who looked like her, moved like her. Not an invisible girl, just a ghost with her body. She shuddered and pulled the shawl closer around her shoulders.

They were close to the top now. Simon felt the change in the air. A little sharper, a breeze stirring through the leaves. Then the ground began to shake and the noise came. The locomotive.

Simon kept on moving, sensing the others behind him, Rosie's prickle of fear, and Jane . . . but he had no idea what was in her mind.

Whittaker was thirty yards ahead of them, picking his way across the ground. His right arm hung useless by his side. The whole sleeve was soaked with blood; Jane had hurt him badly.

Simon waited until the last wagon had passed, the sound slipping away as the train turned the corner.

'Take care up here,' he warned Rosie. 'It's dangerous ground.'

'Where's he going?' she asked.

'I don't think he knows. Away, that's all.' The animal instinct, to run, to survive. 'We'll spread out a little and push him towards the winding wheel.' He pointed at the building on the crest of the rise.

Whittaker turned, feral panic on his face. Wild, hopeless, pulled on by the urge to survive. But he'd seen the truth of the man down at the staithe. The Bow Street Runner, the government agent. All of it stripped away to show a frightened little boy inside a man's body.

It didn't matter any more. The time had come for him to pay what he owed. Simon began to march over the open ground. Whittaker saw him coming and tried to hurry away. But he seemed weary now, every step sluggish and slow. How much blood had he lost from that wound?

A door slammed up at the mine office, the sound carried on the wind. Blenkinsop stood there, hands folded across his chest as he watched the scene, before calling two colliers to him. Whittaker saw it, too, slowly raising his head for a second and shading his eyes with his good arm. He was trapped.

Just twenty yards separated them now.

'You and me, thief-taker,' he called out. 'What do you say?' A challenge made from fear and snatched by the breeze.

'What do I say?' Simon shouted. 'Henry Wise. Margaret Wood.' He kept walking.

'Nobodies. They don't matter.'

'But they do.'

He was aware of Rosie and Jane. Standing with their knives drawn in case Whittaker ran towards them.

Ten yards away. Five.

The man's face was drawn with pain. The arm of his coat was sodden. Blood dripped down; his right hand was red with it.

'You can still give up.'

'What? And hang?' He shook his head.

'At least it'll be an honest death. That's more than you offered them.'

He saw Whittaker's body tense, the toes of his boots digging into the ground. He'd stopped to try and gather his strength, that was all. To give himself one final chance at freedom.

The man breathed deep, then started to run. Straight at Simon. Five yards. Fifteen feet. No distance at all.

Simon stood his ground to the last second, then danced aside, bringing his knife down as Whittaker passed, catching him behind the knee so it buckled and gave under him.

The man shrieked as he fell. Rolling and rolling as he tried to stop the fire in his leg.

All the way to the edge of a bell pit.

Whittaker's knife had gone. He clutched at his leg, groaning. The last trace of colour had vanished from his face. His eyes were begging.

Jane moved first. She stood over him, staring down. 'I told you,' she said. 'I told you.'

She placed her boot on his back and pushed hard. For a moment he was still. But he was too weak to resist. Inch by inch she forced him towards the gap. Slow, gradual, until he was hanging there between life and death. His eyes stared up, beseeching.

'I told you,' she said quietly.

One moment more and he tumbled into the blackness below.

He didn't cry out. Simon heard the soft thud as Whittaker's body landed. He stood on the lip of the hole. Too dark to see to the bottom. The pit might as well have stretched all the way to hell. No cry, not even the sound of breathing.

Rosie gasped and clutched at him. He put an arm around her shoulders and held her tight.

'Do you think he's still alive?'

'I doubt it.'

Jane stood on the other side of the rim. Her face showed nothing.

Simon looked towards the mill office. Blenkinsop was still standing and watching, arms folded.

'It's over now,' he said quietly. 'All done.' He kissed Rosie's cheek. 'You should go home. I'll be back soon. I still have a little business here.'

She nodded but she didn't move. 'Simon . . .' she began. Then: 'It doesn't matter.'

Her face was pale, her eyes filled with a strange combination of pain and satisfaction. She squeezed his hand and began the journey back to town, Jane silent beside her. A final glance into Whittaker's deep grave and Simon walked away.

'You saw it?'

'Everything,' Blenkinsop said. He was smoking a cigar. 'We'll fill that hole. Don't want someone stumbling across him.'

'How deep is it?'

The man shrugged. 'Thirty feet. Maybe forty. Enough.'

Yes, Simon thought. Enough.

'I've seen accidents here before. I've watched men being brought out dead from the ground, but you know, I've never witnessed anything like that. That girl . . .'

'Yes.' There was nothing more to say. He'd seen the way Jane's eyes glittered with the coldness of justice as she pushed Whittaker. A single word might have stopped her, but he'd held his tongue. She was doing something that needed to be done. Maybe he should have been the one to do it. But he knew he couldn't. Not to kill like that.

'Maybe it's for the best,' he said.

'Aye.' Blenkinsop roused himself. 'Maybe it is at that. I'll let Matthew know the business is successfully concluded. He'll be in touch to pay you.'

Simon shook the man's heavy hand.

'If you want a different way into Leeds, wait a while and ride on the locomotive. It'll be back here soon. You'll never experience anything else like it, I'll guarantee that.'

'Thank you, but I'll walk. I need a little time to think.'

'Happen you do. Look out for yourself, Mr Westow.'

Maybe for the best. Quicker than a hanging. As he walked across the coalfield, he couldn't even be certain now which of the pits held Whittaker's body. That one over there, or this near his feet? Did it even matter? The man's tale had ended. Maybe someone in London would stop for a second and wonder what had happened to him. Then he'd be forgotten again, slipping away like mist. No glory in his death at all. But there hadn't been much in his life. A man who found his pleasure in preying on the weak.

No loss at all. That was what he told himself. As long as he didn't have to be the one to finish it.

He started down the path. As the track bent, the scene opened up between the trees for a moment and he could see Leeds spread out ahead of him under its sheen of smoke. Ugly, yes, but curiously beautiful, too. He paused to take in the view, then walked on.

Sitting in the soft sunlight outside Mrs Shields's house, Jane felt at peace. Her wounds had been bathed in cold, fresh water. Soft fingers had rubbed a sweet-smelling ointment on her bruises.

From somewhere, Catherine brought out an old dress that smelled of summer violets. The pattern on the cotton had faded to smudges of lilac and pale yellow.

'Put this on,' she said. 'That old one of yours isn't fit to wear any more. Besides, you've grown out of it.'

It fitted her well, the hem down at her ankles, the bodice curving over her breasts.

'I used to wear that all the time when I was young,' Mrs Shields said. She cradled her wrist in the sling, a wistful smile on her lips. 'I was as tall as you then. That's the thing about age, it makes you small. It withers you before it lets you go. Turn around. Right around. Yes, it suits you, child.'

There was a long looking-glass in the bedroom. Jane stood and stared at her reflection, barely recognizing the person she saw. Not a girl any longer. A woman carrying the marks of the life she lived.

'Do you mean it? I can have it?'

'Of course.'

Jane studied herself in the mirror again, combing her hair with her fingers and letting it fall on to her shoulders. Without thinking, she hugged Catherine.

'Do you really think I look like her?'

'Like I told you: you're the image of her. Every bit as pretty as she was.'

A final short glance and she turned away. For so many years she'd tried to put her mother from her mind, to push everything away until the woman's face had become a blur. But it lived on in her. However much she tried, there was no escape.

'Your arm, child.'

Jane tried to cover it with her hand. The ladder of cuts on her skin. Most of them had healed to faint scars, but the most recent were still raw and scarred.

'That business with Simon, is it all finished?'

'Yes.' No remorse. She'd done exactly what she'd promised, that day in the churchyard when she cut his face. She'd watched as he was swallowed by the silence and felt nothing beyond vengeance for Henry. No sadness or guilt the way she'd felt for Mary Rigton.

'While you were gone, I started to think about a few things.' Mrs Shields sat on the bed. 'You know I told you this house will be yours when I die.'

Jane stood, quiet, attentive.

'You could come and live here now if you like. With me. You could help me. I can't do everything I'd wish these days. We could put another bed in for you.'

'Yes,' Jane answered. No hesitation. Her room with Simon and Rosie was nothing more than somewhere to sleep. It had never been a home. In this house she felt she belonged, that she had a place in the world.

'Thank you,' Catherine said. 'I want you to come and go as you please. To be absolutely free. Carry on your work.' She patted the cover beside her. 'Sit here for a minute.'

Jane obeyed, letting out a slow breath as she felt a hand stroke her hair.

Home. *Home.*

Exhausted. The walk back to Leeds seemed to last forever. The dust on the coal staithe made him cough. But finally he reached the bridge, letting the noise of the town draw him in. Simon saw Jem at the foot of Briggate, trying to hand out his tracts to the people passing. Most of them ignored him, engrossed in their own lives. But still the boy's eyes shone with hope.

He took two pennies from his pocket. 'Here,' he said and pressed them into the boy's hand.

'Do you want one?'

'Go on, then.' It would make the lad feel better. 'Sticking with religion, are you?'

A contented nod. 'Miss Carr's been showing me the way.'

'I'm glad.' He tousled Jem's hair and turned along Swinegate.

The boys rushed to greet him as he opened the door. Rosie stood in the kitchen, a soft smile on her face.

'It never feels right without them, does it?' she said.

'No,' he agreed. 'It doesn't.'

'Business concluded?'

'Yes. Payment coming soon.'

Her eyes flashed with the joy of money.

Without all the books the room seemed larger. Empty. The walls were pale where they'd been; now only two shelves were filled, and loosely.

Emily Ashton sat on a chair, hands folded neatly in her lap, red hair covered by a starched white cap. All the worry and terror had finally fled from her face. She looked . . . what, Simon wondered? Serene? Accepting? Calm, at least.

And Davey looked older, a man who'd learned about himself and didn't like what he'd discovered. He'd regained most of the weight he'd lost in the cells, but somehow he still seemed scrawny. More grey in his hair and time pressing down on his shoulders.

'No more worries for you,' Simon told him. 'You'll be free from the magistrates in future.'

Ashton raised an eyebrow. 'I wish it were that simple. There are more prisons than the one I was in. You know that, Simon. There are the ones we create for ourselves.'

'You're a free man.'

Davey looked around the room. The shelves were empty. Everything gone.

'Do you know why I did it? Gave them away?'

'No.' He'd wondered when he arrived. The books were so much a part of the man. Often he'd pluck one out for a quote or to search for some thread of knowledge. He'd used books to educate Simon about the world.

'I realized that I'm a coward.' He spoke slowly as he levelled the accusation at himself. 'I said all the good and proper things. But fighting for reform takes courage. For a long time I believed I had that.' He tapped his skull. 'Up here I truly believed that. Then they put me behind those bars and I understood' – a hand over his heart – 'that words were all I had. And they don't mean anything without action. I learned I'm nothing more than a frightened man who tried to talk like a giant.'

'Davey—'

'No, please. Don't say anything, Simon. It's the truth, and better to have found it out now so I can see what to do with the rest of my life.' He sat, staring off into the distance for a moment. 'But I'm grateful to you. More than you'll ever know.'

'We both are,' Emily added.

'I told you. I was repaying a debt.'

'If you were,' Davey said, 'then it's all settled now.'

'That's a lovely dress,' Rosie said.

'Yes,' Jane agreed.

'Did you buy it at the market?'

'Mrs Shields gave it to me.'

Simon saw something in her eyes, a hesitation. More, though. Things had changed. He'd heard the news that someone had killed Mary Rigton. But he'd never ask her. Let her carry the secret inside, hidden away with all the others she possessed.

'She's asked me to live there. I said yes.'

'That's wonderful news,' Rosie said. 'But we'll miss you.'

Jane turned to Simon. 'I still want to work with you.'

'I'm happy to have you for as long as you want,' he assured her. 'You know that.'

'Yes.' A smile flickered on her lips. 'Good.'

She had nothing to carry. No bag. All she owned fitted in her hands.

'Tomorrow,' Simon told her. 'Come in the morning. You remember we were looking for Stephen Bullock before any of this start? Someone said they saw him today.'

Jane nodded, turned, and then she was gone, the front door closing with a click behind her. Silence filled the room.

'Let's take a walk,' Simon suggested after a minute. 'The boys can run and play. It'll do them good.'

In the hall, the long-clock chimed the hour.

AFTERWORD

The story of Dodd the spy is very loosely based on the William Oliver affair in 1817. He wasn't so much a spy as an agent provocateur, working for the Home Office. He denounced Radicals in the West Riding, and was only discovered because someone who knew him spotted him talking to the servant of a general before he boarded a coach in Wakefield. It led to a series of articles in the *Leeds Mercury* that did come close to bringing down the government.

The world's first locomotive did run between the Middleton coalfield and the staithe close to the River Aire in Leeds. The *Salamanca* made its debut in 1812, long before Stephenson's *Rocket*. Blenkinsop did come up with the cog wheel design, and it, along with its successors, was built at Matthew Murray's works in Holbeck.

Ann Carr was a real person, one of the few female evangelists of the early nineteenth century and founder of the Female Revivalist Society. In Leeds, she worked in the slums, ran a chapel in the Leylands and built a small community.

I'm very grateful to everyone at Severn House. They all do such a wonderful job, a team that knows and supports their writers. But a special mention to my editor, Sara Porter, who believes in Simon and Jane, and Kate Lyall Grant, the publisher, who understands. And I can't forget my agent, Tina Betts, or Lynne Patrick, who edits my manuscripts so well. Thank you all.

And finally, my real gratitude to all of you who read these books.